MW01533989

Mike Campbell slipped the safety on his M79 grenade launcher, sighted, and shot a grenade cartridge into the main body of guerrillas.

The explosion wiped out several men, frightening the others—long enough for the American merc team to open fire with their M16s. Mike followed with a second shell, scattering the enemy.

"Take cover!" Mike yelled at two of his men, who were standing in the open, blazing away like they were at the O.K. Corral.

They obeyed, fortunately, for a withering hail of lead was gunned their way by the surviving guerrillas. The rebels were gathered in four pockets that still outnumbered the mercs by more than two to one. The question was now, who had who pinned down?

Mike Campbell had an answer to that question. Using the graduated leaf rearsight, he aimed his M79 grenade launcher again....

Also by J. B. Hadley

THE POINT TEAM

Published by
WARNER BOOKS

ATTENTION: SCHOOLS AND CORPORATIONS

WARNER books are available at quantity discounts with bulk
purchase for educational, business, or sales promotional use. For
information, please write to SPECIAL SALES DEPARTMENT,
WARNER BOOKS, 666 FIFTH AVENUE, NEW YORK, N.Y. 10103

**ARE THERE WARNER BOOKS
YOU WANT BUT CANNOT FIND IN YOUR LOCAL STORES?**

You can get any WARNER BOOKS title in print. Simply send title
and retail price, plus 50¢ per order and 50¢ per copy to cover
mailing and handling costs for each book desired. New York State
and California residents add applicable sales tax. Enclose check
or money order only, no cash please, to WARNER BOOKS, P.O.
BOX 690, NEW YORK, N.Y. 10019

VIPER SQUAD

J.B. Hadley

WARNER BOOKS

A Warner Communications Company

WARNER BOOKS EDITION

Copyright © 1985 by Warner Books, Inc.
All rights reserved.

Warner Books, Inc.
666 Fifth Avenue
New York, N.Y. 10103

W A Warner Communications Company

Printed in the United States of America

First Printing: April, 1985

10 9 8 7 6 5 4 3 2 1

The Devil's Gate

ONE of the two men said something to him in Spanish. He couldn't understand a word, but he could see the evil glitter in the man's eyes. It was the fat one, holding the car's rear door open so he could reach in and pull him outside. This was the one who had sat beside him on the drive to this place, holding a lump of lead in his right fist and rapping him on the side of the head with his weighted knuckles anytime he made a move. He was dizzy. His head hurt. His groin hurt. He did not resist as he was pulled out of the car.

They had parked at the summit of an overlook. The city of San Salvador stretched out beneath, and the setting sun looked like a huge ripe peach in the haze of air pollution. The streetlights in some sections had been turned on.

"Cabron!" the fat man spat at him. "Cornudo!"

The thin man jutted a pistol painfully into his ribs. He found himself being forced to the edge of the overlook.

It was not a sheer drop, as at the edge of a cliff. But if he were pushed, he'd surely break something before he managed to hang on to a rock or tussock of grass to stop himself rolling down all the way. And there might be steeper drops farther down which he could not see from up here.

If only they'd try to communicate with him! Were they rightists or leftists? Rightists, he suspected. Yet, he could not be sure and took no chances. One wrong word could be suicide.

He had shouted his name at them, over and over, coming here in the car. He assumed at first it was a case of mistaken identity and that when they realized he was not who they thought he was—but an American citizen—they would release him.

Now he had come to think that these two men knew exactly who he was and had abducted him deliberately. Why?

They seemed to have no wish to make themselves understood to him. That was what was so frustrating! If he was going to be killed, he felt he had the right to know why.

He guessed they were only trying to frighten him. He wished he could find some way of telling them they had already done a great job. That he wouldn't cause any more difficulties for them—if he ever had. That he would even leave the country if they wanted him to. Mañana. Not just mañana, but on the first plane tomorrow morning. He couldn't do any better than that.

He had told them all this in English on the way here. They hadn't understood a word. Whoever was doing this to him should at least have sent along someone who knew a little English . . .

"Monte de mierda!" the fat man snarled at him.

The pistol muzzle snuggled into his left ear, and he felt the thin man watching him with whiplash anxiety—ready to squeeze the trigger at a split-second's notice.

The fat man opened a straight razor. Its stainless steel blade mirrored the peach red of the setting sun.

The fat one took a step toward him, with the gleaming razor dangling casually in his right hand. He took an involuntary half step backward and felt his heels sink as the ground sloped steeply away. He could feel the emptiness of space at his back. The pistol muzzle pressed harder into his left ear.

The fat man now stood directly before him. His blubbery lips were curled back from his decayed teeth in a look of hatred and disgust. No one had ever looked at him with such intense loathing before. There was intelligence as well as dislike in those bloodshot eyes—this man knew who and what he was, and hated him for it. Why?

Faster than he could raise his shirt-sleeved arm to protect his throat, the razor's honed edge struck at him.

The thin edge of tempered steel flicked through the strap of the light meter hung about his neck. The fat man stooped forward and caught the instrument in his left palm before it hit the ground. The fat one looked at it closely for a moment and then sailed it out into the empty air above the city lights.

The motionless, frightened face before him caused a satisfied grin to spread from his thick lips to stubbled jowls. His razor streaked out again.

Before he could react to save himself, he felt the steel blade touch his head above his eyes. It hardly hurt—two light touches from something that was so precisely thin it was beneath the threshold of pain. The straight razor was withdrawn.

He slapped his hand to his forehead. When he lowered his hand, he saw what was imprinted on his palm. A cross of red in blood.

Chapter 1

SALLY Poynings, 20, blond, blue-eyed, sexy, a dropout from posh Smith College in Northampton, Massachusetts, drew all eyes wherever she went in El Salvador. She stepped from the bus she and her boyfriend had taken from the city of San Salvador. They had come to the countryside to see the "real people," as her boyfriend put it. She looked about her.

Cinder-block huts with galvanized zinc roofs formed three sides of a dusty square. An adobe church with huge cracks running up the front, from steps to belfry, lay crumbling on the fourth side. A few withered trees leaned in the center of the square, and a pool of green stagnant water near where she stood gave off a bad smell. She slapped flies from her face and arms. As usual, people stared at her—thin dirty children with big dark eyes, an overweight woman with a basket of oranges on her head, a beggar on the church steps with scaly skin who could be a leper, a few men in sweat-stained shirts and battered straw hats.

Bennett, her boyfriend, panned his movie camera; and she obediently held the microphone in the heat-stricken silence, switching off the tape in time to the camera.

He grinned at her. "Fantastic place."

She smiled fondly back at him.

Then their bus pulled away, the people inside peering down at them through the grimy windows. Sally watched the clouds of dust the bus had raised slowly settle.

"Sally, I got a feeling this place is authentic. These people are real people. What we film is going to be valid."

"Yes, Bennett."

She looked about again. Everything looked so hopeless. A metal Coca-Cola sign was nailed to the front wall of the nearest cinder-block hut. The sign's red color was faded by the sun to pink, and there were clusters of bullet holes about the letter "o" in each of the words, without a single direct hit. Crumpled cigarette packs and orange peels were trampled into the dust at the doorway. Bennett was fooling with the camera again, so she pushed open the wood door with its flaking lavender paint and stepped into the cool, dark interior.

A heavyset middle-aged man sat behind a wooden counter stacked with merchandise. A brown curtain suspended on brass rings from a bamboo pole cut off the back half of the hut. The front half was lit by a window only a foot square—high in one side wall—and the interior walls of the hut were the same as the exterior: naked cinder-block. On a calendar picture, a soccer player was about to kick the ball, and behind glass in a frame a nearly stripped haloed saint was about to have his head chopped off by an axman whose outlandish costume suggested to Sally he was an Indian maharajah. She bought two Cokes, which were warm, and asked the name of the town—things like that were important to Bennett's project; and since he spoke no Spanish, he had to rely on her.

Back outside again, everything had brightness and intensity as if the sun were a strobe that never flickered but just stayed blazing so that her eyes hurt.

"What a dump!" Bennett said gleefully.

He grimaced at the taste of the warm Coke, yet did not complain. Now was no time to bitch about conditions, here in the heart of the Third World. He had come to find the real truth about things in El Salvador once and for all, so he must expect to suffer a little or at least be inconvenienced once in a while.

"Shit, if I had to live in this hole," Bennett went on, "I'd be a rebel too."

"I wish you wouldn't talk like that," Sally said, looking nervously behind her. "Just because you can't understand them doesn't mean they can't understand you. What do we do now?"

This was a reasonable question, since the only other person left in the square at that moment was the beggar on the church steps, and nothing moved except for two small pigs snuffling at the bases of the withered trees. Sally glanced at the pigs and added, "Don't say we should hunt truffles."

Bennett hadn't noticed them. "Hey, you got a good eye, girl. Let's use those pigs. Get in close with the sound."

Sorry she had said anything, Sally adjusted her sound for the low-register grunts and high-pitched squeals of the two pigs. She was about to dart from the shade of the hut, along with Bennett, onto the burning sands of the square, when an army truck careened into the open space at high speed. It stopped, and soldiers jumped down from beneath its canvas covering.

Eight soldiers ran to one hut facing the square. One kicked the door off its hinges and all of them ran inside. Four other soldiers stood around the truck, automatic rifles slung from their shoulders, watchful.

Bennett was filming. Sally hurriedly turned on the sound.

Two men in their early twenties emerged from the hut

with their hands held in the air. A soldier booted the second one in the ass as he came out behind him. Then a woman carrying a baby in one arm and holding a toddler by the hand was followed by a boy about seven and a girl about nine. Two soldiers poked them along with their rifle barrels. Finally an old woman appeared, arguing with the five remaining soldiers who brought up the rear of this procession. The soldier who had been guarding the two young men turned his back on them and returned to talk to the others.

Bennett spoke in that special tone of voice he reserved for the tape recorder. "The soldiers are now deliberately tempting the two men to try to escape so they can gun them down."

The two young men seemed to agree with Bennett's assessment of their situation, because they looked back and waited for the woman with the baby and toddler to join them. After this, all of them were hustled by the soldiers into the back of the truck. Bennett adjusted the lens for a final close-up.

"Senor!" The flaked lavender door of the cinder-block hut behind them opened a few inches. The man's voice inside rattled on hoarsely. Bennett heard the words *muy peligroso*, and even he knew that meant very dangerous. Sally's reaction was to grab him, spoiling a nice shot of the two pigs fleeing in terror across the square in front of the army truck. The driver swerved at one of the pigs with the left front wheel but missed. With all her might, Sally pushed Bennett before her through the lavender door, and the storekeeper slammed it behind them.

After a minute, the man opened the door a crack and peered out. "It's all right, they didn't see you."

"What's he saying?" Bennett asked.

"The soldiers didn't see us," she told him. She switched to Spanish. "What will they do to those people?"

The man shook his head sadly. "Those were very foolish people."

"What did they do?"

"They made fun of the army," the man said, in an awed tone of voice that indicated the seriousness of this offense. "When the guerrillas came to this town two days ago, the regular soldiers ran away."

"The guerrillas were here two days ago?"

"They left early this morning," the man said matter-of-factly. "Those people laughed at the soldiers for running away. They said to everyone that the soldiers were not real men, that they were cowards because they were afraid to fight the guerrillas. It's not good for you to be here with a camera. You had better leave at once. I could drive you back to San Salvador where you will be safe, for one hundred Yanqui dollars."

"You're crazy!" Sally said. "It cost us about three dollars each to come here by bus."

"Seventy-five," the man countered.

Sally thought carefully. She decided to say nothing to Bennett about the rebels having been in the town. If she did, she would never get him to go back to their San Salvador hotel today. This storekeeper was robbing them, but what the hell, money was the least of her problems.

"All right," she said. "Let's go now."

"Momentito. Then I show you something on the way." He pointed to Bennett. "For his camera. It will cost you twenty-five dollars. Altogether, one hundred Yanqui dollars. If you have it."

Sally sighed and produced a crisp bill from her purse.

The Salvadoran whistled in admiration at the unused hundred-dollar bill and slipped it behind the picture of the saint about to be beheaded. Then he looked through the doorway out into the blazing light of the square and beckoned them.

"What's happening?" Bennett asked.

But Sally was already out the door.

They moved at high speed along the road in a battered green 1970 Buick Skylark with no muffler, which made the car sound like a powerboat. A few miles down the road, without easing his speed, the Salvadoran swung off the road into a set of tire tracks across the dust, and the car fishtailed and skidded sideways to a halt. The driver smiled and took off again from a standing start that spun his rear wheels in the dirt before they found traction and rocketed the car forward.

"Great old V-eight," Bennett said with approval. "They don't make 'em like this anymore."

Sally was frightened that if she translated this for the Salvadoran, he would be encouraged to show off more of the jalopy's prowess. She pressed her hands against the dashboard, figuring that two broken arms were preferable to a face disfigured by a splintered windshield.

Round the base of a small hill, they came to the town's garbage dump. The set of tire tracks swerved into the garbage.

"It looks worse than it smells," the Salvadoran said, gesturing expansively at the refuse on both sides of the car. "The sun dries it out after the birds and animals pick over it. The vultures are slow today. Usually they're the first ones here."

He looked around carefully as he drove very slowly, and then pointed to some bright patches ahead that stood out from the camouflage of weathered garbage. He put his foot on the gas and then on the brake as they neared the place. He stopped and switched off the engine, gesturing out his open side window and watching her face closely.

They were the same ones. The two men in their early twenties; the woman still holding her baby; the toddler now about ten feet away from her, one knee bent, lying on his back; the boy; the girl; the old woman . . . they all lay on their backs in the sunshine with bright red blotches on their bodies. Their arms and legs were at odd angles. Their mouths and eyes were open.

Bennett had stuck his camera out the rear side window and was filming them. Sally forgot to turn on the mike, which didn't matter because the only sound to be heard was flies buzzing.

Mike Campbell looked at the sun rise yellow through the blowing sand that beat like rain against the pickup's steel side and roof. He bit on grains between his teeth and tried to lick them off onto the back of his hand. The wind howled, and a lone cactus raised its claw at the sky.

He had pulled the pickup off a ruler-straight road that ran from one horizon of Arizona to the other. On the windward side of the road, the sand had encroached halfway across the traffic lane. Mike had been waiting for daylight before leaving the road, because headlights made everything look deceptive and unfamiliar off a paved surface. The desert could be tricky enough to cross at the best of times.

He switched on the engine, shifted into four-wheel drive and started out across the arid waste. A tall, lean man in his late thirties or early forties, his calm gray eyes contrasted with his restless manner. He had a deep tan, his face was heavily lined, and he had small sharp scars on his neck and arms. Some of them shrapnel. He fixed on a notch in a distant blue mountain range as his marker. After some miles, the dead-flat land began to undulate in small rises and dips; and pockets of soft sand caused the pickup to slew and spin its tires.

The sun climbed in the sky, and the beams of heat from its merciless golden eye would miss nothing later in the day. But now there was still a chill from the desert night lingering in the air. Mike hoped to make it to the first of the canyons before the heat grew uncomfortable. He had discovered the network of canyons by chance when some powerful thermals took his glider over backcountry that fliers normally avoided because of its remoteness. From the air, he had seen the canyons running into one another like cracks in dried mud, till they ended in the river. What most intrigued Mike about them was that he had not known they were there.

He left the pickup in the same place he had left it on previous trips and descended the steep side of a gulch down to a dry streambed at its bottom. Cottonwoods, tamarisks and willows grew among sedges and reeds along the banks that contained only smooth bone-dry stones. As Mike followed the gulch, its walls grew steeper and closer together, until finally he was walking along the dry bottom of a cool, dark canyon about as wide as a deer trail. The walls of the canyon were of smooth sandstone and seemed almost to meet far above his head, leaving only a thin strip of blue sky.

Mike followed this canyon till it joined another wider one, and followed that until it too joined a still larger one almost the width of the two-lane road he had long since left. Some big thunderheads floated in what he could see of the sky. They seemed a long distance off. He had explored this far and up some side canyons on his previous visits. This time he wanted to follow the main canyon, which, unlike the others, narrowed as it went toward the river. As he followed the canyon, the rocks and debris left on its floor made the going hard. He had covered a long, twisting, relatively easy stretch when he stopped to listen.

The sound was exactly like that of a subway train approaching in a tunnel. Mike felt vibrations in the ground beneath him and a great roar echoed down the canyon. He looked back but saw nothing.

A huge snake head of red liquid mud suddenly slithered into view along the undercut sandstone wall of the bend behind him. The serpent of mud twisted back into the center of the canyon and shot forward with deadly speed to consume all in its path.

Mike had time only to rush to the side and scramble on top of some rock debris at the base of one canyon wall. He avoided the direct impact of the flash flood, which would have borne him along, battered him with boulders and ground him up fine along the rocky floor.

The flood swept by, three or four feet deep and almost up to his boots where he stood on the rocks. Then he felt the rocks shift slightly under him from the force of the muddy water. The canyon wall was smooth above him, without handholds. The rocks beneath his feet shifted again.

Then the water level rose alarmingly. In seconds, it was above his knees. He hardly had time to think before it was at waist level. Mike decided not to wait to find out which would give way first, him or the rocks beneath, and he hitched a ride on a heavy tree trunk floating down what was now a swift, muddy river. This proved not so easy as he thought it would be. The trunk was old and weathered, without bark or branches—and the water made it slippery to grip and rolled it in his grasp when he did manage to hold on. He cut one hand. This he could tell by the blood on his skin, for he could feel nothing.

A cottonwood, uprooted by the flood, was carried near him and Mike transferred his hold onto it. Its branches acted like outriggers and prevented the trunk from rolling in the fast-moving waters. He saw two drowned deer float by.

Mike was a strong swimmer and was not greatly concerned by what was happening until the canyon narrowed further and he was swept down two chutes of water. He knew he was getting into waterfall territory. Even a small waterfall could stun and drown him—and he would have no chance at all in a fall of any size. He managed to twist the cottonwood around at a narrow neck so that it became caught securely between both canyon walls. He clung on and let the water break over him.

Very soon the water level dropped. Almost as quickly as the river had come into existence, it began to disappear. Mike let himself dry, sitting on the trunk still wedged between the canyon walls but now above the water. When the flow had diminished to a waist-high stream, he jumped down into the water. He shook the cottonwood tree loose and watched its journey downstream. Then he walked back the way he had come on dry ground alongside one canyon wall.

He climbed beside what was now a ten-foot-high waterfall—it had been a chute when he had passed over it in the headlong rush of deep water—and upstream from that he came across another. This one, about fifteen feet high, was of smooth sandstone and not climbable.

Perhaps he would find an easier way out by following the canyon down toward the river. He climbed back down the side of the ten-foot waterfall and passed the spot where he had wedged the cottonwood between the canyon walls. If he had not pushed the tree back into the water and watched it float away, he could have hauled it back up the lower waterfall and used it as a ladder against the smooth wall of the upper fall. Why had he pushed the tree back in the water? The cottonwood itself couldn't have cared less one way or the other, yet it was almost as if he had been apologizing to it for delaying its journey and helping it on its way again.

Mike continued farther down the canyon along the dry strip by the base of one wall until he came to a dark, misty place where the water disappeared over the lip of yet another fall. Even before reaching it, he could tell by the comparative silence—only a distant muffled plunging of water—that he was not going to like what he was about to see. He peered over the edge.

The muddy river shot clear of the precipice and descended in a long, wavering spout to smash into foam on rocks more than a hundred feet below. The top of the fall, where Mike stood, was an overhang he could have managed with a climbing rope. Beneath the overhang, the walls were sanded smooth by the abrasives carried along in the water over the ages. Mike turned back.

When he passed the place again where he had jammed

the cottonwood between the canyon walls, he was shaken by how close he had gotten to the big fall. His maneuver had been just in time. Then he grew alarmed about his present situation. It might be years before someone came this way and found his bones. By then, more flash floods would probably have carried his bones down the canyons to the river, and from the river into the Gulf of California, to rest on the sea bottom, examined by curious fish, till buried out of sight by settling sediment. . . .

His pickup, in perfect condition in the desert climate, would be his memorial, the only clue to what had happened to him.

He stood for a while, hopelessly, beneath the smooth walls of the fifteen-foot fall, the water shrunken now to the size of a brook, and he could hardly believe it when he saw a big tree trunk with snapped-off branches protrude a few feet over the top of the fall and then come to a stop, the flow of water being insufficient to carry it over. The trunk moved again and rolled; a bit more of the heavy trunk stuck out over the top; then it seesawed a little and at last was eased over the edge. The heavy end hit the pool at the base of the fall, and the trunk remained leaning against the top at an angle of forty-five degrees.

Mike scrambled up it and moved on up the canyon, fast—aware of more thunderheads billowing in full sail across the sky.

Lt. Col. Francisco Cerezo Ramirez, of the Treasury Police in the city of San Salvador, shook hands with the army general. He said quietly, "You may depend on me, Victor."

"I knew I could."

The colonel opened the door of his office and showed the general out. An army lieutenant snapped to attention in the corridor and accompanied his superior officer down the curving marble staircase. The Treasury Police colonel nodded to a bull of a man lounging in the corridor and left the door of his office open behind him. The man's sunglasses added nothing to his expressionless face, and his loose shirt flapped beneath his potbelly as he walked. He closed the door after him.

Broad beams of sunlight shone through the floor-to-ceiling casement windows of the huge office and hit one corner of the enormous rosewood desk. The colonel himself was quite small, and had a neatly trimmed mustache and a freshly pressed uniform, brightened by medals and decorations.

"Turco, it seems we have some left-wing gringo spies upsetting our army friends," the colonel said. "With a movie camera."

Turco smirked. This was his kind of work.

"Male and female, staying here in San Salvador at the Sheraton." Lieutenant Colonel Cerezo passed some papers to him. "No one lays a finger on them till I say so. First we find out what their affiliation is."

"All they need do to get a press pass is rent a car from Avis." Turco's voice was flat and rasping.

"The general thinks this pair has no press credentials."

Turco frowned. "Peculiar."

"Find out who and what they are, and what they've got their hands on so far."

"What did the general say they've done, sir?"

The colonel smiled. "I wouldn't want to spoil your fun by telling you. That's for you to discover for yourself."

Turco's thick lips slowly curled from his green teeth in a grin.

Chapter 2

BENNETT replaced the phone. "He speaks real good English," he said and sank back into an easy chair in their Sheraton room. "He's agreed to give me a half-hour interview, so long as we get there punctually at three. After the interview, he'll take us with him to some kind of meeting."

Sally nodded. "Is this Bermudez an old friend of your father's?"

"An old patient. Every cardiologist keeps a careful record of his patients and tends to follow up on them more than other doctors do. When my father succeeds in keeping someone with a bad heart alive under unfavorable conditions, he doesn't mind taking personal credit for it. When the patient happens to be a politician in El Salvador, naturally my father is doubly interested in the stresses involved. According to my father's instructions, I'm supposed to question Bermudez about his blood pressure, pulse rate, medication and diet as well as on political things. Can you believe it?"

Sally laughed. "Remember that crazy reporter the other night? The one who told us why Salvadorans smoke so heavily—none of them expect to live long enough to develop lung cancer.''

''In the year or so since Bermudez was last in Boston to see my father, there's been two or three attempts on his life. You can imagine the mess he must be.''

They had expected the politician to live in one of the wealthy suburbs where the houses were surrounded by high walls. Instead, their taxi took them to a poor downtown section, one of the few old parts of the city they had seen, where people leaned on windowsills and sat in doorways.

The taxi driver said, ''These people are the best lookouts Senor Bermudez could have. Nobody can come into this neighborhood without being seen. And if they don't like the look of you . . .'' He turned about to look at them in the backseat while he drove and made a noise with his mouth and snapped his fingers simultaneously.

''What's he saying?'' Bennett asked.

''Your friend doesn't speak Spanish, senora?'' the driver asked.

''No.''

''You speak it very well. Better than a lot of us do.''

Sally knew he was referring to her Castilian pronunciation—her European rather than American Spanish. These Central American men seemed amazed by her blond gringa appearance and grammatical, and to them snobbish, Spanish.

''What kind of man is Senor Bermudez?'' she asked.

The driver steered around a peddler's cart and shrugged. ''A moderate. So what can he do? The leftists have guns. The rightists have guns. The moderates are in the middle and have no guns. Senor Bermudez speaks his mind. You have to give it to him that he has courage.''

The houses on the next block all had steel mesh over the windows and the doors were fortified by metal plates. In the middle of the block, one old house was set back from the street behind massive iron railings. Sally paid the driver, and they approached the building under the impersonal stares of four men with submachine guns slung from their shoulders. Bennett paused to film them. They did not react.

"Shit," Bennett said. "I was hoping one of them would at least wave his gun at me."

"Would you dare go around the Combat Zone, back home in Boston, doing what you're doing here?" Sally asked crossly. "Like hell you would. Yet you run around here like you paid the price of admission and now you want to see the show. I tell you, Bennett, I don't like the look of these people and they don't like the look of us."

Bennett smiled tolerantly and kissed her cheek. "It's always a little weird and chaotic doing any movie—especially a documentary. You never know what turn things will take. But that's what gives the final film its charge—the very same things that drove its makers crazy while they were doing it. I'm kind of glad you weren't along for the whale movie. If you'd seen those big bastards breaching right next to our little rowboat, you'd have headed back to port first day."

Sally looked at the ground, hurt that Bennett could be pleased not to have had her with him then. She had already forgotten that he had tried to persuade her not to come to El Salvador and that only her knowledge of Spanish and her role as the film's producer (that is, financial backer) reversed his judgment that she should not come.

They had to walk around a wall of sandbags to enter the doorway of the building, which led through a large hallway to a central courtyard. Here groups of men stood about with rifles and submachine guns. Some had their weapons broken down and were cleaning the trigger assemblies with oily rags and the barrels with twisted pipe cleaners. No one spoke to them.

"You sure this man is your father's patient?" Sally asked nervously.

He laughed. "Of course. I want some footage of these

guys. Since you tell me I'm so damn rude or whatever, why don't you ask their permission?''

She asked the nearest men. Yes, they would be pleased. Caps and sunglasses were adjusted, bellies sucked in, weapons brandished . . .

"And these are the moderates," Bennett said as he adjusted the lens.

He was still running the camera when a man about sixty in a white shirt approached, paused in front of the camera with a big smile and then held up a hand in a friendly gesture to signal enough. Bennett switched off the camera.

"The doctor's son, eh? How is my old friend in Boston? You are in medicine too, no?''

"No," Bennett said.

"Good. Then you won't make me listen to advice about what I should not do. I received your father's letter that you were coming to El Salvador. I wrote by return mail to tell him to stop you.''

"I'd have come anyway, even if he had tried to stop me.''

Bermudez frowned for an instant. "If I was a doctor in Boston, no són of mine would set foot in El Salvador.'' He looked at Sally. "Your wife?''

"A friend," Bennett said.

"I see.'' Bermudez' voice was cold and he looked away from her. She was dismissed.

Latin pig, Sally thought.

"My schedule has changed," Bermudez said. "Meeting first. Then interview. Come.''

They followed him through the hallway to the door to the street, along with a dozen of the gun-toting security men. Two vans were now pulled up in front of the building.

Bermudez gestured apologetically at the gunmen. "I try to be a man of peace as much as possible, but each day it becomes a little more difficult to go the way of nonviolence. Both the communists and the fascists want to kill me.

Why? Because I suggested negotiation and peaceful solutions.''

The Volkswagen van they rode in had metal plates bolted to the inside walls and roof. The window glass had been replaced by inch-thick clear plastic that Sally assumed was bulletproof.

"I try never to confront them with violence," Bermudez was saying, "because each time I do so successfully, I become more like them. That means I have to avoid being attacked, without running away. So I bring my armed security men with me everywhere without making a big show of it, as others do. And I change my routine every day. Often even I do not know where I will be in a few hours' time. That way I stay alive and live to fight another day, no?''

Sally couldn't help admiring him a little for the way he handled himself, in spite of the fact that he enraged her through continuing to treat her as if she weren't there. He's religious, she decided. He probably saw her as some kind of scarlet woman. And he'd have his hand on her knee as soon as Bennett looked the other way. She knew the type.

They came to a supermodern high rise, the kind she disliked in Boston but which, for some reason, looked great down here. Their van and the one following, bringing the rest of the security men, drove into the underground garage beneath the building instead of pulling up before it.

The armed men tumbled out of the second van and looked about among the parked cars in the garage's cavernous interior. Then they assumed positions with their guns swinging at the ready, and one nodded to the driver of their van. It was time for them to get out.

Bennett followed the driver, the two security men next, then Sally, then Bermudez. Bennett panned his camera around the underground garage, complaining of the poor light.

A splatter of what could have been water tore across the

concrete wall behind their heads. The automatic gunfire was deafening in the enclosed space. Bermudez' security men fired back, Sally could not see where. She and Bennett crouched behind a car parked near their van, along with Bermudez. There was a silence after the first bursts of fire. It seemed to go on and on. Bennett was filming. Sally suddenly remembered she had forgotten to turn the mike on and she knew how mad Bennett would be at her about it. She switched it on.

Some of the security men were running from the cover of one parked car to another. One shouted a warning. They heard a metallic clatter underneath the van. The car they crouched behind sheltered them from the blast, yet it knocked them to the concrete floor. Bermudez fell on top of Sally. He kind of grunted and hung onto her.

"Filthy animal!" Sally snarled and tried to lift his unresponsive bulk off her body. She finally managed to heave him off her and looked up to see what was happening. The van lay on its side, burning, and clouds of black smoke rolled beneath the low concrete ceiling. There was a long rattling of many guns. Then silence.

Sally heard another metallic scrape. She looked. About five feet away on the concrete floor, a hand grenade spun slowly on its side. A small iron Easter egg, she thought, cold, malevolent . . .

Mike Campbell pulled into the oasis of sorts that the trailer park created in the Arizona desert. Mike was a solitary man in so many ways, he could live right next to folks and not be much affected by them. He might have been happier living in some tumbledown rancho on a lonely mesa, but his woman, Tina, was having none of that. She needed company, running water, electricity. Trailer park or mesa, it mattered little to Mike much of the time. It had mattered today. He wanted to be alone, so he had gone to the canyons. And almost not come back. Which made coming back now very satisfying.

He left the pickup at one end of his mobile home and climbed out, stiff and tired. A retired couple looked at him from their aluminum lawn chairs, the kind that fold. They usually chose not to speak to him, and they did not do so now.

"He's covered with dirt," the woman observed.

"I can see that, dear," her husband replied.

"Probably been on a drunk for days and lying in a gutter somewhere."

"I saw him leave first thing this morning, dear. He looked all right then."

The woman nodded as if this information just confirmed her worst suspicions. "He's been crawling across the border, bringing in illegal aliens. Or more likely running drugs."

"To me he looks like he might just have been running," the man said.

"Phil, don't take his part in this."

"You were pleased enough to be living close to him when those bikers caused that trouble, dear."

"Even those lowlifes knew enough to steer clear of him." That was her final word on the subject.

Mike overheard fragments of the conversation because working with heavy machinery in the car plants for years had made Phil a little deaf and the woman was accustomed to talking loudly with him. Tina had told Mike often about how his actions were an important part of the camp soap opera that filled in the days for the retired couple. Of particular interest to them was his source of income. "A man of invisible means," Phil's wife liked to intone mysteriously; and she never tired of putting indirect questions to Tina about him, with transparent hints at mob connections and whatever illegal activity Dan Rather had most recently spotlighted on the evening news. The only time Tina had become upset with her was when the old dear developed an obsession that Mike was stealing babies in Mexico for an illegal adoption ring in the States. It had been a TV special, and she was sure she recognized Mike in one of the shots.

Truth to tell, Mike's doings were both tamer and wilder than the old girl ever imagined. He had been a career officer in the Special Forces and had done back-to-back tours in Vietnam. He had been a colonel, already famous as a leader of special missions and search-and-destroy forays all over Southeast Asia, when he quit the Green Berets in disgust at the fall of Saigon. He had wanted to go back in and do it all over again, but this time the soldiers' way instead of the politicians'. Instead he was told to stay quiet and keep his buttons shiny. So he quit.

He thought he had seen every fuckup that politicians could manage while he was in Nam, but he found a whole new nest of spineless wonders when he went as a mercenary to Angola. After that he had been in Rhodesia, then Namibia, in and out of Central and South America, the Middle East, back to Asia. Over the years Mike built himself a rep as a merc to match his legend as a Green Beret colonel. As always, his concern was to keep away from publicity—to strike and be gone before the dust settled and people began wondering what had happened.

Mike waved wearily to the old couple decaying in their garden furniture on their miniature lawn in the desert, among the Michigan shrubs and flowers they forced to stay alive in this alien soil. The ground in front of Mike's trailer ran to sand, cholla and lizards. Tina had picked up the empty beer cans.

Tina was fussing with something in the kitchen and barely glanced at him. Yet Mike knew she needed only a microsecond or so to scan him carefully from head to toe and commit the smallest details to memory. He slumped into a chair.

She stood close before him, handing him an ice-cold can of Tecate. "You have a nice day in the country?"

He laughed and pulled her onto his lap. But she was still suspicious of him, a small, shrewd, pretty woman who knew all about men's lies but whose soft brown eyes and soft looks gave away her love for this man.

"Mike, are you holding back on me? Are you in training for some kind of mission?"

"No. I swear it. I'm not."

"You wouldn't tell me if you were," she accused.

"Wrong. I always tell you when I'm leaving on a mission. I just don't say where or why or when."

She knew this was true. He never lied to her. He just refused to tell her anything, insisting it had to be this way for her own protection.

"You really are only going to Switzerland to look at their army?" she asked.

"When I do tell you where I'm going, don't doubt it."

She wiped off some of his mud from her tank top. "It hasn't rained here for three months. Where did you find this stuff?"

He didn't bother to answer that. Instead he ran his hands inside her tank top and caressed her smooth skin with his fingertips. He held her right breast firmly in one palm and felt its nipple harden.

"You're going to get mud all over me," she murmured.

"I will," he promised.

"Hello, Adolfo," Lt. Col. Cerezo Ramirez greeted the cadaverous man.

A heavy growth of dark stubble covered Adolfo's wolfish jaws. He wore matching sunglasses to Turco's and the same style loose shirt—although, whereas Turco's shirt was barely able to cover his huge gut, Adolfo's shirt threatened almost to smother his emaciated body. He did not respond to the colonel's greeting and placed himself on a chair next to Turco before the rosewood desk.

The colonel ran his eyes over the first two pages of the report Turco had handed him. "Your typing has improved."

"Adolfo did it," Turco said, as if anxious to point out that such office skills were not to be looked for in him.

Gradually the pleased look on the colonel's face faded as he turned the pages. Finally he put the report down. "Bermudez wasn't killed by the grenade. He died of natural causes. A heart attack. A second grenade was thrown. It landed right next to Bermudez and these two Americans but didn't go off."

"Who carried out the attack, sir?" Turco asked. "Theirs or ours?"

"Ours, I'm afraid," the colonel said. "Damn, I wish our side would only have the sense to let the leftists take care of him for all of us. The rightist cause has enough blood to answer for as it is. No need to take on extra work if the Marxists will do it for us. Stupid." The colonel looked defiantly up at Turco's menacing disagreement. "You can tell your friends that, Turco."

A muscle twitched in Adolfo's hollow cheek, but Turco's heavy jowls remained unmoving.

The Treasury Police officer went back to the report. "The girl's father, Dwight Quincy Poynings, owns a chain of television stations and a baseball team. We can't touch her, no matter what she does, not with those norteamericano television stations and millions of dollars behind her."

"She's not the problem," Turco said.

"I agree." The colonel read some more. "Bennett Ward's father is a prominent Boston doctor. This young man won an award for a documentary film on the return of whales to Cape Cod." The colonel looked up, puzzled. "Whales? Can that be right?"

"Yes, sir," Turco said in his flat, certain tones.

The colonel read more and nodded. "So this millionaire's daughter pays the bills for the doctor's son to make movies. He's finished with whales, so now it's us Salvadorans. But we can't spout water through the tops of our heads for him. However, this time he's after deadlier stuff than that—us cutting each other to pieces. No doubt he'll make contact with the rebels and present things from their point of view, like all his sort do. I would normally say a warning to him would be enough: Leave the country in so many hours. But look what he has done already in a single day. In the morning he filmed idiot soldiers taking campesinos into custody and then he filmed the bodies of these same campesinos. Women and children, naturally. Damn communists, all of them. I'd say let these soldiers take the consequences, except I promised the general I'd take care of things.''

"The general has always worked closely with us,'' Turco pointed out.

"Absolutely,'' the colonel said hurriedly. "But that was only this norteamericano's morning work. In the afternoon, as you relate in these pages, he filmed the attack on Bermudez. You do not mention how he came to be with Bermudez.''

"I don't know,'' Turco said. "He's got contacts.''

"Know who he could have caught on film in that garage attack?'' the colonel asked. "The Hernandez Martinez.''

Turco looked startled. The Maximiliano Hernandez Martinez Anti-Communist Brigade was perhaps the best financed and most effective of all the ultra-right-wing death squads. It was named in honor of the military dictator responsible for *la matanza* in 1932, the massacre that had left a deep mark on the country to the present day.

"You know me for a circumspect man, Turco,'' the colonel continued. "I abhor rash and senseless acts of violence. Yet I do not hesitate to strike when the enemy is within the walls. Do not forget the film.''

Turco nodded and got to his feet. Adolfo stood also. Turco headed for the door, and Adolfo followed.

"But not the girl,'' the colonel called after them.

Turco raised a single finger in acknowledgment.

"My God, if that grenade had gone off, we'd be dead now,'' Sally said. "Blown to bits.''

"Either that happens or it doesn't,'' Bennett replied with a shrug.

"I've other plans."

"So, go ahead," he told her.

"You bastard, now you've got my money to make your film, you no longer care whether I'm around anymore."

"Sally, that's not how I feel." He seemed genuinely upset by what she said and took her in his arms. "I want you with me, but not down here. Remember why I asked you not to come? Because it would be dangerous. Now you want me to leave here. Why? Because it's dangerous. But I knew that before I came here and I'm willing to accept the risks. You're the one who didn't think this thing through before you came here. You came because I did. I appreciate that. Yet I can't help feeling that you're being unfair to me by telling me now what I told you before we left the States."

"I just don't want us to get killed," she said, tears welling in her eyes. "And I want to stay here with you. But I'm afraid."

"I'll be more careful in future," Bennett said and squeezed her to him.

As she always did, Sally let him calm and charm her out of her misgivings.

"I'm going to go to that shopping mall before it closes," she said in a while. "Want to come?"

"I hate shopping malls.'

They had seen earlier an American-style shopping mall on the Boulevard de los Heroes. Sally felt the need of something familiar. She didn't know what she needed there. Perhaps nothing except its reassurance.

"Aren't you afraid I'll be molested by guerrillas on my way there?" she asked.

"I think those guerrillas had better watch out you don't molest them. Specially the cute cuddly ones."

She stuck out her tongue at him, picked up her purse, checked herself in the wall mirror and left.

When a knock sounded on the door a minute later, Bennett said aloud, "What did she forget now?"

He opened the door. Turco stepped in fast and kneed him in the groin.

It was more than two hours before Sally got back. When Bennett didn't let her in after she knocked on the door, she had to set down her packages and search in her purse for her key. She opened the door and saw the long ribbons of movie film strewn like fallen party decorations all over the room. She brought her packages in and closed the door.

"Bennett!"

What could have come over him, she thought. She had brought up the subject of her money financing the film when she had been upset earlier. Had he done this just to show her he didn't need her or her money? No. He would do something else, but never interrupt or damage his film.

"Bennett?" Her voice was more uncertain now.

She crossed the room and peered into the bathroom, afraid of what she was going to see. There was no blood on the tiles, no body hanging in the shower. Bennett had disappeared.

Back in the room, she searched about for a note, stepping over the black streamers of film. She wouldn't have been worried at all by his absence had it not been that every inch of film they had brought with them now lay exposed over the chairs, bed and carpet. Something had gone wrong. The two movie cameras were empty but intact. So was her sound equipment. None of the tapes were missing. Then she noticed that the locks on her suitcase were open. That was where they had stored papers, tickets and other things they did not want to leave lying around casually in the hotel room. She had the key to the suitcase in her purse. Its locks had been forced open. But nothing inside was missing.

Another two hours elapsed before she decided to call for help. She had kept hoping that Bennett would walk back into the room with a smile on his face and an explanation. Yet she knew deep down that this was not going to happen.

She even preserved everything as she had found it, leaving the film draped about the room.

Sally called Room Service and ordered coffee. When the waiter knocked, she called, "Come in. The door is open."

The young man's eyes widened in surprise as he looked at the pretty blond American amid the unraveled black film.

"My husband is gone," she said, recalling that they had registered in the hotel as man and wife. Bennett had said it was a Catholic country and they might be forced to stay in separate rooms unless they claimed to be married.

"Your husband gone?" the hotel employee asked warily. "Back to America?"

"No. Disappeared."

The expression on his face changed, and he now looked at the strewn lengths of film as if they told the whole story. "Call the United States embassy."

"I don't want to do that yet." Sally knew that her father would hear of it within hours. He would make it impossible for Bennett to continue with his film here in order to force Sally to leave. Of anyone, her father had to be the last person to know.

"I will give you the phone number of the Human Rights Commission, but you must call yourself." He wrote it for her on a piece of paper. "I hope it goes well for you, senora."

She saw pity for her in his eyes.

Sally sat up in the chair all night after she got back from the American embassy, hospitals, police stations, army barracks. The woman she had spoken to on the phone at the Human Rights Commission had provided her with a list of places to visit without delay. No one had seen Bennett. So they said. It was after two in the morning when she got back to the Sheraton, dropped off in a National Police car. As she sat in the hotel room, she stared at the door, dozed, stared at it some more, dozed off again. She was sure she had not closed an eye all night when she took a shower at dawn and went to hire a car at Avis. The Ford came with a press card in the windshield that read in large letters: PRENSA INTERNACIONAL.

The Human Rights Commission was the popular name given to a church group, the woman had told Sally over the phone, and was not the same as the government's Commission on Human Rights, whose job was to deny there were any problems. The building was small and on church grounds. While Sally waited for the woman, she looked through one of the books of photographs of "the disappeared." They were mostly young men—just a photo, a name and a date for each. She shut the book when she could no longer bear to look at their smiling faces in these family photos.

Alicia—she did not tell Sally her last name—was in her early fifties. She wore no makeup, perhaps in keeping with the grimness of her work. Sally suspected she might even be a nun, because of her simplicity, directness and lack of pretension.

"You have the car?" Alicia asked.

"Yes."

"I have phoned the hospitals, the police forces and the army. They all acknowledged having spoken to you last night, which is something. But they claim they know nothing."

"Thank you."

"They all mentioned also that you speak Spanish very well. Did Bennett?"

"None at all." But Sally now knew the answer to this unspoken question. "He had a movie camera. All the film in our hotel room was exposed."

Alicia nodded. "First we drive to the morgue."

Sally took a sharp breath.

Alicia touched her arm. "It will not be easy. But you have to be sure he is not there before we try elsewhere."

She was aware that Sally and she probably meant different things by the word *elsewhere*.

There were five new bodies of young men at the morgue. None matched Bennett's description, and Alicia spared Sally the trial of looking at them by doing so herself. Sally gave her a photo of Bennett.

Alicia came out to the car, shaking her head and smiling. Sally breathed more freely again.

"Where do we go now?" Sally asked. "The hospitals again?"

"El Playon and Puerta del Diablo."

Sally's face tightened. El Playon she had heard about—a lava field where assassins dumped the bodies of their victims. The Devil's Gate was new to her.

"What is Puerta del Diablo?" Sally asked.

Alicia took this as Sally's choice of destination and gave her directions. After they got going, she added, "Puerta del Diablo is more than just a body dump. The locos in some death squads use it as a kind of ceremonial execution place."

Sally had a cold foreboding about the place. An overall view of the city could be had from the surrounding hills, called Los Planes de Renderos. She drove to the highest peak in Balboa Park. There was a space for cars at an overlook on the top.

"They shoot them here," Alicia said, standing at the edge, "and the bodies tumble down."

The city lay spread out beneath them in a shroud of smog. Sally looked down the steep slope of angular rocks on which grew clumps of ferns and mountain plants. "We have to climb down to see?"

Alicia nodded. "Follow me."

Sally tried not to look down at the huge drop below her. It was not a sheer drop; and if she had slipped, she would have fallen fifty feet at the most. The two women climbed down slowly, and Sally carefully followed Alicia's directions about footholds, handholds and slippery places.

Alicia pointed. There were some white rib bones and arm or leg bones—Sally did not know which—along with two human skulls. One skull had a bullet hole above the right eye socket.

When they found him, Sally knew it was Bennett right away from his shirt and pants, before Alicia pulled the body over to see the face. A cross was slashed on his forehead, and one on each cheek. He had been shot through the left ear.

Chapter 3

THE same pool of green water gave off the same
bad smell in the village square when Sally got off the bus
from the city. The beggar was not on the church steps and
there was no sign of the two small pigs by the roots of the
withered trees in the center of the square. Otherwise the
place was the same as when she and Bennett had arrived
the morning before. She even recognized some of the
children in tattered clothing. They all seemed to know her.

"Buenas dias, senora!"

She smiled at them.

Sally felt the loss of Bennett deeply as she repeated their
actions of the previous day, this time without him. She went
to the cinder-block hut with the Coca-Cola sign and pushed
open the door with the flaking lavender paint. The middle-
aged man sat behind his counter by the dim light of the tiny
window high in the wall. Sally wondered if he sat like this
all day. The soccer player on the calendar still had not
kicked the ball and the maharajah still had not beheaded the
saint in the holy picture. But Bennett was gone. Forever.

"Senor, I want you to take me to the guerrillas."

He flinched as if she had thrown scalding water on him.

Then he spoke very carefully. "The guerrillas have gone. Up into the mountains."

"I'll pay," she offered.

"Where is the senor?"

"Dead."

"I'm sorry. Was he disappeared?"

"Yes, they disappeared him," she said, using the verb common in El Salvador, "but we found his body."

"The situation . . ." He shook his head.

That was what everybody in El Salvador called their civil war, "the situation."

Sally wondered for the first time if Bennett had been murdered at least in part for what had taken place in this village, and whether this man might have informed on them. Up till now she had blamed his death entirely on the Bermudez incident. She looked closely at the shopkeeper and thought it very possible he had informed on them. Yet she could feel no animosity toward him. She and Bennett had intruded on his life. Then again, the way he had been startled by her mention of the guerrillas indicated to her he was in some way connected to them or at least in sympathy with them. But would that be enough to prevent his informing on them to the army? For his own safety? After all, she and Bennett were just foreigners. Yet it was this man who had shown them the bodies, given Bennett his chance to make his film of them. Had someone else in the village informed? Or was it connected solely with Bennett's filming of the attack on Bermudez? She would never know and she was too weary to care. If this man was an army informer, she'd give him something to tell them this time.

Sally realized she had been standing there staring wordlessly at the shopkeeper. She hastily pulled a Kleenex from her purse and wiped away her tears.

He fumbled beneath the counter and handed her a lukewarm Coke.

"Thank you."

He looked at her suitcase. "You wish to stay with the guerrillas a little while?"

"Yes."

"And you wish to hire me to take you to where they are?"

"Yes." Sally took a hundred-dollar bill from her purse and placed it on the counter between them.

He ignored it.

She was unsure whether he was holding out for more money or displaying his Hispanic male dignity.

"I could take you to where the rebels are," he said after a little while. "What if they decide you are a spy?"

"They can check for themselves that the senor was killed by a death squad at the Puerta del Diablo."

"They will check, senora. If they suspect a trick, you will die."

"It's no trick. I only wish it hadn't happened."

"Sad, very sad." He patted her arm. "We have become too accustomed to such things here. You must forgive us if we seem unfeeling."

"Everyone has been sympathetic. Even the police."

As they left the cinder-block hut, he slipped her hundred-dollar bill behind the holy picture and winked at her. "Don't tell the guerrillas you gave me filthy Yanqui dollars."

The old Buick sped along the road for a while before turning off onto a dirt road that led into scrubby foothills that reminded her of those in Southern California. The shopkeeper drove at the same speed he had on the paved highway, despite how the car now dipped, lurched and clanked on its broken front suspension. Sally at times kept her side window rolled up to avoid choking on dust, and at other times rolled it down to avoid being baked alive in the closed-up car. The Salvadoran raised and lowered his own side window in accord with hers, a Central American male courtesy she found particularly irritating.

His gallantry deserted him after they had gone a way into the hills. He stopped the car and turned off the engine.

"Let it cool," he said.

He seemed furtive. She did not know what to expect.

He produced a large, spotlessly clean white handker-chief from his pants pocket. After smoothing the wrinkles and folds, he tied it carefully by two corners to the top of the car's radio aerial. He fished into his pants pocket again before slipping behind the steering wheel and pulling out rosary beads. He kissed the crucifix and wound the beads around the stem of the rearview mirror so that the crucifix dangled and swung. Then he crossed himself and turned the key in the ignition.

The car's progress was slow now, and he stopped every once in a while to look about or perhaps let himself be seen. Sally realized he was now so preoccupied with his own safety, he was hardly aware of her anymore except as an object to be delivered. He did not speak, and neither did she.

He braked the car and turned off the engine in a broad valley with fields of young corn in the bottom and, on the slopes, many bushes, which she supposed were coffee, beneath taller shade trees. For the next fifteen minutes, the only things they saw move were some butterflies and a big hawk quartering the upper end of the valley.

"Here they come now," he said and pointed through the windshield at the side of a hill.

At first she could make out nothing. Then she saw a man's head and shoulders. He wore a green peaked cap and a green army shirt, and he was hardly visible as he walked through the chest-high bushes and growth. She saw another man to his left, and another and another. In all, she counted eight men walking abreast down the hill toward them, with perhaps twenty yards between each pair of men. Their movements were calm and deadly. Sally felt suddenly very much afraid.

The shopkeeper had put her suitcase at the side of the road. He was now holding her door open for her and saying something to her.

"You must get out, senora. Please, senora."

She did as he said and stood with her suitcase by the side of the road.

The Buick made a dust-raising U-turn off the road into a field and back onto the dirt road again. The driver's mood seemed to have grown suddenly lighter, and the white flag flapped cheerfully on the radio aerial as the old car bounced away, gathering speed.

Alone, Sally turned to face the eight men advancing toward her down the side of the empty valley.

"I can't carry it any farther," Sally said petulantly and dropped her suitcase.

Her guerrilla escort stopped and waited for their leader to speak.

"Pick it up and come along," he said.

"I can't. I'm exhausted."

"Maybe you should have hired servants to look after you out here," the rebel suggested sarcastically.

"I'd carry the damn suitcase if I could," she snapped. "I'm not physically strong enough."

"Then you shouldn't have brought it. You should only bring into the mountains what you can carry yourself, instead of expecting others to do your work for you."

"Will none of you help me?" Sally asked plaintively.

"We're permitted to carry only essentials and aids to the revolution."

She opened the case and stuffed some pairs of jeans, panties, bras, T-shirts, a sweater and sneakers into a nylon laundry bag. Her toothbrush, hairbrush and a few other items completed the bundle.

"You should be able to manage that," the guerrilla leader said patronizingly.

"But what about all these beautiful clothes?" Sally almost sobbed as she looked at the rest of the suitcase's contents.

The men laughed.

"Our women wear combat fatigues," their leader said shortly and set out again.

After one last regretful look at the Norma Kamalis and Ralph Laurens she was leaving behind, she followed him.

With no further complaints, she climbed the steep slopes, stopped and kept still when told to, watched and listened like the others. It was she who heard the sound of the engine first.

"A helicopter," she said.

"Down!" the leader shouted. "Everybody down!"

They all threw themselves facedown in the long grass on the hillside. The helicopter passed a couple of hundred feet above the top of the hill they were climbing and disappeared over its far side.

"A Huey," one man remarked.

"Reconnaissance," another said.

After they had started out again, the leader dropped back and walked with Sally for a moment before wordlessly taking her laundry bag and carrying it for her. She assumed this was a reward for her sharp hearing and prompt warning of the government helicopter's approach. She was aware that the rebel was glancing at her curiously.

"You came to fight?" he asked finally.

She just looked at him as if he were crazy.

"I'm Antonio," he said.

"Sally."

"Sa-lee," he said a few times, getting the pronunciation worse each time. "You came here on a...sudden decision?"

She knew he had been about to say "whim." Obviously men down here had much the same opinion about blondes as they did farther north. She told him about Bennett.

"Won't the United States embassy be upset when you don't appear as planned?"

"I stomped off in a fury when a National Police officer suggested that his men search for a weapon at Puerta del Diablo because it looked to him like Bennett had committed suicide. Can you believe it? Slashed himself on the forehead and cheeks with a blade, then stood on top of a mountain and shot himself in the left ear! He could have done all that in front of the television set back in our room at the Sheraton.''

''Why did he want to make contact with us?''

''To make a fair film. He had to present both sides.''

The rebel was silent for a minute. ''But you brought no camera with you.''

''I couldn't make a film. I just held the microphone while Bennett did everything.''

''So you're not here to fight and you're not here to make a film. What are you here for?'' The question was asked gently.

Sally did not hesitate. ''What else could I do? Go home and admit it was all a tragic failure? Bennett felt we could find out the truth. I feel the least I can do is still try. I owe it to him.''

''I don't think you do,'' Antonio said simply and walked on ahead of her again.

The group came to a halt on top of a ridge. Sally gratefully sat on the grass. The leader dispatched six of the men in three teams of two.

''We will go to our camp while the rest of the patrol complete their rounds,'' Antonio told Sally. ''Leon will come with us.''

Sally nodded to Leon, who was a shifty-eyed, open-mouthed country boy. He did not look her in the eye and played nervously with his automatic rifle.

The three of them passed through a narrow defile that a stream had cut through a long ridge, and emerged at the edge of a huge pine forest that stretched away to the mountain peaks in the distance.

''Wait here with Leon,'' Antonio said, handing back her laundry bag, and he disappeared into the trees.

Sally sat wearily on the soft cushion of dead pine needles. ''Is the camp far from here?''

''Not far.''

The tension Leon put into these two words caused Sally to look at him. He was watching her strangely.

"Is something wrong?" she asked, puzzled.

He licked his lips. "It's lonely for a man here in the mountains." His eyes flicked away from meeting hers.

Sally laughed. "Come on, Leon. You can think of a better approach than that."

"It's true!" he shouted with such force and vehemence he frightened her.

"Aren't there women up here?" Sally asked, hoping to get him talking now and steer his mind onto other things. "Antonio said there were."

Leon spat. "They're dirt! Either they have a man already or they want none. You heard Antonio say they wear combat fatigues. And boots. And guns. Some of them are so ugly and deep-voiced, you'd swear they were men anyway—specially the ones with mustaches."

As she saw him hungrily eyeing her body, Sally wished she were wearing combat fatigues instead of tight designer jeans and a T-shirt.

"You're the first real woman I've been near in twelve months," he gasped and licked his lips again. "The women here are all dried-up bitches!" He came at her, dropping his rifle and unzipping his pants. He waved his erect dick in her face as she sat in the shade of the pines.

"I've seen better," Sally remarked coolly.

He hooked two fingers in the neck of her T-shirt beneath her chin and ripped the entire garment from her body. He hooked the same two fingers under her bra between her breasts and tore it from her, revealing her perfectly formed mounds and their pink nipples.

Sally stared in horror as his swollen member, right before her face, exploded in a welter of blood and ruptured tissues. Her face and breasts were splattered with the gore. Leon clutched his hands to the stump of his penis and, screaming in agony, half-ran and half-danced away.

Sally looked up to see a somber-faced young woman in combat fatigues holding a huge automatic pistol in her left hand. A curl of gray smoke rose from the gun's muzzle.

The woman said to Sally, "I'm one of the dried-up bitches Leon was telling you about."

Andre Verdoux, Mike Campbell's buddy from the bad old days in Angola, met his plane at Zurich. The city was deep in snow.

"It's beautiful," Mike said with all the wonder of a desert-dweller.

"That's the trouble with Switzerland," Andre complained. "It looks like a color photo of itself. You may not think so kindly of it in twenty-four hours' time when you're tramping around in the snow with a pack on your back. Eat, drink and be merry, for tomorrow we climb."

After a day in the city of Zurich, capped by a huge gourmet dinner, they retired to their hotel rooms at ten. Andre phoned Mike's room at three-thirty in the morning, and by four they were driving westward out of the city in pitch darkness and at a temperature well below freezing.

Andre was in his mid-fifties. The older he grew, the fitter he stayed, and his constant attempts to prove he could still hack it with the toughest sometimes got on Mike's nerves. Andre, a Frenchman, had been with their forces in Indochina and had survived the Viet Minh assault on Dienbienphu. He had been with the French in equatorial Africa and with the Belgians in the Congo. After the Portuguese abandoned Angola, he and Mike had fought with Holden Roberto's forces against the Cuban-led leftists until the CIA abandoned Roberto. It galled them both that the American-backed anticommunists there had been forced to quit, while the anticommunists led by Jonas Savimbi in the southern part of the country—backed by South Africa— held out to the present day against the Cuban-dominated Angolans.

Andre and Mike had been together as mercenaries on a

number of missions since then. But now Mike felt it was time for Andre to hang up his guns and grow old gracefully. A man past his prime can get too many of his comrades killed with his slow reflexes or lack of drive. For Andre, this was what he had always feared. He would prefer a blade of tempered steel pushed slowly into his heart to suffering the colder steel of icy rejection for his being "too old" to go on a mission.

Andre had persuaded Mike to take him along on a recent mission inside Vietnam. Mike had been unwilling at first, but finally gave in because of Andre's special knowledge of the area's languages and customs. Andre had proved himself a valuable member of that team.

Mike guessed Andre's invitation to him to spend a week inspecting the Swiss army in training was intended to soften his expected future resistance. Mike did not know what Andre's status with the Swiss army was. Andre told him only that he was finishing a two-month stint as a "consultant." When Mike agreed to go, two days later he received in the mail an "honorarium" of $5000, to cover his airfare and expenses. The check was from a Swiss merchant bank in New York City.

Andre swept the BMW smoothly along the dark road. The snow was pushed into walls on either side of the road, and they loomed whitely in the headlights. The inside of the car was very warm. Mike was suffering from the multiple effects of the previous night's celebration and jet lag. He fell into a deep sleep, strapped into the bucket seat.

It was bright daylight when he awoke. His ears popped. They were in the mountains, about to enter a picture-postcard village. Mike saw that the signs above businesses were in French—he should have guessed Andre would locate himself westward in the French-speaking part of Switzerland. The BMW pulled into a schoolyard. About thirty men stood about, next to their packs and weapons, stamping their boots to keep their feet warm.

Andre wasted no time on introductions. He outfitted Mike and himself in a green windproof jacket and pants, a peaked cap with earflaps and rubber-soled boots. Sausage, raisins, cheese and chocolate were stowed in their backpacks along with maps and a medical kit. In short time, the men were climbing single file up the steep slope behind the village. On the far side of the slope lay country with pitching valleys whose walls were too sharply angled to hold snow. The international set did not come here to ski. The army officer came down the line of men and spoke to Mike in slow, straightforward French.

"What would you like to see?"

Mike grinned. He knew that Switzerland had only a tiny regular army and that all these men were civilians putting in their three weeks of annual compulsory training. So far this morning he had not seen two men walk in step. There was something about the way the men slouched unwillingly along the mountain that reminded him of kids on a school trip. He would not be too hard on them. He'd ask for something vague and let the officer order what he thought the men could deliver.

Mike pointed across a shallow basin to a sharp ridge. "I see enemy helicopters make a surprise sweep over that ridge and land combat troops."

The words were hardly out of Mike's mouth when the officer shouted, "Helicopters landing enemy troops!" He pointed at rock outcrops. "There! There! There! And there!"

Rifles rattled. Mike could see rock being chipped by the live ammunition. A three-man team ran beneath the hail of automatic fire toward one rock outcrop. All three threw grenades and blasted chunks out of the rock outcrop. If it had been a chopper, it would now be twisted metal.

Another chopper was taken out seconds later with more grenades, but Mike's attention was caught by a two-man team attacking an outcrop to his left. One man carried a rocket tube strapped to his back. He threw himself flat on the ground so that the rocket tube was aimed at the chopper, and his partner fired the projectile.

The outcrop exploded in a great orange ball of flame and showered down in fragments on all their heads.

"How was that?" the officer yelled at Mike.

Both were half-deafened by the gunfire and explosions.

"Very impressive," Mike yelled back. "It would be a credit to an elite squad of full-time professionals."

The officer nodded, pleased. He said, "I'm a chef in a hotel kitchen."

Dwight Quincy Poynings left his office on Federal Street, in downtown Boston's business district, punctually at seven minutes to five. He liked to give his executive secretary, through his absence, a few minutes for personal things before she left for the day at five. He strode briskly along Franklin Street, following his accustomed route into Bromfield Street, rounded the Park Street Church to continue along the edge of the Common to reach Beacon Street and then Walnut Street; and from Walnut it was only a matter of a few hundred yards to his house on Chestnut Street and the relative privacy and peace of Beacon Hill before the tourist season.

He had just entered Park Street, by the Common, when a short, dark person of foreign appearance accosted him.

"I don't think I know you, sir," Dwight Quincy Poynings informed him and hastened onward. One of the amazing things about some foreigners, Dwight reflected, was that they seemed to have no qualms about approaching a perfect stranger. Since Poynings was six-two and the stranger about five-eight and half his weight, the Bostonian was reasonably assured that robbery or assault was not the motive.

"Mr. Poynings, I have a message for you."

The damn fellow spoke English with an abominable accent, Poynings thought, but it was undeniable he knew who Dwight was. It could be an urgent business matter.

The man sounded Spanish. Perhaps he was related in some way to one of the Hispanic players on his pro baseball team, although they all had agents and managers, as he knew to his cost. He slowed just enough to allow the little foreigner to trot along beside his great strides.

"I'm from the Nicaraguan embassy in Washington," the man explained.

Poynings was amazed. "I didn't know they let your sort into Washington. Nicaragua, you say. Whereabouts is it?"

"Central America—"

"Dammit, man, I meant your embassy in Washington."

"Sixteen twenty-seven New Hampshire Avenue," the man said.

"I'll look into it. The fact that you people frolic on the diplomatic cocktail circuit here in America might make a nice news item."

Poynings noted that the foreigner had the insolence to smile at this. What was Boston coming to? Here he was being harassed by a smiling communist on a spring evening next to the Common!

"I wish to speak to you about the treatment of Marxist countries on news programs aired by your chain of television stations. Your extreme antileftist views—"

"I have heard enough, sir!"

"—your extreme views may have to be modified now that your daughter Sally has joined the brave fighters in El Salvador's glorious struggle for freedom."

Dwight Quincy Poynings stood absolutely still for a long time. Then he started breathing again.

"I didn't know . . ." Poynings' voice trailed off.

"Your State Department hasn't told you?" The foreigner clucked his tongue as an adult might over the behavior of a naughty child. "Those people can be so unreliable."

"I don't even know if this is true." Poynings came back on the attack again. "Why should I accept your word for it?"

"You already have, Mr. Poynings."

Dwight did not try to deny it. "And what's this? Extortion? You want something in exchange for her freedom?"

"I am not here to bargain with you, Mr. Poynings, nor have I the power to do so. Your daughter has joined the leftist guerrillas in El Salvador. She is not in Nicaragua, and has never been, so far as we know. Aware of the family bonds that must bind you together, the Nicaraguan government, out of simple humanity, is bringing you news of your daughter's whereabouts—which is more than your own government is apparently willing to do. We have nothing to trade with you. This matter will remain confidential until you or your government chooses to publicize it, even though news of a nationally known conservative's daughter joining the worldwide struggle for workers' freedom would be, as you might put it yourself, a feather in our cap."

"What is it you want?" Poynings insisted.

"Nothing more than a somewhat more favorable presentation of TV news on Nicaragua and Cuba, and less favorable treatment of the rightist Salvadoran and Honduran governments."

"You and I become pals, right?" Poynings asked sarcastically.

"Sally is such a pretty young girl, Mr. Poynings."

The little bastard turned out to have a better grasp of English than he had first thought, Dwight decided as he watched the foreigner hurry away. Dwight wondered if what the Nicaraguan had said about family bonds between him and his daughter was a deliberate insult. He hadn't seen or heard from Sally in more than six months. Or was it a year?

Chapter 4

HARVEY Waller couldn't go home to Flemington, New Jersey, anymore. Some nights when he couldn't bear the loneliness, he'd drive there and just slowly move about the streets he had grown up on, keeping the car windows rolled up in case someone recognized him. The FBI had made his life a nightmare: questioning people in the town who had known him, coming back again and again with more questions and blurred photos that might and might not be of him—no one could tell—giving them emergency phone numbers to call if they should ever see him again, in Flemington or anyplace else in the world. Some of his friends had told him what was going on. He had thanked them and ordered them to do their duty as good Americans—phone the FBI and say they had seen him.

Harvey still had friends here. He knew what they said about him—that he had come home from Vietnam funny in the head. He could agree with them that he was now a different man than he would have become if he had stayed put in Flemington, New Jersey. He had left as an innocent small-town kid and come back a hardened veteran with his eyes opened to what was really happening in the world.

Harvey could see how ridiculous it must seem to someone who knew nothing but small-town life (although Flemington was hardly the boondocks, being close to both Philadelphia and New York City); he could readily see how ridiculous it must seem in the eyes of such a person that the Soviet Union had agents and sympathizers in key positions at every level of American life.

His certain knowledge that the Soviets were on the verge of subverting America through their cunningly planted agents was what distinguished Harvey, in his own view, from the common herd. He might be one of the sheep, but he at least knew he was being driven and who was driving the herd or flock or whatever. Almost every day, he saw some other subtle thing that added to the evidence against the Russians.

The patriotism of the vast majority of his fellow Americans was something Harvey did not doubt. They just did not see what was being done to them, and would not see what was happening till it was too late. Thus it became the sacred duty of the farseeing few to protect the many—and not by words alone but by action.

This was where Harvey Waller stood up to be counted. Where others hesitated and were lost, he strode forward bravely and took up arms against the enemy.

Chips Stadnick glanced at the photo in his hand and knew he had his man, Tuesday morning, coming off the New York shuttle at Boston's Logan airport. Chips was big, had a flat face and a broken nose, knew he stood out in a crowd, so he hung well back and gave the man a very loose rein. The man took a taxi, and Chips followed in a hired Dodge Dart with a missing cigarette lighter, which meant he had to light one Marlboro off another since he had no matches. The taxi came out of the tunnel and headed toward the harbor along the Fitzgerald Expressway. It pulled up outside the McDonald's near the Tea Party ship. Stadnick stayed in his car and waited.

He had found himself a nice source of work, a constant trickle at high fees that paid the rent and the child-support payments. And the liquor store. He could charge his expenses and no one gave a fuck, because this was TV and nothing was real anyway. Like they have these big show-biz lawyers, he was now a show-biz private investigator. He even had an appointment to meet the big boss at three that afternoon—the great Dwight Quincy Poynings himself. Chips had shaved and put on a tie for the occasion. He hoped he'd be done with this creep by then, otherwise Poynings would have to wait.

What was the weirdo doing? Flying from New York City to take a taxi to a McDonald's in Boston! Maybe he should follow him in. No, he couldn't risk that. If he was noticed there, he'd be spotted later when he tried to tail him. The banana had arrived at the airport with a shabby raincoat that looked as if it had been to a laundromat instead of the dry cleaner's, a *Wall Street Journal* and a perfectly furled black umbrella that would have pleased the British ambassador. And ended up in McDonald's at nine in the morning.

Of course, this crazy had already tried to kill one of the TV news investigative reporters last Tuesday. Which was where Chips came into the story. Poynings had lost a reporter at his Nevada TV station to some hidden interests in a Reno gambling casino. There had been a phone call from Chicago to explain everything, and they had never found the body. After that, when things looked dangerous, Poynings' orders were that the newsroom hire outside help. This was liberally interpreted by some station news producers as meaning that when the job was tedious, call in Stadnick. Chips didn't mind. He was paid good bread, and there were no kickbacks involved.

The news people had been tracking this present weirdo

in Philly, New York and now Boston. They had seen him by chance at Logan airport one Tuesday morning, and he had shown up the next two Tuesday mornings also. This was his fourth known Tuesday arrival in Boston. He had given them the slip each time. The news department had definitely tied him to a bunch of mercenaries—some kind of kamikazes that the State Department didn't want to hear about but hoped would die quietly in some dismal swamp far away from newsmen and cameras.

But this was only a part-time occupation for this one. The news people claimed he was assassinating communists as another of his sidelines—and not old folk-singing commies from way-back-when-in-the-dust-bowl, but big-time powerful bolshies that the FBI could pin nothing on. The guy's source of information was near the top, so it was said. He had made some mistakes, wasted innocent people, but his batting average was high for hitting real spies in sensitive places. Come to think of it, the weirdo had taken out one of the Russkis with a baseball bat.

Harvey Waller chewed his Egg McMuffin and peered out the window at the Dodge Dart that had followed his taxi from the airport. This was his seventh Tuesday trip to Boston and he intended this to be his last. Jesus, if this went on any longer, the FBI could pick him up for loitering. Who had they got on him today? Only one? Some hotshot, he supposed. Maybe a dumb guy to distract him, take up his whole attention so the smart guy could succeed in staying on his tail this time. Harvey had put the fear of God into the little jerk who had been tailing him last Tuesday, nearly catching him between a wall and his car. He could have caught him, of course, but that was not what Harvey intended, because he admired FBI agents as good Americans who were doing their duty. He and they were on the same side! Fighting the Empire of Evil. Pity they couldn't know it and work with him. But Harvey had been warned, a hero's work is lonesome.

He didn't even want to make these FBI men look foolish or feel bad because they lost him every week. He tried to let them down lightly. But they weren't much good as field operatives, so far as he could see. This one seemed a real dodo—like those TV-series private eyes who are so goddam obvious they even hold their cigarettes in their mouths a certain way. This one chain-smoked. Nervous. Or stupid. Maybe both. Harvey wouldn't hurt him.

Chips Stadnick had a list of thirteen known aliases for this guy, so he preferred to think of him by no name rather than a useless one. The guy came out of McDonald's and crossed the bridge toward the Tea Party ship.

I can't believe this shithead, Chips was thinking. Next he'll be going to the aquarium and then maybe Paul Revere's house.

The Tea Party ship was tied to a small wharf that was at right angles to the center of the bridge. The guy passed the entrance to the wharf and continued across the bridge. Stadnick hurriedly left the car and followed on foot.

The man walked around the southern end of the Federal Reserve Building, a huge metal box on metal legs that always reminded Chips of the walking fortresses in the second *Star Wars* film that they tripped with steel cables towed by those little flying saucers. He had taken his son . . . Enough of that. The weirdo was walking along Summer Street toward South Station—maybe he was going to take the train back to New York after his breakfast at McDonald's! Instead, he ducked into the Red Line subway. Stadnick ran.

He stood on the platform in his rumpled raincoat, reading his *Wall Street Journal*, with his formal umbrella tucked under one arm. When the train came, Stadnick entered the same car as his quarry, at the other end. Bozo was too deep in his stocks-and-shares news to notice much. Stadnick was not greatly surprised when he got off the train at Harvard. He followed him as he walked hurriedly from the subway station to the Harvard Coop. He followed him inside the store. He looked around for him. He wasn't there.

Once inside the Harvard Coop, Harvey Waller rushed to an alcove display of sweatshirts and T-shirts, pulling off his raincoat as he went. He dropped the coat, umbrella and newspaper behind a display case and rapidly pulled on a wig of wavy brown hair and stuck two heavy brown mustaches to his upper lips. He heard a giggle behind him.

A young salesclerk at a cash register had seen everything, and she was very amused. Harvey grabbed a wine-red sweatshirt with a white Harvard crest on its front and brought it over to her.

"Your right mustache is crooked," she said.

He looked in the mirror next to her and quickly adjusted his appearance.

"That's a *little* better," she said.

"It doesn't have to be perfect," Harvey answered.

"It doesn't look very real. And this sweatshirt has to be at least three sizes too small for you."

"I'll take it anyway," Harvey said. "Can you wrap it in a hurry?"

She did and he paid.

"Do me a favor?" he asked.

She smiled.

"Gift-wrap my umbrella."

She laughed and wrapped it in store paper when he brought it to her.

"Don't forget your coat and newspaper," she called after him.

"I'll be back for them in five minutes," he said. "I'll tell you what this is all about then."

"Okay." She guessed it would be some corny joke, and

this guy was old enough to be a professor. But she knew all about *them*.

Harvey deliberately strolled right in front of the poor dumb bastard from the FBI, who had lost his cool and was running this way and that searching for him. But Harvey was now a longish-haired, heavily mustached college type with no coat and two parcels. He glanced at his watch. Twenty minutes or more to while away.

Walking away from Harvard Square, along John F. Kennedy Street toward the bridge over the Charles River, he turned down some steps into the Boathouse Bar. Crossed oars, racing skulls and insulting remarks about Yale hung about the place. A few solitary jocks sat along the bar, glowering into their beer. Maybe Harvard was having a bad year.

Harvey at one time would have been intimidated by a university atmosphere, thinking he was too stupid to open his mouth—or even if he knew what he was talking about, he would be afraid of sounding stupid because he didn't know the right words to use. He had no time to waste on such crap now. He went where his work took him. If anyone meddled with him, he stomped all over them. He even liked Cambridge. People here weren't goddam over-friendly. They let him alone.

Twenty minutes later he was out on the street, walking toward the river. On the grass edge along the river, occasional people with notebooks walked briskly. It was too cold not to wear a coat, but he had no choice about that. Harvey strode along like a health fanatic taking in the river air. He passed one old boy, a dignified professorial type with a stoop, thick-glassed spectacles and a bulging briefcase. In a couple of minutes, Harvey turned and followed him.

He gauged his walking speed so he caught up to the man at the bridge. He crossed over on the bridge's side-walk behind him, the traffic heavy in both directions over the bridge. Harvey tossed his packaged sweatshirt over the bridge wall into the water. He unwrapped his umbrella and threw the paper over the wall. Then he unscrewed the metal tip of the furled umbrella and flicked that into the water.

Walking only a few feet now behind the man with the briefcase, Harvey tested the half-inch hypodermic needle at the tip of the umbrella. He held the needle shaft and pressed it in very slightly so that the hidden rubber bulb exuded liquid at the needle's sharp point. Like a snake's fang. He had taken the umbrella from a Bulgarian in Gaithersburg, Maryland, who would not be needing it anymore. They were at the center of the bridge. A lot of cars. No other pedestrians on their side.

Harvey walked a few quick steps directly behind his victim and poked him in the right buttock with the tip of the umbrella.

"Yikes!" the old fellow howled and dropped his briefcase. He waved his arms and shouted and cursed in Russian at Harvey.

"I'm very sorry, mister," Harvey told him. "I thought you was someone else."

The Russian switched to excellent English. "Even if I were someone who had the misfortune of your friendship, that umbrella of yours delivers a painful jab."

Harvey looked contrite and threw the offending umbrella over the bridge wall into the water. "I'll never do it again, sir."

Surprised at Harvey's gesture, the Russian nodded. Harvey picked up his briefcase and handed it to him.

"Thank you," the man said.

"Commie motherfucker," Harvey said pleasantly to him and continued quickly across the bridge.

He looked back from the Harvard Business School side and saw to his satisfaction that the old geezer had started to stagger a bit, as if he had had one too many.

Dwight Quincy Poynings had no true need for an office except as somewhere to go during the day when he hadn't any particular plans. A reception area, a conference room and his private office made up the suite. An executive secretary answered the phone and typed his occasional letters. Family lawyers and accountants watched over the family businesses. The enterprises that Dwight had initiated himself—the TV stations and the major-league baseball team—were managed by professionals who made it clear to him they would resign instantly if he encroached upon their areas of responsibility. This he did now and then, till he grew bored and had to rehire the people who had walked out—often having to pay them ridiculous increases in the process. If it weren't for his ocean-racing yacht and his political views, Dwight felt he would be lost. And first time he won either the Bermuda or the Fastnet, he was going to start building a boat for the America's Cup.

Two sons at Dartmouth, one daughter married, and then there was Sally. He never could make head or tail of that girl, even when she was little. Even so, this El Salvador business was a bit much. What could she have in mind?

He was depending on Harrison Sloane Dudley to enlighten him. Dudley and he had been to Dartmouth together in the old days. Now that Dudley was a leading light at the State Department, Dwight felt he would get reliable inside information. In addition, Dudley had been terribly embarrassed by the fact that Dwight had heard first from those awful Nicaraguan people about Sally's whereabouts. Dwight sat in his office and waited for him, without much to do. The baseball season hadn't started yet, so there was nothing but women's programs on TV.

The two old friends greeted each other heartily.

"Sorry I couldn't make lunch, Dwight, because I've a heck of a schedule here in Boston today. Gave them your office number here, in case something comes in. I hope that's all right."

"Of course. How're things in Washington?"

"What's not tying itself into knots is unraveling,"

Harrison Sloane Dudley said without too much concern. "Pity about this wretched thing with Sally. They found her suitcase with her passport inside. It was left on some hillside, apparently. The Salvadoran army thinks it's been planted there to trap them and they refuse to send troops into the area. Which may be a blessing in a way, because they seem to cause as much harm as good whenever they actually get around to doing something. No note or anything like a message in her hotel room. But unlike Bennett Ward, who seems to have been abducted at gunpoint from the hotel, she left of her own free will. Very confusing. The Ward boy's body will arrive here in Boston tomorrow."

"I've spoken to his parents," Dwight said, "and of course I'll attend the funeral. It's decent of them to keep Sally's name out of this. I must say I appreciate your efforts also."

Dudley looked uncomfortable. "You can't allow yourself to be blackmailed in this matter."

Dwight looked at him in surprise. "But I'm not. I was the one who told you about that Nicaraguan's demands."

"Quite so. However, any softening of your position as evidenced by the content of newscasts from the TV stations you control could create major tax, licensing and other difficulties for you."

Dwight's mouth dropped open in indignation, and a red flush crept over his jowls. "Are you threatening me?"

"Passing along a message and not mincing my words, as promised. Sorry."

"Now that we know what's required of me"—Dwight's voice trembled with anger—"what the hell are you people doing about my daughter's plight?"

"Nothing."

"That's about as I guessed."

"I'm being straight with you," Harrison said. "Next time she shows, we'll go all out to rescue her. But as you know, we can't do much because of possible political repercussions—the U.S. Army is in El Salvador solely in an advisorial role, and the hands of the CIA are tied. I just hope we don't have a Patty Hearst–type scenario here, Dwight.''

Poynings looked aghast. ''Sally would never do that to me.''

This was enough to confirm in Dudley's mind that Sally very likely would.

The executive secretary buzzed. ''Call for Mr. Dudley.''

He was on the phone for a time, and Dwight moved politely out of earshot. If his old friend Harrison Dudley could sit there and threaten him with income-tax audits and the loss of his broadcast licenses, it was imperative he take action on this mess himself. What could the girl be doing down there? He understood about the boy's wanting to make films and that. But what was she doing now?

This Chips Stadnick person who was due at three would be a start. Certainly Stadnick was his only contact in this rather shady area, although he had never met him.

Dwight looked at Harrison impatiently. They had nothing more to talk about. If at all possible—meaning that if it did not interfere with Harrison's own interests—he would look out for Dwight. That did not need to be stated between them. What friends are for. Dwight wished the fellow would get off the phone and go.

Harrison finally replaced the receiver and stood. ''Have to be off. You won't forget you've all sorts of people looking over your shoulder, will you, Dwight? By the way, there was a little news item that might interest your TV people. I'll tell you, but don't reveal your source. Seems that Russian scientist who died at Harvard earlier today didn't have a heart attack. He was killed with poison, perhaps with a dart from a blowgun. In Cambridge, of all places. You can't say you weren't the first to get that news from us.''

As Dwight walked his old friend to the elevator, he saw what looked like a retired pro-football player with a flat face and a broken nose sitting in the reception area. He had no doubt that would prove to be Chips Stadnick.

When Dwight came back, he ushered Stadnick into his office before him, closed the door after him and went alone to the conference room to phone his news team with the information Dudley had given him on this Russian's death. They loved things like poison darts and blowguns.

"How are things going?" Dwight asked cheerfully when he came back to his office.

"I'm afraid I lost him, sir," Stadnick said.

"Who?"

"The subject I was assigned, sir. The man who tried to kill your reporter last Tuesday. But I'll get him for sure next week."

"Good. Good."

Dwight had other things on his mind. He did not associate the Russian's death with the man they had under investigation, and Stadnick did not mention he had lost his quarry in Cambridge.

"He's a tough nut to crack," Chips said to break the silence that had developed. "But we got a real lead on him now for the first time. One of your reporters remembered seeing him in old footage taken in Thailand after those mercenaries grabbed the Vanderhoven grandson in Vietnam."

"He was one of them?" Dwight asked with interest. "Who was that man they said was commander of the group? A Green Beret they called 'Mad Mike,' wasn't it?"

"Right, sir. Mike Campbell. If you ask me, he's probably some kind of wacko maniac—"

"But he does get results."

"Yes, sir. So I hear."

"That's what's important, Mr. Stadnick."

"Yes, sir. I'll do better this Tuesday."

"I want you to leave tomorrow for El Salvador."

Stadnick recoiled as if hit. "Oh, no. Not me."

"I'm going to tell you something which I want kept very quiet. But first we'll discuss economics. Mr. Stadnick,

I know you've heard the phrase 'Money is no object.' That condition applies here. Succeed or fail, you will considerably enrich yourself by going to El Salvador for me tomorrow.''

Dwight almost smiled at the look of greed on Stadnick's broken face. This man would be a good start. If he could find Sally without undue publicity, Dwight would not have to hide his face from his political friends. Most of all, he would not have to tell his wife their daughter was missing and have to live through her emotional hysteria. He could feel he was getting events back under control. There were so many other things Sally could have done. Why this?

Mike Campbell joined Andre Verdoux on a grassy bank some distance outside an alpine village after passing around bottles of beer and wine to the rest of the company. They had just climbed from the village, laden with shopping bags of bottles. Since Swiss soldiers on maneuvers were forbidden to enter stores to purchase things for themselves, the presence of two foreign observers provided them with a convenient loophole in these regulations.

Mike had phoned Tina in Arizona while they were in the village. He said to Andre, ''I think she's finally begun to believe I really am in Switzerland with you, like I told her. She knows I'd never contact her during a real mission.''

''She sounds like a fine woman,'' Andre said. ''I notice you take care that I never meet her.''

Mike smiled. ''Not because I'm afraid she would fall for your Gallic charm, Andre. It's just that I think she'll be safer if she knows nothing—absolutely nothing—about my mercenary activities, including who else is involved in them.''

''I agree with you. Try some of this—it's not at all bad, for a Swiss wine. Not up to our French standards, of course, but palatable.''

They washed down cheese, smoked sausage, nuts and Swiss chocolate with two bottles of tart white wine and looked at the jagged snow-capped peaks all around them. A warm breeze blew on them from the direction of Italy.

This pastoral serenity was suddenly shattered by a jet fighter that swooped down upon them without warning from behind a rock face, bent the tall grass about them with its wind as it screamed overhead, crawled like a lizard up a mountain face and disappeared over the top.

The soldiers laughed and one shouted, ''I bet the top brass will let us know they have aerial photos of us drinking beer and wine on a hillside while we're meant to be defending our country.''

This drew several toasts of an obscene nature to the top brass and more laughter.

Andre said, ''That man is not exaggerating when he says they will have photos. There's a story of a Swiss air show at which the American, Russian and Chinese military attachés, along with those of twenty other nations, were settling themselves in the grandstand for the show when a Mirage came in the back door, almost scraped the hats off the men in the grandstand and did a backflip over a mountain. When the show ended, each attaché was presented with an aerial photo of himself looking up with a startled expression.''

Mike laughed. ''You forgot to mention, Andre, that Mirages are French-built.''

''I did? We French are so modest.''

''Yes, indeed.''

''In the late fifties, the French army had a group of us training with Mirages in the Charente,'' Andre said. ''The countryside there, all around the town of Cognac, is gently rolling hills with a lot of vineyards. The planes would fly just above the ground, moving up and down with its contours, at incredible speeds. Sometimes the Mirages had to search for us while we advanced from one point to another, both points known to the pilots. Some of those fliers could almost cut bunches of grapes off the vines with a wingtip. They dropped canisters of dye on us and took photos. At other times the planes worked with us against a designated target or a moving enemy. They moved too fast to be of much use for that—helicopters were better.''

"I think the Russians would take a bigger hammering here in Switzerland than they are taking in Afghanistan,'' Mike said, and added, "if they were dumb enough to try conventional warfare in these mountains.''

It was time for their company to move on. As they passed over a bridge that took the only road over a ravine, Andre and Mike looked over the side till they found the unobtrusive metal door in its ferroconcrete side. They knew that inside that locked steel door explosives had already been set in place to blow up the bridge. Everything was ready to go. And some local men back in the village they had just passed through had the keys and necessary instructions.

It was said that every key bridge, tunnel and pass in Switzerland was similarly mined and ready to blow on short notice. The Swiss could make their mountains impassible in a couple of hours.

The Russians would almost certainly choose some easier way around them, as had the Germans in World War II.

Mike was glad he had come. He realized what Andre had wanted him to see—a well-armed and well-prepared populace determined to fight, if they had to, for their freedom and way of life. Not a bunch of freeloaders hoping that politicians would keep their vague promises to them.

Rosita insisted on driving. "Please, Chips, let me. I am very good driver.''

The hired car was insured, so Stadnick did not care how good she was. He gave her the keys. He had picked her up the previous night in a hotel cocktail lounge and paid her to spend the night with him. Besides being pretty and being a good lay, she spoke reasonable English and knew her way around. She gave him what sounded to be a reasonable three-day rate.

She wasn't bad as a driver when she remembered to keep her eyes on the road. They were leaving the city of San Salvador, passing through its outer ring of shanties, hovels and lean-tos.

"Are these the people who have come in from the rural areas to escape the violence?" he asked, remembering something he had seen on TV that, so far as he could recall, had been about El Salvador.

"Yes," Rosita said, waving a hand. "They come for work, but there's so little work for anybody. These people are not as poor as others."

Chips looked at the miserable conditions about him and wondered what being really poor here must look like. Odd-shaped pieces of lumber leaning against each other like houses built of playing cards, sheets of plastic, scrap metal, running children, bony dogs, scorching sun.

"Look down there," he said. "They're living in a dried-up river gulley."

"That's what we call *barranca*."

"Doesn't it flood them out?" he asked.

"Sometimes, in the rainy season."

"You grew up in a place like this?"

"Yes, it was a nice place, lot of friendly people," she said. Then she smiled and touched his knee, taking her eyes off the road to look at him. "I prefer living in luxury hotel."

He pointed out that she was veering left into oncoming traffic.

A minute later she cut off a guy in a big car, who blew his horn furiously, then raced after and overtook them. When the driver saw it was a pretty girl who had cut him off, his anger changed to laughter and the two cars had a friendly race, side by side, that made Stadnick's hair stand on end.

Rosita laughed and slowed down. "You come all this

way to El Salvador, Chips, and it is not the guerrillas who kill you, it is a woman driver.''

After an hour, they pulled into the small town's dusty square.

''It's the one with the Coca-Cola sign.'' He pointed, checking once again the typed instructions that had been ready for him at the American embassy.

Inside the cinder-block hut, the heavyset man behind the counter politely bade them good day.

Rosita told him in Spanish what Chips had told her to say. ''This norteamericano works for the blond girl's father, the one you drove out to the guerrillas. We know it was you who took her. The National Police reported it to the American embassy. The embassy has insisted that you be allowed to remain free.''

''Nobody here wants to harm me. The soldiers are my friends.''

''It seems to me you're playing a dangerous game,'' Rosita commented.

''And you?'' he challenged.

She laughed. ''I do it for money. Here is the name and hotel in San Salvador of my norteamericano. He says the rebels should contact him there so they can talk.''

''That will cost him a hundred Yanqui dollars.''

Rosita raised her eyebrows in appreciation and said to Chips in English, ''He say he want one hundred Yanqui dollar.''

''A hundred dollars!'' Chips rooted in his pocket. ''Here, give him this twenty.''

The shopkeeper held up a hand and shook his head.

''Fifty,'' Chips offered.

''Cincuenta,'' Rosita translated.

''Ciento,'' the man responded.

Rosita began in English, ''He say—''

''I know, I know.'' Chips peeled off another four twenties from a wad, added them to the fifth bill and handed them to the man.

He sensed Rosita's eyes following the thick wad of bills from which he had peeled the five twenties, and he allowed it to float under her nose a moment to arouse her desires.

Seven members of the Clara Elizabeth Ramirez Metropolitan Commando sat on wood boxes beneath the banana-leaf thatch of a shack in a barranca near the San Salvador football stadium. They were secure here with the poor as their watchdogs. A lone policeman or soldier would meet a bullet or steel blade within minutes in this barranca, and the arrival of an armed force would raise an alarm a mile around them. And this was not a place where strangers chose to wander and spy. Not if they wanted to live to see another day.

"We have to wait for Paulo for orders on what to do," an intense young man argued. "He knows the whole story. We don't."

There was much grumbling about this.

"These Cubans think they are better than us," another said. "We always have to wait for Paulo or one of the other Cubans to tell us what to do. I say we take action for ourselves."

"What action do we take? No one in El Salvador knows what's going on, rightist or leftist. At least the Cubans and Nicaraguans have outside contacts and access to hard information."

"They feed us what they want us to believe," the first shot back, "and leave out anything that doesn't suit their purposes. You ask what we should do. I'll tell you. Let's find out what this Chips Stadnick has to say. What harm can that do?"

"Sounds reasonable," another concurred.

"We'll wait for Paulo because we're under orders to wait for him. I don't like Paulo Esteban any more than you do, but as members of this commando we obey orders, not give them."

"I want to hear some reasons this time," another grumbled, but they all stayed where they were.

After a while, two young boys ran into the shack. "He's coming!"

"Good. Make sure he was not followed."

The kids ran away again.

Paulo Esteban had a big head on a broad pair of shoulders, and his large, thin-lipped mouth gave his face a serious judgmental look that went well with his piercing eyes. Fidel Castro was supposed to have said of him that he was a perfect blend of brains and brawn. Paulo sensed his lack of welcome among the seven members of the commando. They had to be made to realize that the revolution had no time for their feelings.

"We have to make up our minds how to deal with the norteamericano Stadnick."

Paulo gazed at the man who had made this statement. So they were going to show him their independence by making it sound as if they were calling the shots. He could go along with that. He took his time in pulling up a crate before he sat on it.

"Some of us think we should find out what it is this Stadnick has to offer. He says he works for Poynings."

Paulo nodded. "So he says."

"You think he's CIA?"

"I didn't say that." Paulo raised a big hand. "Maybe he does work for Poynings."

"Then we talk with him?"

"Why?" Paulo asked.

"To find out what he's here for!"

"I could tell you that," Paulo said. "He's here to finger you for the police and the army."

"How do you know, cubano?"

Paulo ignored the unfriendliness. "You heard that the Nicaraguans contacted Poynings in Boston for you? They'll convey all your demands to him up there. So what's this Senor Stadnick doing down here? You trust him more than you trust our Nicaraguan friends? You want to talk with this gringo?''

Paulo was pleased to hear a respectful silence.

He went on, ''Even if this Stadnick has been sent here by Poynings to make an offer to you, why would you think it was genuine if Poynings had to go behind the backs of the Nicaraguans to do it?''

Another silence.

Paulo now spoke in a rapid, toneless, matter-of-fact voice. ''The members of the Revolutionary Committee for San Salvador Province have decided not to deal with this Senor Stadnick. They recommend making this clear to the people who sent him as an emissary here.'' He paused and looked at them one by one. ''I'll leave it up to you, my friends, how best to make it clear.''

Chips Stadnick left the Sheraton, in the western out-skirts of the city, and caught a taxi on Colonia Escalon back to the Metrocenter business and shopping complex where his hotel, the Camino Real, was located. He left the taxi on Boulevard de los Heroes and decided to walk around for a while in the cheerful newness of the city. There was nothing grim, dark and historical about the place at all, which was a real plus in his eyes. Chips had none of the New Englander's veneration for musty monuments—he liked glass, aluminum and elevators that worked. He didn't notice the small motorbike that mount-ed the sidewalk some distance behind him.

The noisy little bike was hardly more than a toy, yet carried two grown men. Chips stepped to one side as he heard the scutter of the bike's exhaust come close behind him, and he looked to make sure he was clear of its path.

The bike stopped next to him on the sidewalk. The man on the pillion stuck a little .22 automatic in Stadnick's face and fired five shots into his head and another four into his body as he fell to the pavement.

Then the bike wove between a tree and a garbage can,

squeezed between two parked cars and carried its two riders away into the anonymity of moving traffic.

After a quick look at the face to see if the body was that of anyone they recognized, pedestrians hurried on about their business.

Chapter 5

THE snow had melted clean away in the south-western corner of Vermont; the runoff was still trick-ling from the Green Mountains; and the ground was soggy in the daytime and frozen hard at night. This was one of the few times of the year a man could find nothing much to do in this part of the world. It was too early for farming or fixing up the house, too early for trout fishing, too late for snowmobiling or hunting, too muddy for walking about, with most people a mite stir-crazy from the long, dark winter. It was the season Bob Murphy called good drinking weather.

He pulled his Jeep into the dirt area before a clapboard house. A large sheet of plywood nailed to the front wall was clumsily lettered in red paint: TOM'S. A neon sign for Genesee beer was suspended in the window. Bob noticed that most of the cars and pickups parked outside had been eaten with rust holes caused by road salt. It had been a bitch of a winter.

The barkeep nodded and wordlessly poured him a triple Chivas over ice.

Bob Murphy always had to remember to keep in check

his Australian high spirits and loud talk when he first walked into a Vermont bar, even in one like this where he was well known. His New England neighbors liked to greet each other with a few suspicious looks and careful nods before they got around to exchanging conversation. Like dogs sniffing each other.

Not that anyone was going to cause trouble for Bob if they didn't like the way he behaved. The Australian had wide shoulders, long, powerful arms and huge gnarled hands on a short stocky body. His straw-yellow hair was cropped short, not much longer than the several days' growth of yellow stubble on his red face. His crooked nose and blubbery lips showed he hadn't won all his fights—or if he had, he hadn't won all of them easily. It surprised people, especially women, to find that his eyes were brown, soft, mild and unthreatening.

"Been a big pool of water near four foot deep down back end of my yard near on two weeks now," one man at the bar announced mournfully.

"Maybe it's catfish you should be farming instead of them fool cows," another said.

"With catfish, you'd get to stay abed in the morning," a third put in. "Be as good as marrying a rich woman."

Bob paid no heed to this jibe at him. His wife, Euniee, was from an old-money New England socialite family. Eunice would never have thought of describing herself as anything so vulgar as "a rich woman," being of the opinion that "a woman of independent means" sounded more dignified. Bob Murphy couldn't give a curse one way or another, which made him independent of both the rich and those that envied them, like the man at the bar who had made the remark.

One of his wife's friends had once remarked that Bob was the only thing in Eunice's life she could not control. Naturally, most of her friends assumed that Bob had married her for her money, since Eunice was no beauty. Only a few realized that she and he were really happy together—the uptight daughter of old Puritan stock and the son of an outback sheep farmer proud to trace his lineage back to an Irish rebel exiled down under as a felon.

Talk in the bar had now turned to a local drunk who had frozen to death on his own doorstep after being locked out by his wife one night a few weeks previously. Bob left the bar and took his Jeep up a side road into the mountains. He felt he needed company but didn't want to talk. He'd go sit and watch Clem Watkins awhile if he was in his workshop. Clem was. He never had much to say to anyone, yet he was generally regarded as friendly and welcoming. If a man had something to say, Clem would listen as he went about his work. If his visitor had nothing to say, Clem still went about his work.

Bob had ordered a hunting knife from him. Clem hadn't started making it yet—in fact, Bob knew it might be months before he got a start on it. So he sat in his workshop and watched him cut a 9½-inch-long strip from a piece of old gang-saw steel blade, 5 inches for the knife blade and 4½ for the handle. He cut, ground and hammered on the steel while Bob thought back on his meeting with Dwight Quincy Poynings. When Bob heard that Poynings, an old family friend of Eunice's, was coming, he was about to take off in order to avoid him.

"Dwight wants you and your friends to rescue his daughter in El Salvador," Eunice told him urgently.

Bob looked at her, surprised. To Eunice, his mercenary activities belonged with his drinking, hunting, fishing—things a woman had to tolerate in a man. To her way of thinking, his combat missions with merc groups were boyish adventures in the woods. She had been to Washington on peace marches while he was in the Australian army in Vietnam. She never could get it straight whom he had been fighting in the jungles of Malaysia along with the British army.

"Bob," she said, "Dwight needs your help. I never protest when you rush off to aid some undesirable types halfway round the world. I think that just this once you might consider helping someone close to me."

For anyone else, this would amount to a fairly restrained request. For Eunice, it was equivalent to going down on her knees and scraping the ground before him. She had been brought up not to ask things of people but to be self-sufficient in all and beholden to none. Not even her husband.

Bob smiled and kissed her. "Certainly, my love. Of course I'll go. But you know what I think of your friend Dwight, don't you?"

"Please don't say it to him. He was quite upset the last time at that charity dinner when you called him an asshole."

"It stopped him talking," Bob said. "That's all any of us wanted."

Dwight came to their house, and Bob listened, along with Eunice, to his tale of woe. Then Bob phoned Mike Campbell in Arizona, only to be told he was in Switzerland with Andre Verdoux. Bob left an invitation for Mike and Andre to visit him on their way home—Tina was expecting him back in a few days, and she said he would call first. Bob added, in what he hoped was a meaningful way, that it was essential for Mike to contact him whatever he was going to do. Bob was pleased to get a call from Mike in Switzerland not many hours later accepting his invitation, and not so pleased at Andre's acceptance also. He had not expected Andre to come, since he and Verdoux had taken an instant dislike to each other when they had first met. This dislike had not interfered with their soldiering on the mission to Vietnam, because both men were professionals and would not allow personal disputes to affect their working as a team. Bob guessed that the Frenchman scented a mission in the offing and knew that if he did not come along, he probably would be left off the team. Certainly Bob would be pleased to leave the sharp-tongued frog behind.

Bob followed the knife-maker to his gas-fired forge in

one brick-lined corner of the workshop. The steel had lost its tempering due to the cutting and smoothing. Clem started up the flames and held the handle end of the steel strip in a pair of tongs. He dipped the blade end into the flames and held it there until the steel turned blue with heat. He kept the steel in the flames till it had changed from this shade of blue to a lighter shade, then whipped it from the flames and plunged it into cold water, which boiled about the metal for a few seconds.

"You'll find some that will heat the steel past blue into yellow or red before they quench it," Clem said, speaking for the first time. He fingered the newly tempered blade. "Me, I never go beyond the light blue color you saw just now. That way the steel don't get too brittle."

Bob nodded.

These were as many words as he had ever heard Clem hook up together all at one time.

Sally looked at the rows of green tents under the cover of the forest trees.

"They are all U.S. Army tents," Gabriela told her. Gabriela had saved her from the rapist, who had since died, Sally had heard, from shock and loss of blood. "The Pentagon supplies us. Look, our men walk about in U.S. uniforms and boots, they carry standard-issue M16s, they eat made-in-U.S.A. rations."

"You captured all this from government soldiers?" Sally asked.

Gabriela laughed. "Not exactly captured. They run away and leave it behind. Some of it we buy from them."

"That must make everyone in Washington very happy."

"I don't think they know what goes on any more than anyone here. It's crazy."

Sally was pleased to exchange her designer jeans and skimpy tank top for camouflage fatigues, and to hide her blond hair in a bush hat. However, she drew the line at wearing heavy boots and kept her running shoes. She also refused a rifle or pistol, and accepted a knife only when told she would need it to cut her food. Gabriela and she shared a tent.

Feeling that she had gained some anonymity, if not acceptance, in her fatigues, Sally wandered about the camp alone and talked to the others. No longer looking like a tourist, she was no longer treated as one. Careful not to ask probing questions, as a reporter would, she kept her conversations polite and unintrusive. A few had Marxist-Leninist replies to the most casual observation, but most talked and behaved exactly like their fellow-countrymen did in the city of San Salvador and the villages she had been to. It made Sally wonder if some private tragedy like her own had caused each of these people to come to this rebel camp.

They seemed in no hurry to interrogate her. First, as she had been warned, they would check the details of her story as she had told it to Antonio and repeated it to Gabriela. No one prevented her from going where she wished. No doubt, if she did not pass the interrogation, she would not live to tell anyone what she was now seeing anyway.

"Are you a communist?" Sally asked Gabriela at one point.

"Maybe."

"I suppose that means yes." Sally looked curiously at the serious dark-haired girl, who was about her own age. Sally decided that if they had been at high school together, Gabriela would have gone to the library while she went to cheerleading practice. "But you can't be a real communist, with all that Stalin and Mao stuff and not letting people do what they want. Is that what you hope will happen here?"

Gabriela looked away. "The government disappeared my father and my brother. Like they did your friend Bennett. My father was a professor at the university, and they closed that down. My brother was a student."

"I'm sorry," Sally said. "Is that when you became a guerrilla?"

"Not at first. I was too afraid. But in a while, my anger grew. Now I'm a freedom fighter." She looked at Sally sympathetically. "That's why I understand what you are going through now. At first you feel powerless, helpless, think there's nothing you can do. But that changes."

So that's what you aim to do, Sally thought, turn me into a guerrilla fighter. I may be dumb, but I'm not that much of a turkey.

Poynings came to lunch the day after Mike Campbell and Andre Verdoux arrived at Bob and Eunice Murphy's large house in Vermont. They sat at a long mahogany table with a silver service, cut-glass goblets and sprays of flowers in vases. Eunice had assumed, for no particular reason, that a formal lunch would be the best way for all of them to get reacquainted and to meet Poynings. It was a disaster. Andre complained about the sauce on the lamb. Bob called Andre an asshole. Dwight tried to make peace between the two and got insulted by both. Mike talked with Eunice, who believed him to be an avid bird-watcher or, as she said, ornithologist. Mike knew only three birds—sparrow, roadrunner and hawk, not counting seagulls— but since Eunice knew even fewer, they got along quite well.

In spite of their seeming lack of interest and Bob's rude interruptions, Dwight Poynings persisted till he got his story told, relating everything he knew, including the State Department's attitude to him and also Chips Stadnick's death, who had been described in his obituaries as a journalist. By the time coffee was served, Dwight looked gloomy and had obviously decided that things were not going to work out for him with Campbell & Co.

"You have a million to spare?" Mike asked him casually.

Dwight blinked. "I don't toss my money around any old how, Mr. Campbell. Although it's not a widely known fact, holding onto one's money once one has got it can be just as difficult as earning it in the first place."

Mike patiently rephrased his question. "Are you willing to spend a million to get your daughter back?"

Dwight thought about that. "Yes."

"I pay the team members a share of one hundred thou each, win or lose," Mike explained. "I take two shares. The rest goes on expenses. Might run you more than a million."

Dwight nodded his agreement.

"Bob doesn't need his hundred thousand," Eunice put in brightly. "He'll do it for friendship's sake, won't you, Bob?"

"No, he won't, Eunice," Mike said firmly. "I make the rules, and those rules say Bob gets his share and holds onto it. No givebacks. Clear?"

"Absolutely," Dwight said.

Bob said with an evil smile, "Hell, the whole lot of us ain't costing Dwight what a medium-good pitcher would demand for a season on his baseball team."

"Yes, but that's an investment," Dwight replied. "I'd earn it all back and more in ticket sales."

"You trying to say your daughter Sally isn't a good investment?" Bob needled.

"That's a low blow, Bob. But I suppose I do look upon my children as emotional investments, and I could say that Sally has not been a good emotional investment."

"You put your money in and expect affection back?" Bob continued to goad him.

"Bob, please stop," Eunice pleaded.

"Eunice, thank you, but I'm capable of taking care of myself," Dwight put in. "Whatever inadequacies I may or may not have as a father hardly concern you gentlemen as a paramilitary group."

Mike handed him a piece of paper. "That's the account number and bank, in Georgetown on Grand Cayman, where you deposit the money. We'll need recent photos of your daughter, a signed statement from you authorizing us to rescue her and anything else at all that you think might help us. The most important thing you can do is maintain secrecy about having contacted us."

"You mean to say you'll definitely go?" Dwight asked, delighted.

"Bob and I will go, but that's the only guarantee I çan offer. The odds will be against us."

Andre was aware he had not been included. He sipped his coffee reflectively. As if his mind were still on the food, he said, "Bob, by any chance was that awful sauce on the lamb one of your Australian specialties?"

After almost a week at the guerrilla camp, Gabriela woke Sally Poynings one morning before dawn.

"We have to move out at first light," Gabriela said. "Get yourself ready."

"But where are we going?" Sally asked, rubbing her eyes.

"I don't know. Somewhere more secure."

"I'm not sure I want to go," Sally announced.

Sally had said nothing yet to Gabriela of her feelings that things were not working out as she had hoped. After all, she had come to find the truth, to find answers. She had now decided there were no answers to be found living in a tent on the pine-covered slope of a mountain. The sound of car horns on the Boulevard de los Heroes would be sweet music in her ears at this moment.

"I think I'll stay on here another day or so," Sally said, "then take a trip into San Salvador and see how that feels."

Gabriela looked at her for a moment and then went away without a word.

Sally was returning to the tent after having washed her face when Gabriela came back with Antonio.

"Senorita Sarah Quincy Poynings," he said in the very formal tones he used when irritated—calling her by her correct name Sarah, which she hated, "when you are in a military camp you obey orders, unless you are in a position to give them."

"I feel like a couple of days in the city, Antonio," Sally said. "Have some hot tamales from a street stall. Spend fifteen minutes in a hotel shower. Then I'd like to try the coastline you guys hold in the province of La Union or Usulutan. I mean, why be a rebel in the mountains when you can be one on the beach?"

Antonio gave her that sarcastic smile she remembered from the time he had made her leave some of her favorite clothes behind in that suitcase in the valley. He asked, "Should I phone ahead to make reservations for you and make sure they take American Express?"

"Don't be mean, Antonio," Sally said. "What's the problem?"

"We have no problem, senorita. We have orders. You move out this morning."

"Are you coming too?"

"No." Antonio's coldness melted. "I would like to, Sally, but I can't."

"And Gabriela?"

"If you want her to go with you, she will go."

"Yes," Sally said without hesitation. "All right, Gabriela?"

"I'd like to, Sally."

Sally noticed the momentary glance exchanged between them. If Sally wasn't exactly their prisoner, certainly Gabriela was some kind of guard over her. But Sally was used to that, and she felt safe with Gabriela around and liked her as a person.

"Better get your coffee and have something to eat, Sally," Antonio said. "You leave in thirty minutes."

As she watched him walk away, Sally regretted not having had a chance to talk with him more over the past days. He was always so busy, and she knew that he had deliberately kept away from her so as not to become distracted from his rebel activities.

She, Gabriela and two men force-marched through the mountain forests nearly all day till they reached another camp. They left that at dawn the following day, with eight new recruits. At the end of three days' constant trekking through the mountains, they had collected twenty-seven recruits along the way and were told that next day they would reach the camp of the legendary Comandante Clarinero.

Sally was excited. Here at last was the real thing! The big time! Comandante Clarinero was the Robin Hood of the guerrillas. He swooped down on government forces, captured them and sent them home gunless to their mothers or wives and children with a stern warning to find a better line of work in the future. He announced raises for workers on the coffee fincas; and the big landowners had no choice but to pay them, even when they had government troops on their land. Comandante Clarinero talked to the *New York Times* and CBS News and so forth on a regular basis. He was banned from her father's chain of TV stations. Now Sally would get to meet him in person! Things were definitely looking up.

They reached the camp about noon, and everyone but Sally spent the next three hottest hours of the day resting in the shade of the forest pines. She pestered many of the comandante's guerrillas with conversation and explored the camp. People began to move about again when the heat abated a little. She heard Gabriela calling her name.

"The comandante wants to talk with you," Gabriela said.

Sally already knew that the biggest tent in the camp was the comandante's office, but that he slept in a small tent too, like everyone else. She had steered clear of his office till now, when she followed Gabriela toward it.

Four men sat behind a folding table under a canopy near the large tent, like judges at a bench. One had thick folders stacked before him on the table, and although he clearly modeled his appearance on that of Pancho Villa, he looked more like a harassed schoolteacher who has just realized he is now going to have to read all these homework projects. He was handsome and young, and Sally's heart skipped a beat as he was introduced to her as Comandante Clarinero. Only one of the other three men made an impression on her. He was a brutal, powerful man with piercing eyes, with a large cigar in his mouth and a big revolver on the table in front of him. His name was Paulo Esteban, and she could tell by his accent he was not Salvadoran. Gabriela told her later that this Cuban had been picked personally by Fidel Castro as his advisor to the comandante.

Sally told her story in great detail. They seemed less interested in her than in Bennett's films and how he knew Bermudez. To her surprise, they never questioned her motivations. Was she of such little importance it didn't matter why she had come? Her annoyance at this was overcome by her awareness that she still could not have given them a clear answer if they had asked. But they didn't.

"Is that all?" she said to Gabriela as the two women left.

"I suppose so."

"But don't they need to know about my political stance and life-style and—"

"No," Gabriela said shortly. "All they need to know is which side you're on. We're all here for our own reasons. After we win and take power, maybe then we'll see what differences lie among us."

"That's when the communists will squeeze out the moderates and socialists in order to grab power for the party," Sally observed acidly.

Gabriela smiled. "It often seems to turn out that way."

Sally welcomed the quick descent of night because she was exhausted after her three-day trek and had taken no rest during the hot part of the day. She and Gabriel had been assigned a tent, and she was just about to creep into it when she heard the notes of a trumpet playing a strange and mournful tune. She sat outside the tent awhile and listened to old-fashioned dance measures and marches with all sorts of decorative trills that might have sounded very ordinary played by a full brass band but which had an eerie quality played on a solitary horn at dusk in a mountain forest.

Sally walked toward the sound. She saw the handsome young comandante sitting alone on a rock playing a battered silver cornet. The cornet's notes were softer, more buttery, than the sharp, sweet notes of a trumpet. She sat at a distance, watching and listening to the melancholy old airs until it was completely dark. At the end of one tune, the comandante got to his feet without warning and walked back toward the tents.

Sally almost called after him, aware that he had not seen her there listening to him. But she did not. She made her way slowly back to her tent in the darkness, her head full of sensual brass glissandos and diminuendos, knowing she would dream about the comandante.

Early the next morning, the comandante led his men from the camp on a series of raids. Apart from Sally and Gabriela, only thirteen were left behind in the camp, and these were some of the recruits who had arrived with them. Gabriela was placed in charge.

A few hours after the others had departed, Sally heard shouting as she walked with Gabriela among the tents beneath the pines. This camp was much more extensive than the others she had seen, but the cover offered by the pines here was not so good as at the first camp in which she had stayed. The trees were bigger here but more thinly spread on the ground. The men shouting were pointing up at the sky, a calm and peaceful blue in gaps in the branches overhead.

"Push-pull! Push-pull!"

"Stay still!" Gabriela yelled at the men who were running about and shouting.

The big automatic pistol appeared in her left hand and she fired two shots over their heads. That stopped them.

"Don't move from where you are!" Gabriela ordered. "Next man who moves, I shoot him!"

No one moved.

Gabriela muttered to Sally beside her, "Damn raw recruits. Where do they come from? They should know better."

Sally didn't have time to dwell on Gabriela's sudden transformation, as the Salvadoran woman's voice was drowned out by the roar of an aircraft flying low overhead.

Gabriela shouted to Sally above the noise, "See the propellers both fore and aft on the engine mounts? That's why we call the plane a push-pull. It's an O-2, an observation craft you Americans give to the Salvadoran air force. They often work with A-37s."

Sally did not ask what an A-37 was. The recruits had stopped panicking and were looking a bit shamefaced. Gabriela put away her big pistol.

"They must have seen something," she announced in a loud voice. She pointed. "Shout to those men over there to keep still. That plane will make a repeat pass."

Sally looked around. Earth had been thrown on the fire the previous night—no smoke rose from it. The tents were green, and everything else was either green also or camouflaged. She had already been told that any brightly colored object that stood out from its background—even an object as small as the notebook with a bright red cover that one recruit was carrying at the time—could be seen quite easily from the air, particularly if it was moving. Sally ran an anxious eye over everything, ironically aware of how she was slipping into the role of a guerrilla and learning survival tactics.

They heard the plane's engines again, coming from the same direction it had approached before.

"He's circled around and he's coming in this time

higher than he was before," Gabriela told them. "You can bet he's spotted something if he's afraid to come in low."

The plane did not continue its flight path, but cut to the left and began to climb in a tight circle directly above them.

"Bastard has seen us!" Gabriela yelled. "He's calling in the A-37s and marking our position for them!"

She ran to a nearby supply tent and came out carrying a four-foot metal tube with a scope mounted on it. In her left hand she carried an energy pack and trailing wires. She hooked up the tube to the energy pack, placed it on her right shoulder and sighted up at the plane through the scope. And waited.

"Damn," Gabriela muttered.

"What's wrong?" Sally ventured.

"I'm waiting for the sound signal that tells when the missile homing system is engaged. This is a Redeye, one of your American surface-to-air missiles. Its infrared homing device zeroes in on the heat given off by the aircraft's engines. I hope the energy system has been maintained."

Gabriela waited for the sound signal, balancing the tube on her shoulder and sighting the O-2 plane through the scope as it circled higher and higher overhead. Sally backed away from her slowly, holding her fingers in her ears.

There was no explosion—only a whistle as the four-foot missile was launched from its carrying tube. Twenty feet above the ground, the missile's main motor took over from its booster and the projectile shot toward its target at supersonic speed.

The two women and the recruits watched the missile streak up to the plane, now very high above them. Five seconds passed, and the streaking dart of high explosives was almost upon its prey when the aircraft dipped its right wing and tumbled out of its flight path.

The missile quivered in midflight, but its force drove it

on past the plane. The projectile rose a little higher, slowed and then dropped like a spent arrow.

"He saw it coming," Gabriela said through her teeth. "We have another, but he's near three thousand meters— almost out of range—as it is." She pointed to one of the recruits. "You, take this norteamericana away from here. Keep her out in the open, away from the trees."

Before Sally could protest, the recruit grabbed her by the left wrist and dragged her after him to the edge of the pine forest. She heard the distant explosion of the Redeye missile hitting the ground and felt the heat of the sun beat down on her as they left the shade of the trees. She followed the recruit down a slope, half-running and half-falling after him, dragged by one arm. He stopped, pushed her down behind a large rock and lay on the ground beside her, looking fearfully up at the sky. The push-pull observation plane continued to circle high above the location of the camp.

A green drab military jet screamed low over their heads, and its racing shadow on the ground passed over them.

A huge billow of flame—blue and white at its core, radiating out to boiling orange with black smoke fringes—lifted giant pines by their roots high into the air. Second and third blasts followed the first in quick succession.

The jet disappeared, but the O-2 came in on a wide circle to inspect the damage. The entire part of the forest where the camp had been was now a roaring fire that was spreading with the wind up the mountain slope. Apparently satisfied with the results, the push-pull plane completed only one pass and flew away.

Sally and the recruit, whose name was Miguel, waited until the fire burned itself out. They ran among the charred trunks, across thick smoldering beds of dead pine needles, to where the tents had been. Trees were still burning around the first bomb crater, and were it not for the cooling breeze from behind their backs, they could not have stood the heat all about them.

They kept moving, running from one less scorched place to another, smeared now with ash and carbon, sweat seeping from every pore of their bodies. There were big flames in the trees higher up the slope as the fire moved uphill away from them, with loud crackling sounds of its burning and choking smoke floating everywhere. They could not find where the tents had been.

"Look!" Miguel pointed.

The bodies lay about the blackened forest floor with only fragments of burnt cloth adhering to their scorched flesh. The smell of cooked meat revolted Sally as much as the sight of the charred corpses, but she forced herself to walk among them with Miguel. She knew that none could possibly be alive, but felt she owed it to Gabriela to look for her, on the remote chance, somehow, something . . . She did not know what, and went on looking.

Sally found the empty Redeye missile tube that Gabriela had fired. Another tube, this one loaded, lay next to a body charred beyond recognition—burned even beyond her being able to tell whether it was male or female. The guerrilla fighters wore no dog tags. Sally could not bring herself to move the flame-shriveled human remains with her foot in order to examine the corpse more closely. She felt cold and empty—too much in shock to grieve for her friend Gabriela—and began walking toward the edge of the burned-over area so she could feel grass under her feet again, get away from the heat and the smell of burning. Miguel followed.

"They are all gone," he said once they were downhill of the burned forest, "the friends I came here with, all gone now. I cannot stay here without them. I will return home."

Sally panicked. "Take me with you!"

"I am only a campesino from a small mountain village," Miguel said. "What would I do there with a blond norteamericana? The soldiers would hear of it and come. Either them or the guerrillas. I can't take you with me."

"But you could drop me off in San Salvador at the Sheraton, on your way," Sally pleaded urgently.

"San Salvador! The Hotel Sheraton!" Miguel laughed. "I have seen pictures of these places. I have never been to a place like a big city. I live in the mountains—in a place like where we are now—a few days' walk from here. I will pray for you, senorita."

"Thanks a lot, Miguel," Sally said bitterly and watched him go.

The sun was getting low in the western sky, and she trembled at the thought of night coming on, with no one for company on this mountain slope except for a dozen bodies bombed and then barbecued in a forest fire. The pines were still burning farther up the mountain, and smoke from the fire stretched away over the valleys and slopes in a long yellow-gray cloud.

Sally thought of Chestnut Street on Beacon Hill. That was the real world. For the first time, she began to believe that she might never see it again.

Chapter 6

"Why not put it bluntly?" Andre Verdoux asked Mike Campbell. "Just say to me, 'Andre, you can't come with us because I think you're over the hill.'"

"Andre, you can't come with us because I think you're over the hill."

Verdoux shook his head. "Mike, you have to say it with conviction—as if you believed it."

"I do believe it!"

"I wonder what you will do when the team gets in a tight spot and you find you can't rely on these younger, inexperienced men. You'll regret not having me by you then. Remember the time in Angola when—"

"Forget it, Andre," Mike interrupted. "If it were just you and me going alone, that would be okay with me. But I can't endanger the lives of the other team members by taking along one man who, through no fault of his own, can't hack it with everyone else. You got more guts maybe than any of the rest of us, but you've put a lot of mileage on your engine and body parts, Andre."

"I'm in better shape than that lamebrain Aussie there," Andre said, pointing at Bob Murphy.

Bob looked away, embarrassed for Andre. He had no liking for the Frenchman, but he respected him as a soldier and did not want to see him humiliated.

Andre himself grew embarrassed by the way Bob did not return his insult through feeling sorry for him. He muttered something in French and lapsed into silence.

Mike went to work to ease his own feeling of guilt at having to treat Andre this way. Mike had let Andre down easy several times, and that hadn't worked. Letting him down hard didn't seem to be working any better.

They sat in the gun room of Bob's Vermont home, sipping twelve-year-old Scotch and looking out through large windows over the lawn to where Eunice and a gardener were hacking at rhododendron bushes.

The peaceful slopes of the Green Mountains rose on the far side of the extensive gardens and a large field with show-jumping fences.

Mike opened that day's *Wall Street Journal*. "It's a good paper for Harvey Waller to use, since you can get it almost anywhere in the country. Though I find it hard to imagine Harvey reading it."

Mike said no more, because only he knew of Harvey's heroic record as a Marine in Nam; his rejection in his hometown as a warmonger and "baby-killer" after he came back; how this, on top of bad combat experiences, had all gotten too much for him, so that now he associated with what Mike regarded as the loony fringe of patriots who saw the Russian KGB messing with mom and apple pie and spreading gypsy moths and elm disease.

Mike flipped the newspaper pages till he came to the classified ads. "Here's the section—BUSINESS OPPORTUNITIES—in which he says he has all his contacts put their ads. Seemingly he knows who it is by the kind of business, plus key words. You know what he assigned to me? ARIZONA DENTAL PRACTICE—Root Canal Work a Specialty—Partner Wanted."

Andre smiled grimly. "That man is emotionally disturbed. I find it interesting you value him more highly than me."

Mike ignored him and turned to Bob. "Can I use your phone number here in the ad?"

"Hell, no," Bob said. "I don't want crazy Harvey calling me here. Use your own number in Arizona."

Mike smiled. "I don't think I will. For the same reason as you."

"You may give him my New York number," Andre said coldly.

Mike phoned Tina to say he would be back in Arizona the next day. But only for a few days. Then he had to take a trip.

"I see," Tina said in a disappointed voice. "For how long?"

"I don't know."

"And it's not Switzerland this time."

"No, it's not."

She found the phone number for him for the Bunch o' Shamrock saloon in Youngstown, Ohio. It was eleven in the morning, but he made the call on the off chance.

"Shamrock," a gruff voice answered.

"You the bartender?" Mike asked.

"That's what I started out as this morning."

"Joe Nolan there?"

"Naw."

"Will you see him later?"

"Sure."

"Tell him I called. Just say Faraway Hills, all right?"

A pause. "I get it. The Call of the Faraway Hills. You're some joker, fella."

This hadn't been Mike's idea—it was Joe's. "Just tell Nolan. Can you write down this New York number for him to call?"

"Sure."

Mike gave him Andre's number.

*   *   *

Like a lot of other people in Youngstown, Ohio, Joe Nolan was out of work. Some of those who had loaded up their cars, said good-bye and left for a new life in what they called the Sun Belt had come back to the grime and spring cold of Youngstown—preferring to be out of work among friends than strangers. A man who has spent fifteen years ladling molten metal from a smelter does not turn in the twinkling of some economic eye into a computer programmer tapping coded jargon onto a keyboard about people's credit status in a twenty-sixth-floor glass-shrouded "controlled environment."

Joe was thin, moved fast, and his face was long and sad. He had very bright blue eyes, long teeth like a dog and light brown hair. He didn't mind being called "mountainy," because his folks had come north from Kentucky during World War II to work in the plants; but when a man called him a "hillbilly," he had better mean it as a compliment—and not too many did.

Joe didn't mind what he had to put his hand to to turn a buck. He had messed with dope-selling, but since that meant dealing with assorted creeps at high risk, he was seeing if he could stay out of that type of employment. Lack of economic security had not hit Joe hard, as it had most of his friends. Since coming back from his stint as a Green Beret in Vietnam, Joe had gone from job to job, woman to woman, drink to drink. . . . When there were no jobs, there were always women and drinks.

From his mission to Vietnam with Mad Mike Campbell, he had taken home what would amount to three or four years' pay for many workers in Youngstown. He hadn't blown it as he'd intended, but had paid for hospitals, funerals, weddings, christenings, charter buses—everything imaginable—for his family, cousins, close friends, fellow union members, the guys down at the bar. Not one bottle of champagne, no visits to Playboy clubs in New York or Chicago, not even a new car. Now the money was gone.

Had been for a month. But his family and friends had not forgotten how generous he had been when he had it. So in Joe's eyes, the money had not been wasted.

There was only one side effect of his generosity that disturbed him: it made him a respected member of respectable society. He had always been a floater; the last thing he wanted was to be a pillar of anything. He hated the way people smiled at him as if he weren't a crazy son of a bitch anymore.

Well, he had found his opportunity now to show 'em that the bad old Joe Nolan they all hoped was dead and buried was still alive and kicking.

His cousin Tommy was retarded, a big harmless slob of eighteen who shambled around the neighborhood with a smile on his vacant face and drool running from his mouth. Occasionally Joe had kicked someone's ass for making fun of Tommy. People who didn't know Tommy were often scared of him, but the locals all had a few kind words for him, and he went through enormous quantities of homemade cookies and Kool-Aid.

"I reckon maybe it was Tommy's own fault he got hit by that truck," his mother told Joe at the hospital, "but that don't mean it's right for the driver to take off and leave him lying there on the road."

Both Tommy's legs were broken, his right hip fractured and some ribs cracked. According to the doctors, he'd be on his back two months minimum.

"And we don't have no medical insurance that covers him now that his father took that non-union job on the building site," she went on. "If that driver had done the proper thing, his insurance company would take care of everything. I'm not asking you to help out, Joe," she added hurriedly. "You done enough for us already, and I heard you're as broke as the rest of us these days."

" 'Fraid so," Joe said. "Tommy told me he recognized the truck and driver. Hit-and-run is a crime. What did the cops say? Tommy said they had been to see him."

"The officer came and wrote down what Tommy said. But the driver denied it." The woman's face clouded with shame. "The officer tried to put it nice to me when he said poor Tommy's word wouldn't count in a court of law; that his evidence would be ruled . . . not regular."

Joe himself talked to the driver of the truck, a loud-mouth who ran metal bars from Youngstown down to Wheeling, West Virginia, five times a week and who liked to highball along a two-lane highway between the plant and Route 11, scaring the shit out of oncoming traffic. Joe spoke to him, and the guy didn't even bother to deny it was he who'd hit Tommy. He told Joe to fuck off, and stuck the barrel of a Smith & Wesson .38 in Joe's neck to make his message clear.

Joe let two days go by so he could simmer down and put in a little thought on how best to straighten out this cowboy. He sure as hell didn't want to go to the pen for eight years on a manslaughter rap.

The trucker shouldn't be hard to locate. He had a big mouth and a CB radio in the cabin of his truck tractor. Joe parked his Chevy on the shoulder of the two-lane highway between Route 11 and the plant a little after 10:15 in the morning. He knew the voice on the truck's CB long before he saw the blue-and-white rig. The driver's handle was "Bullhead," and he was talking up a storm.

Next morning Joe borrowed a friend's Ford Escort and fixed a pair of New York plates on it, a pair from a collection he had taken from car wrecks on Route 80 in the bad old days when he had need of such things. He waited on the shoulder of the two-lane road, listening on his CB and carefully watching the occasional trucks that roared by at more than 70 mph on this deserted stretch. He heard Bullhead mouthing off to all and sundry, right on time, a little after 10:15.

Joe started his engine and pulled onto the road. He would meet the truck head-on. He rolled down his side window all the way and pressed the gas pedal to the floor.

Bullhead's voice came loud and clear over the CB, with only short pauses for replies.

The blue-and-white rig came into view down a long straight that they had to themselves, waterlogged empty fields beyond sunken ditches on either side of the road. Joe goosed the Escort and came down the straight at about 80 to meet the tractor-trailer, which was highballing along at more than 70 itself. Joe reached down with his left hand to the side of his seat and hefted a red building brick.

West Virginia license plate. As the rig barreled toward him, towering over the Ford, Joe flipped the brick up in front of its windshield on the driver's side.

He was doing 80; the rig at least 70. Which meant the brick would take out Bullhead at 150 mph. Be like being hit with a fucking rocket. They'd have to scrape Bullhead off the inside walls of the cab.

In his rearview mirror, Joe saw the rig leave the road. The tractor went down in the ditch; and the trailer jackknifed, jumped the ditch and fell on its side in the field. Last look he got, it hadn't burst into flames or anything dramatic but just lay there quiet, like some big dead animal.

Joe dumped the New York plates in a pond for safety's sake, though he was a hundred percent sure there had been no witnesses. He returned the borrowed Escort and went for a beer.

"Hey, Joe," the bartender said, "some weirdo called for you awhile ago—said something about the prairie and left a New York number for you to call."

When Joe phoned, a recorded voice told him, "This is Andre Verdoux. At the sound of the tone, please leave a message and I will get back to you as soon as I can. Au revoir."

The name Andre Verdoux was enough for Joe to know the score. The tone sounded.

"Andre, this is your old friend from Youngstown. Count me in. Whenever."

*   *   *

Lance Hardwick put down the phone in his West Hollywood apartment. He was getting his big break! His opportunity to break into professional soldiering!

He glanced at the unopened letter from his mother. "Dear Miroslav," it would begin. She even addressed the envelope to Miroslav Svoboda c/o Lance Hardwick, refusing to accept his stage name in any form. She was crazy and stubborn as always. Imagine calling her kid born in Minneapolis by a name like Miroslav Svoboda and expecting they would all go back to live one day in Czechoslovakia when things changed over there. Yeah, he could admit that his stage name, Lance Hardwick, was as much of a joke as his real name, but it suited a stuntman.

That was how he had met Mike Campbell. The famous merc known as Mad Mike was a consultant in the shooting of a war movie. Lance and a few others filled in for the stars every time the action got rougher than toddlers playing in a sandlot. It was a laugh. In the final version of the movie, Lance and the other stuntmen had more actual camera exposure than the stars who were credited with the action roles.

Campbell had advised the director on the authenticity of the action shots, so there were no huge globs of plastic explosive and technicolor blasts fifty feet high in order to destroy a simple bamboo bridge. Neither did the enemy blast away with machine guns at good old USA choppers and never seem able to hit them only fifty yards away! Mike had insisted on realism, and the movie had been a huge success as a result of that. Helped along by Lance's stunts, of course.

Lance had asked Mike outright for a chance to go on a mission. "Look, Mike, you seen me do my stuff here. I know it's only stunts. But you can check on my army record. I been a Ranger. I never got to see any action then, either, so it was like being a stuntman then too. But that wasn't my fault, was it? Not that I'm loco for a firefight or crazy or reckless, 'cause I'm not. You seen the way I handle myself. So far in this movie, I don't have a scratch; and that fucking director has me practically humping the barbed wire. You seen I can do what people tell me, exactly like they say, but also how I can think for myself and make suggestions." Lance remembered how Mike had let him go on and on like this and then had burst out laughing at him. Lance had been pissed, but kept it to himself.

Then Mike had suddenly turned serious and said, "I agree it might be good for you to test the real thing against the make-believe. I think you'd handle it just fine. And I'm a good judge of character."

"So you'll give me a chance."

"I didn't say that," Mike responded.

That was all Lance had managed to get from him, but he had never given up hope Mike would call the number he had given him.

Here it finally was! Be in New York City in three days. Call this number when you get there. You will receive instructions. No word of this to anyone. One hundred thousand dollars will be placed in your bank account. Be sure to make a will.

The *real* thing!

First thing he'd do was something he'd been waiting to do for four months now: feed a lion to the Christians. Stunt work had been slow. Not slow. Dead. They were shooting movies on location these days, and practically no work was being done in L.A. In fact, it seemed as though half the movies were shot in Mexico, no matter what their locale was supposed to be. These runaway productions were supposed to cut down costs. And there was always some local half-assed daredevil ready to perform genuinely dangerous stunts at almost vanity rates for the sheer glory of it. The producers didn't need professionals like him anymore, except when the insurance companies insisted. And they could only insist when they knew what was going on. And in North Dakota or Chihuahua, no one knew or cared. Muscle was cheap.

Lance had been doing some work as a bodyguard. Mostly for an English rock singer with a luxury place—lawns, walls, fountain, stables, the lot—in Pacific Pallisades. The guy couldn't sing concerts anymore because of the bad habits he'd picked up, but on good days in his private sound studio he could get enough on tape for the sound engineers to doctor. The more the singer went to pieces, the cleverer the audio technicians became. They kept the LPs rolling, and each LP always delivered at least one hit single that often went gold or even platinum.

The rock star was a monster when he was having the horrors, and when he wasn't he was a louse. He paid everyone three times what they could get for the same work anywhere else, and treated them three times worse than they would put up with anywhere else. If the singer had a real genius for anything, Lance decided, it was for working up personal hatred for himself in others.

Some months previously, an article had appeared in *Rolling Stone* that put the Pacific Pallisades estate and its inaccessible occupant in a scenario fit for the residence in Paraguay of Dr. Mengele or some other Nazi hotshot. Guard dogs, electrified wire, electronic surveillance, armed guards, martial arts experts . . . His record company picked up on this by putting out a video on the place—the only video to appear on MTV that did not show a shot of the star musician—and an LP cover to match. The kids took two days to find the place, and carloads began arriving for beer busts and much more. As often as not, they threw the empty cans over the wall after leaving a message in spray paint.

These were the Christians that Lance intended throwing the lion to. He drove down after getting his call from Campbell, turned off the alarms, opened the gates and told the kids to call their friends (one of them called a radio station)—it was open house, he said, as he waved everyone in.

The gate was out of sight of the house, so Lance missed out on seeing what went on. That could not be helped, he reflected, directing in what had now become a steady stream of cars. It was his gesture that counted.

Although Campbell was often known as "Mad Mike" because of his wild exploits, those who knew him well— those who had worked with him, put their lives in his hands on a mission—always said Mike calculated his risks better than any other military man they knew. Campbell himself, always amused and puzzled at why he should be called Mad Mike, had been through the mill. While in the Green Berets, he had gone on his share of missions under orders of superior officers who did not know enough about what they were doing. Mike knew the feeling very well of having to obey orders by putting his life on the line against his own better judgment. He had never refused to obey, but had simply gone out and done what he could in his own way under the circumstances—and been made a colonel for it in the end. But it had been an arduous journey before he made that rank—though not long, because he had risen in rank under combat conditions.

The chief reason Mike ran his own merc operation was because that way he knew for sure what he was getting into or staying away from. If there were any big mistakes, they would be his own; and Mike felt that if he had to die because of anyone's mistakes, he would prefer them to be his own.

Things hadn't always been this clear in his mind. He had worked for others as a merc in Africa, and between assignments there he had come back to Florida once to make a run to Cuba. He knew the mission was CIA-backed, and it had been hinted to him that it wouldn't hurt to have worked for the federal government on a few occasions if he should ever have future troubles regarding his status as a mercenary. So Mike "volunteered."

The purpose of the mission was to eliminate a communications expert who was doing his job too well. All Mike had seen were some aerial photos and the location on the map of the communications surveillance station at which the man worked. He drove an old yellow Citroen, which showed up in aerial shots in a parking lot between electrical transformers and a dish antenna. Mike knew the man's name and had been shown two grainy telephotos of him. He knew nothing more.

Things went wrong from the start. The fishermen who were supposed to pick up Mike and another man from the U.S. Coast Guard cutter off the north coast of Cuba did not appear. Having been told he could rely on the other man, Cesar Ordonez, for everything, Mike decided to go ashore under cover of darkness in one of the cutter's aluminum dinghies. Since they had no time to scrape off the boat's Coast Guard identification numbers, they sank it in fairly deep water and swam and waded ashore.

"Where to?" Mike asked Cesar Ordonez.

Cesar looked surprised. "Man, I translate for you and stick with you no matter what, but no more."

"Shit, I don't need a translator. I can speak Spanish. You're a Cuban and this is Cuba. That's why you're along."

Cesar shrugged. "Tell me what you want to do."

It turned out that Cesar, who Mike understood knew all the details about their target that had not been supplied to him, hadn't even been told who or where their target would be.

If it hadn't been for U.S. government involvement, Mike would have aborted the mission there and then. Not for the first time, he allowed his love of country to persuade him to undertake what good sense forbade. Cesar Ordonez turned out to be so fanatically anti-Castro, he was willing to buck the odds too—just so long as it gave him a crack at a Cuban communist.

They slept in bushes by day and traveled by night till they reached the communications outpost, farther west along the north coast. The yellow Citroen arrived at 10:00 A.M.

Ordonez grinned. "With the communists, the boss arrives latest."

Security was tight. Mike and Cesar had nothing but revolvers, and would hardly be able to get in close enough to use those. Even if they did, they would not stand a chance of escaping after the attack.

Mike's attention focused on a long toolhouse. Its windows were barred, and an armed guard stood at its door. However, the man's duties seemed to consist more of signing tools out and in than actually guarding the building, and his Kalashnikov assault rifle was slung by its strap across his back in a comfortable but not readily accessible position. He often wandered away to talk with whoever was getting into or out of cars in the parking lot.

Mike had some ideas floating around in his mind. Things would have to depend on what he found in that toolhouse. When the guard wandered off for one of his little chats, Mike and Cesar ran in a crouch through the bushes till they got to the rear of the toolhouse, then ran along its side and through its open door. Cesar stood inside the door, watching in case they had been seen. Mike searched about inside.

"Damn, Mike, he's coming back by a different way," Cesar whispered loudly. "He'll see us if we try to leave."

"So we stay," Mike said unconcernedly, pulling a long roll of heavy cable from a shelf.

Cesar backed away from the door. A minute later, they saw the shadow of the guard as he stood outside on duty again. Cesar looked at Mike. Mike put his fingers to his lips and pulled out his revolver. If the guard came inside, he would see them right away, for there was no place for them to hide—just a long open space with a floor of rough boards and walls of shelves loaded with light tools and supplies.

Mike gestured at the cable and tools he wanted them to take. Cesar nodded. When the guard left next, they would take them and sneak away.

The guard coughed. They saw his shadow move; then blue cigarette smoke wandered in along the shaft of light through the open door. Then his body darkened the doorway and he stood there looking at them for an instant.

He leaped out again fast as a deer and slammed the door after him. Mike heard a bolt being shot home as he reached the door too late, and then another. The guard yelled an alarm and was answered by others.

Mike and Cesar looked about them. They were prisoners. The windows were barred. The walls, floor and ceiling were constructed of wide, rough-cut boards. They had revolvers. The guard had an automatic rifle. More guards were coming. Cesar cursed. Mike winked. He handed Cesar a jimmy and took one for himself.

Four other guards joined the one outside the door. They checked the safety catches on their Kalashnikovs and nodded to him. He slid back the two bolts and pushed in the door. The guards went in fast, rifles held at hip level, ready to empty the magazines into the intruders.

No one was there. Just a long open space with shelves. They watched, amused, as the guard who had raised the alarm walked the length of the toolhouse and looked, mystified, at the barred windows.

"Know where the gringo spies have gone, amigo?" one of the four said. "Back to your house to make love to your wife."

The others laughed and one said, "Look under the bed."

They left and were followed outside by the guard in charge of the toolhouse. He was apologizing.

As in an old horror movie, a hand rose from beneath the

floor and raised a board. Mike climbed up from beneath it, replaced the board fast and tiptoed up behind the door. When the guard walked in again after the others had gone, gun at the ready, to look things over, Mike brought down the steel jimmy on the back of his head.

"Okay, Cesar," he called.

Another floorboard rose and Cesar appeared. The guard's skull was stove in, and they put him beneath the floorboard after relieving him of his rifle and spare magazines.

They carried the cable and tools outside to the bushes at the edge of the parking lot. The yellow Citroen was parked close to the undergrowth, so Mike was able to conceal the two cables he attached to the car's bodywork and run them back through the bushes toward the electrical transformers. He climbed the Hurricane fence around the equipment, having checked for the presence of guards, and Cesar threaded the two cables through the fence to him and then climbed over himself.

Mike bared three feet of heavy-duty wire at the end of each cable, then he took one and Cesar the other. Mike pointed to the place for Cesar to let the bared end of his cable drop, and at his signal, both wires fell simultaneously onto the high-voltage contacts. Huge sparks snapped like pistol shots, a smell of ozone spread in the air and the heavy copper wires melted like chocolate over the steel contacts. But they held.

The car should now be part of this high-voltage circuit, insulated from the ground by the rubber and air of its tires—ready to zap a load of power through anything that connected it to the ground.

Mike and Cesar climbed back outside the fence and positioned themselves in the bushes with a clear view of the Citroen.

Mike looked at his watch. "Ten minutes to twelve. I'm betting he drives into the town for lunch at twelve sharp. Let's hope they don't start up a search for the missing guard before then."

But no one was looking for equipment from the tool-house this close to lunch hour. Mike and Cesar saw three figures enter the parking lot from the far end.

"He's early," Mike whispered to Cesar. "He's the tall one in the center." He readied the Kalashnikov. "Let's hope the right man touches that car first. If I have to use this rifle on him, we won't stand a dog's chance of escaping from here in the middle of the day."

"Fire if you have to," Cesar ground out coldly.

Mike smiled. "I'm betting on their confusion to give us a good start. It'll take them awhile to figure out what's happening if I don't have to use this rifle."

The three men neared, and Mike and Cesar watched in silence.

The tall man reached with his key to insert it in the door lock. Sparks flickered about his hand. He stiffened and his mouth opened in a silent scream. His eyeballs rolled back in his head and he sank slowly to his knees, his right hand still glued to the car door.

His nearest companion shouted something and tried to lift him by his armpits. He too writhed about, but as he fell, he lost contact and broke free of the flow of electrical power. He lay on his back on the ground, unmoving, his eyes closed.

The third man looked from him to the first, now huddled motionless against the yellow Citroen's door. A ribbon of back smoke curled upward from where his clothes and skin burned on contact with the steel. The third man looked about him wildly and then ran.

"Let him go," Mike restrained Cesar.

Both of them retreated deep into the cover of the bushes in the direction of the coast. Some distance from the communications center they holed up till after dark. Mike used the Kalashnikov to commandeer a small fishing craft, and they made their rendezvous offshore with the Coast Guard cutter. Mission complete.

Mike had done occasional things since then for a couple

of other federal agencies, and as a result enjoyed a limited immunity from government interference. So long as he stayed away from sensitive areas. El Salvador was a very sensitive area. The powers that be would slap him down real fast if they had any notion he was moseying in that direction.

Campbell had been in El Salvador twice before, each time as a point of unobtrusive entry to somewhere else—once to Honduras, the other time to Guatemala. He knew he needed someone very familiar with what was happening there, yet who could be relied upon because he was not personally involved. In other words, he needed someone who understood Salvador but was not Salvadoran. Cesar Ordonez. Mike knew his phone number in Miami. Their paths had crossed several times since their trip to Cuba, and Mike had tried twice unsuccessfully to enlist him on merc assaults in Africa. Cesar was less a soldier of fortune than an anti-Castro fighter. He had told Mike he would have gone with him to Angola to fight the Cuban reds there. The Salvador guerrillas were getting Cuban aid. Maybe he would go there. It was worth a try.

"This is Mike Campbell. Remember me?"

"Sure, Mike. Go ahead. You can talk on this line."

Mike recognized his voice but did not want to say too much. "I'm going somewhere I expect to run into some Cuban technicians and advisors. I thought you might like to meet them."

There was a silence at the other end of the line, then a laugh.

"You wouldn't shit me, Mike?"

"No guarantees, but I hear they are in this place. Money is good too."

"I don't care about the money and I don't care about the place."

Mike gave him Andre Verdoux's number.

After Mike had hung up, Andre said to him, "Looks like you're stuck with me, like it or not, Mike. It seems

I'll be organizing our training camp and taking care of logistics.''

Mike laughed. ''I couldn't have a better man for the job, Andre. Stateside we'll need all the help you're willing to give. No deal overseas, though.''

''Understood, mon vieux, understood,'' Andre purred. ''Where will we train?''

''Where Washington will least expect us,'' Mike answered. ''Right in D.C.'s backyard.''

Chapter 7

    MIKE Campbell pulled the pickup next to his mobile home. Tina rushed out to meet him. They embraced long and hard, to the amusement of the old couple in the aluminum lawn chairs on the next lot in the trailer park. Tina helped Mike carry in the loaded shopping bags. As soon as they were inside, she jumped him.

Mike caressed her long black hair out of her eyes, stroked her cheeks and kissed her lips. He felt her soft body press close to him in a kind of wordless plea for him not to leave on this mission. He felt himself rise to the warm provocation of her belly and thighs. Then he gathered her shapely body into his arms and carried her to their bed.

The old folks in their lawn chairs shook their heads at the rhythmic shaking of one end of their neighbors' mobile home.

"Going at it real good for this early in the day," the old boy commented with a wink.

"That man is an animal," his wife said disapprovingly. "I can't imagine why on earth that woman tolerates him."

Mike set up ten separate medical kits, each one independent of the others, the extras to replace lost or damaged kits or to be given to friendly forces in the field. He wanted to bring as little as possible of a suspicious nature through the El Salvador customs—but he could not compromise on medicines. Weapons he knew he would find in abundance there, but quality medical supplies were often not to be had abroad for any kind of money. Each team member would bring his own kit in with him.

He packed the bottles and packets tightly into coffee cans and snapped on the plastic caps. Two broad-spectrum antibiotics, tetracycline and ampicillin. Chloroquine and primaquine against malaria. Flagyl, as an anti-amoebic. Paregoric and Lomotil against dysentery, and Metamucil against the opposite, constipation. An electrolyte solution in case of dehydration. A bottle of pure alcohol to rub on arms and legs to disinfect and ease the itch of cuts and insect bites, which tend to fester quickly in the tropics. Band-Aids. Ointments against eye and ear infections. Merthiolate as an antiseptic and germicide. Vitamins, salt tablets, aspirin, Tylenol #3, codeine, Novocain, morphine . . . Cortisone against swellings and asthma, Benadryl and epinephrine against allergies. A surgical mini-kit including sterile-sealed scalpel, tweezers, mosquito clamps, sutures, needles, gauze pads and bandages. Scotchcast, a fast-hardening plastic for making casts for broken bones. He made notes to add things he had forgotten to buy.

Each kit contained a small quantity of every item, so the kit's bulk was not so great as a list of its contents might indicate. The experienced men would not bitch about having to carry what inexperienced men might regard as an oversupply. The importance of having an adequate medical supply was one of the first grim lessons Mike had learned as a merc. He and others with only regular army experience behind them had not realized how much they had depended on the backup forces a regular army provides as a matter of course. The irregular soldier, whether merc or guerrilla, more often than not cannot depend on any backup. Mike had seen mercs die slow and agonized deaths in Africa for want of some drug no one had thought to bring into the bush—or succumb to African river blindness, transmitted by black flies, for want of the little white pills taken only twice a week.

He packed the kits into three cardboard boxes. He would send them by UPS to Andre Verdoux in New York on his way to the airport in Phoenix. Mike had booked a flight to New Orleans and a connection from there to Mobile, Alabama.

Before leaving, he phoned Andre to warn him not to leave it up to the men themselves to get their shots. Verdoux promised to personally ensure that each man received the inoculations Mike had decided on.

Andre was going to be a problem. He was being sneaky and keeping a low profile, making himself indispensable. Mike knew his game and couldn't do anything about it. Because Andre *was* indispensable. Bob Murphy or any of the others Mike would trust in a firefight, but if he sent any of them to Woolworth's for a ball of string, he'd be willing to bet they'd come back with something else. He could depend on Andre. Pity he was over the hill.

A soldier needs a gun. This is often a problem for a merc who wants to infiltrate unnoticed into a designated zone. If he tries to bring the hardware in with him, he increases his chances of being detected before he ever even gets started. If he waits till he is positioned where he wants to be, he may have to use second-rate equipment and find that his promised supplier proves less dependable than he had believed. Another problem is that a man who sells armaments is often also willing to sell information, so that the existence of a mission becomes known through its requirement of weapons.

Other things also combined to make ordering and picking up military-grade weapons one of the big areas of vulnerability for the soldier of fortune, not least among them the very possession of weapons of this grade. It is kind of hard for guys with rocket-propelled grenades and a kilo of plastic explosives to claim they are after deer.

Often a mission doesn't take shape till the weapons pickup is made—it's only a conspiracy till then. Thus the professional soldier never knows how secure his arrangements are until he has a gun in his hand, and it's mostly too late to make changes at that point.

Mike Campbell solved these difficulties by dealing through Cuthbert Colquitt. Cuthbert believed that a gentleman kept his word; and he dealt only with those he believed to be gentlemen, regardless of what nefarious activity they might be up to. Colquitt's code of honor was simple: the customer paid what, where and when he promised, and Colquitt in turn delivered what, where and when he promised. It was up to each side to overcome its own surprise difficulties without disturbing the business arrangement. Cuthbert was known to have a number of associates, anything but gentlemen, who were willing to see that no one took advantage of his good nature.

Colquitt Armaments consisted of a small office building and large warehouse in an industrial estate on the edge of Mobile. The place had a bland look—it could have been trading in wholesale Bibles. Neatly cut grass with PLEASE KEEP OFF signs, sprinklers, trimmed shrubs and strictly arranged flowers created a button-down look despite the frivolity of Southern spring. Mike left the taxi he had taken from the airport and entered the glass double doors to the offices.

"Hi, honey," a leggy blonde with a husky voice said to him. "You have an appointment?"

"Yes. Mike Campbell is the name."

"Okay, Mike." She popped her gum. "I'll see if Cuthbert is free." She picked up the receiver and pressed a button. "Sugar? Mike's here." She listened a moment, then dissolved in giggles.

Mike headed for the door to Cuthbert's office. Colquitt

always hired pretty girls who weren't sharp enough to get too nosy about his business. He seemed to go through quite a few of them, so maybe working for him fell short of being a dream job.

Cuthbert was cradling the phone between his shoulder and the rolls of fat on his neck when Mike walked in. His big paw clutched a gold Cross pen, and his square white teeth, spaced far apart, were clamped on a cigar.

"Gotta go," he said into the phone, hung up and heaved his great bulk out of the chair to greet his visitor. "Hey, boy, you're lookin' real good. I sit here and age and worry while hound dogs like you go out and chew on the world, havin' yourselves a fine old time."

"Cuthbert, men like me toil so that men like you can sit back at your ease."

"That ain't the way it is here with me, Mike. Look at me, worn away to a frazzle"—he stuck out his huge belly and shook his loose red jowls like a turkey cock—"just a shade of my former self. Work and worry. Worry and work. You look younger all the while. Touch of good bourbon?"

He sloshed the amber liquid over ice cubes in two cut-crystal glasses the size of jelly jars.

"You off on one of your little vacations, Mike?"

"El Salvador."

Cuthbert shook his head. "I'm afraid to go to Chicago, and you go to places like that. I don't mind telling you, Mike, I meet a lot of men on their way to dangerous places, but you're the only *repeat* customer I have who goes all the time. And it's not that the others don't come back again because they're dissatisfied with my services. They don't come back. Period. You really want to go to El Salvador?"

"Looking forward to it, Cuthbert. Any problem there for you?"

"None at all. Business ain't big there for me because the U.S. government sends them arms for free, and the

pols and army boys down there sell the guns off to anyone
who wants to buy. I can't compete with that. What I do
sell there is what I'm going to recommend to you. If you
carry M16s and other American weapons there and get
caught, you could be charged with stealing them or with
being equipped by Washington on top of everything else.
If you're caught with Eastern-bloc weapons, they'll claim
you work for Nicaragua or Cuba. I sell nice neutral
European guns—from Germany, Belgium, Sweden, Israel,
France—to people who don't want any misunderstandings
to arise. The weapons are mostly for guards who patrol
private houses in wealthy sections of the cities.''

"Sounds reasonable,'' Mike confirmed. "Let me tell
you what I expect. The north of El Salvador has poor soil
and small farms. There's a lot of hills which grade into
mountains up to five thousand feet high at the Honduran
border. The guerrillas more or less control this area, but I
don't expect to be coming up against personnel carriers
and certainly not tanks. A few Jeeps maybe, but not much
more in the way of vehicles. So I don't need anything
armor-piercing, and I don't want my men to have to drag
around awkward launch tubes that would only increase
their visibility. We'll be up against highly mobile groups
which travel light and know the country. It's not jungle, so
we may get into some open firing. I think I'd prefer a
battle rifle rather than an assault rifle like the M16 or
Kalashnikov. The assault rifle is great for automatic fire at
close range, but it has its limitations beyond thirty or forty
feet. A battle rifle will be better. And since we won't have
to carry food or equipment, each man can carry a backup
submachine gun like a Uzi.''

Cuthbert held up a chubby hand. "Best battle rifle you
can buy today is the FN-FAL Standard.''

Mike grimaced. "It's a little long to handle.''

"Take the Paratroop version. That has a grenade launcher,
which the Standard doesn't. It uses the same 7.62 mm
ammo with a twenty-round detachable box magazine.

The Paratroop model has better protection of the rear sight and has a really good folding stock that locks into both open and closed positions with no give or looseness at all. I'll take you out back and let you see for yourself."

"The Paratroop has the folding cocking handle?" Mike asked.

"That's the one. There's no gouging, and as you know you can operate it easily without removing your firing hand from the trigger group."

"Give me six of them. No, make it seven." Mike realized he was adding one for Andre Verdoux. Not that he intended changing his mind about bringing him along. But just in case . . . and anyway, a spare weapon could come in handy.

"Same with the Uzi?" Cuthbert asked.

"Sure."

"Only complaint I ever heard about the Uzi was that there's no bolt hold-open device, which I think is a valid objection. Personally I prefer the Thompson over the Uzi any day."

"The Thompson is a foot longer and five pounds heavier," Mike pointed out. "I'm asking my men to carry this gun in addition to a rifle in tropical heat."

"No argument, old boy," Cuthbert said. "I keep my Thompson under the dashboard of my car."

Mike smiled and surrendered his glass for another bourbon. "Pistols? Semiautomatic."

"The Heckler & Koch P9S is used by the German police. It takes 9 by 19 Parabellum in a nine-round detachable box. It has a delayed blowback system like that of the G3 rifle. You know, the delay is achieved through the use of locking rollers which must be driven down angled faces to the unlocked position before the bolt can make its major rearward excursion. The angled faces and the return faces together present a resistance that results in a very small initial bolt movement while the chamber pressure is high. You'll get to fire one out back.''

"Sounds good," Mike agreed.

"Beautiful craftsmanship. The barrel has polygonal rifling, which improves accuracy and makes it easier to maintain. And the loaded-chamber indicators can be detected by touch.''

"I'm sold, Cuthbert," Mike said in concession, knowing that the Southerner could go on in an endless filibuster about the qualities and workings of any weapon.

"Seven?''

"Yes.''

"Think you'll need to shoot down any helicopters?'' Cuthbert asked solicitously.

"I hope not.''

"Grenades, old boy. That's what you need. Grenades.''

The way Cuthbert said "grenades," he made them sound like vitamins. You knew they had to be good for you.

Comandante Clarinero, as he was known popularly because of his cornet playing, commanded a brigade of more than 180 guerrillas, the Padre Ernesto Barrera Brigade. It was called that in memory of a priest who had been killed in 1978 while he was with the guerrillas. The brigade had six companies, each containing thirty or more men, commanded by Clarinero's lieutenants. Each company had three platoons of ten men or more, with a sergeant in command. The platoons consisting of trained and combat-hardened men were divided into squads of two, three or four members; and each squad specialized in a certain activity, such as blowing bridges. It looked great on paper.

Clarinero's big trouble, however, was that many of his troops were only fifteen or sixteen years old and far more liable to shoot each other or themselves accidentally than pick off the enemy as sharpshooters. Balancing this was the fact that the government forces were equally young and inexperienced. Many had joined the army solely because of its pay, which was good at two hundred colones a month, about eighty dollars, and because of the regular meals, which they could not depend on getting elsewhere. Needless to say, the less these men had to fight for their pay and food, the happier they were.

When a young man turns down a comparatively soft life in a barracks to live as a fugitive in wild places, knowing he can never return to his family and village unless his side wins, he has mostly been forced into the decision. He has an ax to grind—a family death to avenge, an eviction or some other injustice to settle, a seething hate to release.... The field of combat is a very effective training ground. A man learns fast or he goes under fast.

The brigade had attacked a small town and held it for two days until a superior government force arrived. They had then retreated and seized another town, which government soldiers had to retake with heavy losses later in the day. The guerrillas fled to the mountains, pausing only to burn the tobacco-drying sheds owned by a powerful right-wing family. As always, the army soldiers were reluctant to follow the guerrillas into the dense cover of the foothills. They liked to stop fighting well before dark so they would be back in camp in plenty of time for their evening meal. Besides, most of their officers had to bathe before their dinner engagements.

It was not until nearly midday the next day, having been away four and a half days, that the guerrilla companies began returning to their burnt-out camp. Comandante Clarinero himself found Sally Poynings. The comandante was touched by the sight of the pretty blond girl all alone by the side of a mountain stream, not far from the blackened cinders of his bombed and burnt forest base. Clarinero had seen too many things gutted by flames to be either particularly impressed or surprised at the remains of his camp. What he had never seen before was a beautiful foreign woman who, as sole survivor, waited helplessly on a mountainside for his return.

Sally in her turn was struck by the handsome young comandante with his Pancho Villa mustaches and decorative silver work on his black leather riding boots and gun belt. He was being so gallant and treating her like a damsel in distress, she decided not to tell him how she had found undamaged food stores and a sleeping bag and had taken off on her own. He seemed to want to believe she had sat by the edge of this stream like a wilted flower waiting for his return. When a man formed a romantic notion like that, Sally was not the kind of girl to spoil his illusion.

Of course, what had really taken place was quite different. Sally had said to herself, after her first nervous traumas had subsided, that this whole country was only a little bigger than New Jersey and was crawling with people. All she had to do was walk down from these mountains and hitch a ride to San Salvador, which couldn't be more than fifty or a hundred miles away. Even if she had to walk that distance, it would be better than being stuck up on a mountain with charred corpses for company.

She carried food and drinking water in a canvas bag and made her way down the slopes. Before she emerged from the timber belt, she heard male voices. Instead of running toward them for help, something made her conceal herself in some bushes. The voices came nearer along a forest path.

Four campesinos walked together, armed as always with their machetes, passing a bottle among them which she guessed was cane liquor. Sally broke out into a cold sweat as she realized she would not have survived this encounter if they had seen her. She knew for certain they would have raped her, killed her and hidden her body in the forest. Why she was certain of this she could not explain, even to herself. Hands trembling, she stayed hidden till long after the men's voices had faded in the distance. She determined she would not approach any man—she would stay out of sight until she spotted women working in the fields and go to them.

Sally had noticed that in El Salvador it was always easy

to find women working and men resting. The first woman she approached would not speak to her. A pretty girl about her own age, who was picking coffee beans with the others, called to her.

"She can't help you. She's already lost one son; she doesn't want anything else to happen to her. Talk with me. I have nothing to lose."

Sally walked over to where she worked. "I don't want any of you to suffer because of me."

The pretty girl laughed bitterly. "Norteamericana, you run from the guerrillas or the army? Maybe from both. Anyway, they both blame us for helping you to escape. You see what is happening here? I am the only one who is talking to you. Everyone can point her finger to me and say it was me who helped, not she."

"Thank you for talking to me. I hope it won't get you in trouble. All I need to know is how to get to San Salvador from here."

The woman shook her head. "Impossible. The guerrillas hold this area. They and the army are fighting everywhere. If the soldiers catch you, maybe they shoot you, maybe not. It does not matter who you are—they are loco and no one will ever know. The guerrillas are different—they will give you a trial and then shoot you for certain. As a spy. They think everyone is a spy. I won't ask you how you came here—but that is your only way out of here."

The other women mostly kept their eyes on their work, glancing at her quickly but listening to every word. Sally felt they were sympathetic to her but lacked the young woman's nerve. Women everywhere are so easily intimidated, Sally thought angrily.

"What if I go east, over the mountains into Honduras?" Sally aked.

The woman pointed to the high mountains. "These are baby mountains in El Salvador. In Honduras they have big mountains. Cordilleras. And you would have to cross the river Lempa at the border. A foreign woman by herself would be stopped. No. You must go back the way you came in here.''

"I understand."

Without letting the other women see what she was doing, Sally removed one of the hundred-dollar bills from the wad she had kept hidden from the guerrillas. The woman's eyes grew round in wonder at the sight of such a valuable banknote. Sally crumpled it quickly and dropped it on the earth.

She winked at the woman and said, "Gracias, senorita." She turned and waved to the other woman. "Hasta luego, senoras."

A chorus of farewells followed her as she walked away.

As Sally climbed back up the mountains toward the burnt-out camp, she felt strangely elated. This was something she would not have been capable of doing only weeks previously—admitting to herself that something could not be achieved the way she wanted and backtracking in order to wait for another opportunity. No sulks. No rages. Only a calm determination to see this through. Sally decided that she was becoming a mature woman.

She slept in the forest that night, terrified of the sounds that night creatures made, expecting at any moment to feel the fangs of a jaguar in her flesh or of a vampire bat on her neck. Apart from a few mice, nothing came near her. Back at the destroyed camp the next day, her determination weakened and she lapsed into a depression. After she swam and washed her hair and combat fatigues with real soap in the stream, she felt better.

When Clarinero returned and fussed over the languishing maiden, she enjoyed every minute of it. She had almost forgotten the pleasures of male attention.

"I am sorry about the death of your friend Gabriela," Clarinero told her.

"She was my guard as well as protector," Sally said. "I liked her, but I didn't cry any tears for her. In fact, I was kind of surprised at myself for not being more upset. I've even totally recovered from Bennett's murder, and I know I wouldn't have yet if we'd been home in Boston and he had been killed in a car accident on the Massachusetts Turnpike. I would have been distraught for a year. Here I seem to harden myself and move on."

"One has to, in order to survive," Clarinero said sympathetically.

"Do you think freedom is worth all this death and violence?"

"We've always had murder and injustice here—they didn't arrive with the guerrillas. We believe that our fight for freedom will bring a just and peaceful society. After we win."

"Are you a communist?" Sally asked.

He shook his head vehemently. "Certainly not. The guerrillas are every shade of the political spectrum—we even have some in the far right. I know your American media always refer to us as left-wing terrorists, but that is not true."

"Not everyone who fought on Castro's side was a communist, and a lot of the Sandinistas in Nicaragua weren't either, yet guess who ended up in control."

Clarinero held up a hand. "That will not happen in El Salvador."

"Famous last words." Sally laughed. "That's part of their plan—let the moderates recruit the fighters and bear the brunt of the fighting, then the cadres move in and get rid of the moderate leaders after they've won. That's what they did in Moscow. The Bolsheviks didn't overthrow the czar like they'd have everyone believe. The moderates did. Then the Bolsheviks and Mr. Lenin sneaked in and took over, along with Comrade Stalin."

"Never in El Salvador," Clarinero said.

"Bullshit!" Sally said in English, since the Spanish language lacked a word to convey so neatly her exact meaning.

"Those troubles we will have to leave until it's time to

face them," Clarinero said in perfect English. He smiled at her surprised look. "My father at one time was a diplomat. I went to high school in Chevy Chase and spent two years at Princeton. I made the rowing team there and had my own Ferrari." He gestured about him at the burnt-out camp. "This is how I repay my parents."

"Your family was one of Los Catorce?"

"One of what are called 'The Fourteen,' yes, although there are really about fifty families in the ruling oligarchy. About two percent of the population owns more than sixty percent of the land in El Salvador. Our families are very aristocratic, proud of what we claim is our pure European blood. We regard the slightest concession to the illiterate campesinos as pure Bolshevism. You've seen the campesinos for yourself, Sally. They have little to lose, whatever they do; and it's true that they are exploited by communist agitators. You Americans say, 'Have a fair vote and a democratic government.' But democracy depends upon the middle class, and here the middle class is small and weak. There are some things wrong that I do as a guerrilla, Sally, but I would be an even greater criminal if I sat back, grew fat on the misfortunes of others and did nothing."

Sally hardly knew what he was saying anymore. He spoke English . . . Princeton . . . handsome. . . . She gazed in his eyes and trembled when his fingers lightly brushed her arm.

Mike Campbell flew from Mobile to Atlanta and changed planes for Washington, D.C. He hired a car, crossed the bridge from Annapolis to the Delmarva peninsula and took Route 50 down Maryland's Eastern Shore. Knowing how they could be stopped entering El Salvador on a single word from the U.S. government, Mike had decided he could not risk any weapons training. If the FBI spotted three known mercs together with shotguns after rabbits, they raised a multistate alarm.

He followed 13 south and turned off for Chincoteague. The road ran along the edge of the Wallops Island rocket base, picturesque and smooth as a golf course, giant dish antennas peering up into the sky next to dark woods. A few trawlers were being unloaded at the dock at the town of Chincoteague, but otherwise there was not much happening. The tourist places were still shut up this early in the year. Mike asked directions to the campground at the edge of town, and this proved to be almost empty too, except for seven one-man tents beneath pine trees in one corner. Mike had seen this campground in an otherwise boring home movie that one of his neighbors back in Arizona had made on a trip east. As he drove up, Andre was exercising the team. They all wore running shoes and green track suits with blue lettering: MURRAY HILL TRACK AND ROAD CLUB.

Each morning, not long after dawn and a breakfast of eggs, bacon and sausages cooked over a camp stove, Andre drove them in his rented station wagon across the bridge to Assateague Island National Seashore, and they ran, jogged and walked for miles along the deserted Atlantic beach. They got back to the station wagon about midday and drove to town to a restaurant by the docks for a meal of seafood and beer. Then a couple of hours' siesta in the tents, followed by a couple of hours' running in the marshes, scrub and grasses on Assateague Island. Dinner in the restaurant—with a lot of beer this time to relax sore muscles—and sack out gratefully in a sleeping bag with a hole scooped in the ground beneath for the hipbone.

Mike ordered the same routine every day, knowing that routine and boredom both created and tested a team's discipline. Andre Verdoux called the shots, and Mike worked out as a regular member of the team—sometimes, to their amusement, cursing Andre out as a stern taskmaster.

"You notice anything about Lance Hardwick?" Andre asked Mike one evening.

"Hell, no. I have enough trouble looking out for myself," Mike said. "He seems gung ho. He's sure got more energy and enthusiasm than any of the rest of us."

"That's what I mean," Andre said. "Where's it coming from?"

"Sour grapes," Mike responded with a grin. "When you and I were kids, we were just like that."

"Watch him," Andre said dryly.

Mike did. Lance was a rookie at the merc game, so it was reasonable for him to show more enthusiasm than any of the others. Besides, he was the only man on the team without real-life combat experience, so he had to prove something to himself and the others.

Just as Andre might be trying to make a place on the team for himself by insinuating things against Lance.

At dinner that night, Mike announced they would not be hitting their usual routine on Assateague Island the next day. Instead, they would go to the Blackwater National Wildlife Refuge in Dorchester County on the Eastern Shore. He passed around an ordinance map of the area and a compass to each man.

"Each man sets off at twenty-minute intervals from this point, where Route 335 crosses the water," Mike told them. "The X marked in ballpoint on the blue highway east of the refuge is the pickup point where Andre will wait for us with the station wagon. I think it's illegal to cross the refuge the way we are going; and if you're caught by park rangers, you're eliminated. It's against the rules to ask anyone the way or get help, though I doubt you'll meet anyone while crossing these marshes. However, you may follow another man if you can, or team up if you want—but remember that of any two men finishing together, the one who started latest is the winner. There'll be only one winner. The rest of us will be losers."

This sounded like a holiday to everyone after Andre's relentless daily grind on the beach—at least it did till they saw the Blackwater Refuge next morning from the bridge on Route 335. It was a gray, cold day and the waves slapped on the inland water as if it were the Atlantic. Tall reeds grew in icy water as far as they could see across the flat horizon, interrupted only by isolated hummocks sporting a few wind-tattered pines. No house could be seen in any direction.

Unexpectedly, Mike took over from Andre and lined the men up by the side of the road. "Strip!" he roared at Lance Hardwick.

"Mike, in this cold!" Lance protested. "You gotta be crazy!"

"Strip."

Lance untied his running shoes and unzipped his track suit and stood in the buff by the deserted road, shivering.

Mike picked up the track suit and searched its pockets. He found only the map, compass and a packet of raisins, which he emptied out on the road. He picked up the right shoe and found nothing. Then the left. A clear plastic packet of white powder fell out.

"Get dressed," Mike said. As Lance did, Mike asked him, "Coke?"

"Right. You want some?"

Mike waited till Lance had tied both shoelaces and stood erect. Then he hit him on the mouth, drawing blood, and again caught him with a right across, which decked him.

Lance rolled away from his attacker and came to his feet again in one fluid movement, hands held before his body, feet apart.

Mike lunged at him, allowing Lance to think he was making an enraged charge. Instead, Mike drew back just before contact, swiveled on one foot and delivered a chest-high kick. Lance managed to twist away from the full impact of the kick and rode with its force, being thrown to the ground again but again rolling back effortlessly into a fighting stance.

Mike saw that Lance was good enough to spar and roll with anything that was thrown at him. Which was the sort of stuff he could learn in a gym. Close-in fighting for real was probably something he knew less about, and something in which Mike excelled. Mike stepped in fast, feinted, and stepped inside the range of Lance's kicks. Mike drove the base of his right palm beneath Lance's nostrils, snapping his head back on his shoulders, nearly tearing the nose off his face. Mike followed with a straight left knuckles-up karate punch to his solar plexus, which drove the wind from his lungs and left him bent over, choking on the blood from his nose. A side kick in his ribs leveled him and left him retching and writhing on the roadway at Mike's feet.

Mike glanced at his watch and pointed at Joe Nolan. "First man away!"

Joe headed into the marsh without a word, and Andre fussily noted the time on a clipboard.

Harvey went next. Cesar. Then Mike himself. Bob Murphy uncapped a flask of coffee immediately after Mike had gone and helped Lance to some. Without getting up from the roadway, Lance gratefully sipped the hot liquid. Bob fetched him a plastic basin of water and a roll of paper towels so he could wash the blood from his face and neck.

"Andre will drive you to Cambridge and give you money to get home," Bob said. "I got to go, kid. Take care of yourself."

Lance nodded, dejected.

After Bob set out, Andre called to Lance, "Let's go."

"No."

Andre shrugged. "So be it."

He drove away.

Bob Murphy finished with the best time by far, reaching the pickup point before any of the others, even though the first man had a start of an hour and twenty minutes on him.

First to start, Joe Nolan came in last. "If you guys had to cross Baltimore or Wilmington, I'd have won hands down. Trouble here is all this damn green stuff blocking the view, and it all looks the same."

Bob said, "What this place needs, Joe, is a thick coat of asphalt and maybe some birdbaths and stuff so you don't have to leave your car to see the wildlife."

They had a celebration dinner that night, at which Bob claimed to be the top man in the group, much to Andre's annoyance. Bob beat the waiter at arm wrestling, which he claimed confirmed that he was the champion specimen of manhood on this part of the Atlantic seaboard. He spoiled this by throwing up out the station-wagon window on the way back to the campground.

Next morning it was back to the daily grind on Assateague Island. They were eating breakfast at the picnic table in the campground before setting out when they heard the zipper on what they had assumed was Lance Hardwick's empty tent.

Lance crawled out in his track suit, battered and bruised but ready to go. He said nothing to anyone, sat at the table and helped himself to a paper plate of eggs, sausages and bacon. From one pocket of his track suit, he produced a Fresca can flattened and folded to the size of a fifty-cent piece.

Bob took it. "Hey, that's mine. Remember, Andre, you were pissed off because I disturbed the ecology by throwing it away at the pickup point?" He looked at Lance. "So you did make it there, after all."

Lance nodded.

"It's sixty or seventy miles from the pickup point to here. You hitch?"

Lance nodded again. Next he pulled out a clear plastic bag of cocaine, much larger than the one from the day before. He placed it on the table before Mike, who tore the bag in half and let its contents run into the sand.

Mike nodded to Andre to pour Lance an enamel mug of coffee.

Nothing more was said.

Chapter 8

ON Campbell's orders, they flew from Washington to Miami, bought a ticket there to Guatemala City, and another ticket in Guatemala City on a local airline to San Salvador. Mike and Cesar flew the first morning, traveling separately but on the same planes. Andre left alone in the afternoon. Next day the four remaining all traveled separately, with orders that on no account were they all to arrive on the same plane from Guatemala City to San Salvador.

Six rooms had been reserved at the Ritz Continental, downtown on Avenida Sur, not one of the most expensive and luxurious hotels and therefore, they hoped, free of journalists and other pests on expense accounts. The rooms had been reserved for "Mr. Hillman's party." No one was to give a false name, but was to write illegibly whenever possible and avoid handing over his passport.

Mike had asked Andre to come as far as San Salvador with them. He had a room reserved at the Parker House, even less pretentious than the Ritz Continental and not far away. He was to keep apart from the others as their ace in the hole if things went wrong in the city. After they left for the countryside, Andre was to remain in the city of San Salvador as their anchorman. He was not enthusiastic but took what was offered.

Orders were for everyone to lie low for a few days, see the sights, relax—and stay out of trouble. They could hang out together in pairs if they wished; but not more than two at a time, since three or more foreigners together were more likely to attract attention.

The big draw on their second day in San Salvador was a soccer match.

"We've got to see this game," Bob told the others. "I don't know who El Salvador is playing—Ecuador or Paraguay or somebody, but it's an international match, and in my book any game between any country and El Salvador has to be worth watching."

He waited for Nolan, Waller or Hardwick to ask why. They didn't, being content to sit back and drink very good Salvadoran beer, cane spirit—which they called by its Spanish name *espiritu de cana*—and Atlacatl rum. They sat in Bob's hotel room, figuring that Mike's prohibition of gatherings of more than two applied to outings in public only. Between drinks they munched on *gallo en chica*, which was cockerel cooked in hard cider, and *pupusas*, small cakes made of corn, some filled with ground meat and some with cheese.

"I think this goddam soccer game is going to be worth watching," Bob proclaimed. "Let me tell you what happened when El Salvador played Honduras in 1969. They had the 'soccer war.' The players kicked the shit out of each other on the field; the fans fought each other in the stadium; the TV and radio picked up the quarrel; politicians traded insults across the border; and the generals rushed back to their barracks to bring their troops out to settle the final score. The war lasted only four days—"

"Mike said stay out of trouble," Lance butted in.

Bob looked at him with disgust. "Look at who just found Jesus."

"Hey, I'm on probation," Lance said. "I ain't going to blow it over some fucking soccer brawl. I'll put my bucks down for the Rams and the Vikings, but I couldn't give a shit for Pele and fancy footwork."

Bob grunted. "So stay home and watch TV."

At the moment, *Hill Street Blues* was on the set. The guys at the precinct house rattled at each other in Spanish not even closely synchronized to their lip movements.

Lance laughed. "Okay, I'll come."

"I'm going to find me a lowdown whorehouse tonight," Joe Nolan said, "but I got nothing against good clean fun in the afternoon."

"Who did you say El Salvador was playing?" Harvey asked suspiciously.

"I don't know for sure," Bob said. "I think Paraguay or Ecuador."

"They communist countries?" Harvey asked.

"Damn, no, Harvey. You think I'd take you to see pinko faggots play ball?" Bob asked with a straight face. "Is that what you think of me?"

"Okay, I'll come," Harvey said, thus reassured.

A huge mob swarmed outside the stadium. Long lines waited at ticket windows. Scalpers held up tickets and shouted prices. The cheap seats were in the sun, the more expensive in the shade. The scalpers with the most expensive tickets picked on Bob and Joe. Although Bob was wearing a guayabera, the appliquéd shirt-jacket that many Salvadorans wore, he was easily spotted as a foreigner by his Aussie slouch hat, khaki in color and complete with puggaree and chin strap. Joe Nolan looked like someone who had gone for a walk in the Appalachians and, through some kind of space warp, found himself inexplicably in Central America. A scalper grabbed Joe by the arm and held on, sticking tickets into his face and screaming into his ear.

Joe pointed at the man's fingers clutching his arm. He

shook his head at the man and said "No" loudly several times. The scalper gave Joe the idea he was not going to let go of his arm till Joe bought the tickets. If this was his intention, it was the wrong way to go about persuading Joe.

Joe picked the scalper's little finger off his arm and bent it back, breaking the man's grip as the other fingers were torn away to ease the pressure on the little finger. Joe forced the man's hand back past his shoulder and pressed him down to his knees on the ground. The ticket scalper screamed, more in terror than in pain, and his sudden high-pitched howl, like that of a stuck pig, instantly quieted the noisy mob outside the stadium. This sound was something they recognized, something powerful enough to frighten them into momentary stillness.

Then the crowd began shouting at Joe and Bob. The ticket-seller wandered away, nursing his fingers, but a dozen men lingered, shouting things at them which they assumed were curses. One tried to knock off Bob's slouch hat.

"Motherfucker!" Bob yelled and booted him in the gut.

He crumpled like a paper bag.

Two of the downed man's friends jumped Bob, who shook them off his broad shoulders and kicked one on the side of the head. The guy went out like a light.

Someone stood over this man and said something, of which Bob understood the word *muerto*.

"He's not dead," Bob bellowed, "but you assholes will be if you don't get the fuck away from me."

He went at them, fists swinging.

Joe joined in, shouting, "Kangaroo, it's you 'n me agin this whole country!"

Which was how it seemed at first, with two men against a crowd of thousands, although a lot of these did not know what was going on. Lance Hardwick and Harvey Waller saw the disturbance and waded through the crowd at the double, pushing men out of their way, in order to help their buddies.

"Kick ass! Kick ass!" Harvey was yelling, smashing any face he could reach as he came. "God bless America!"

All four traded blows with everyone around them, yelling encouragements to one another and obscenities at the roiling mob about them. A large number of Salvadorans seemed anxious to prove that four gringos could not intimidate four thousand Salvadorans. Bob and the others would doubtless have been beaten and stomped to death had not a mean-looking individual that Lance had managed to belt a few times hauled out a pistol from next to his big belly under a loose sport shirt and loosed off three shots into the air.

Everyone stopped fighting and looked at him. He flashed a badge for all to see, and the crowd slunk off except for a dozen or so who had some trouble getting up off the ground. These were helped away, and a large space was left around Bob, Joe, Lance, Harvey, the man with the gun and badge, and an emaciated character who seemed to be the cop's sidekick.

"You speak Spanish?" the badge asked in Spanish, tucking the gun into his bellyband beneath his shirt.

"I do," Lance said. "They don't."

"You all together?"

"No, him and me came to help these two when we saw they were in trouble with the crowd. We figured on helping two fellow Americans."

"You do that all the time?" the cop asked. "Help your countrymen in trouble?"

"In foreign places, sure," Lance said.

"How did you know they didn't speak Spanish if you never saw them before?"

Lance gestured. "They wouldn't have got into a fight if they'd been able to speak Spanish."

"You think so?" The cop looked him over. "I'm going to give you good advice. Don't go in that football stadium.

I'll stop a taxi for you over here and you all go back downtown. Tell your friends.''

Lt. Col. Francisco Cerezo Ramirez, of the Treasury Police in San Salvador, climbed the curving marble staircase, and when he reached the corridor above, noticed Turco peel off the wall and follow him. The colonel had a somewhat acid stomach this morning, and his henchman was the last person he wanted to see, yet he was afraid to send him away. This was what things had come to. Here he was, Lieutenant Colonel Cerezo, fearful of dismissing a lackey. But Turco had the ear of many important men and personally led one of the death squads financed by the Escandell family. The colonel was married to one of the younger Escandell daughters, and he represented the family's interest in the Treasury Police. His own family was much less well-to-do and powerful than the Escandells, and his father and mother were proud of their son's link to the ruling oligarchy. He had been promoted to his present rank a month before his marriage.

Turco followed the colonel into his office, closed the door behind them and waited respectfully for the officer to sit before he did so himself. Despite his uncouthness, Turco had had a strict military training and never stepped out of line in matters like respect to his superiors, although all knew Turco did as he pleased when their backs were turned. Turco waited politely for the colonel to wish him good day.

The Escandells had three sons with the rank of general, one in the air force and two in the army. They had cousins and in-laws, like him, and those beholden to them at every level in all branches of the armed and security forces. Didn't they trust him? Is that why Turco had been assigned to him? The colonel knew that Turco had the ear of the three Escandell generals, which was more than he, their brother-in-law, had. They were often patronizing to him.

This Turco was continually digging up problems that

needed immediate attention. The colonel had to be wary with him because Turco was careful always to get authorization before proceeding. When Lieutenant Colonel Cerezo did not set limits on what he permitted Turco to do, the man ran amok and claimed to be operating under Cerezo's orders.

"Buenas dias, Turco," Cerezo finally said, twitched his mustache and posed authoritatively behind his big desk. "Como esta, amigo?"

Turco murmured a courteous reply and handed the officer some papers.

The colonel sighed and impatiently looked through them, obviously waiting for a chance to dismiss Turco from his office.

"From what I can understand," Cerezo said, "these four norteamericanos involved in the disturbance yesterday at the stadium are all staying at the same hotel in rooms reserved by a Senor Hillman after two of them denied to you that they knew the other two; that this Senor Hillman himself has not appeared; and that the passports of these gentlemen have not been properly registered. Also you say that another norteamericano, and a Hispanic whom you have not seen, occupy another two rooms reserved by Senor Hillman. So? Get their passports properly registered. Threaten the hotel manager for not following procedure. What do you want of me?"

"Colonel, the desk clerk thinks the Hispanic member of the group is a Cuban."

"A Cuban!" The colonel's system sent a dart of acid into his already sour stomach. "Why didn't the desk clerk report his presence before this?"

"Because she is not completely certain. She heard him speak only in English. She is an educated woman and careful of her opinions. But she is sure enough he is Cuban."

"Possibly Cuban," the colonel amended, by now fully awake and thinking hard. "Five norteamericanos who seem to want to hide their identities and a possible Cuban . . . not good, not good. Do they have wild hair and beards and wear peace buttons?"

"No. These ones are dangerous. They are clever, and when they look you in the eye, you can see they are not afraid."

The colonel wondered for an instant what Turco saw in his eyes when their looks met. "Where are they now?"

"In their rooms at the Ritz Continental. Still recovering from last night, I would say. Adolfo is in the lobby, watching for them."

"Don't approach this . . . possible Cuban. You don't speak any English, do you, Turco?" The colonel was pleased. His own English was good. "Too bad. It limits your capacity. You mentioned that one of the norteamericanos at the stadium spoke Spanish. You and Adolfo talk with him."

Turco stood immediately on getting the authorization he needed.

The colonel held up a hand for him to wait. "Turco, I said *talk* with him."

Lance heard the rap on his door as he lay on his bed wondering which had been the cause of his hangover—the rum, the beer or the espiritu de cana. The rapping became more insistent. He decided it was probably one of the others looking for aspirin.

"What do you want?" he called.

"Coffee, senor," a male voice called from outside the door.

He didn't remember ordering any, but now coffee sounded like a good idea. He pulled a dressing gown over his shoulders, opened the door and saw the hollow-faced man who had been with the cop at the stadium the day before. The emaciated man held his right hand close to his hip. Lance saw that it held a small automatic, a .22 or .25, with a silencer attached that was longer than the gun itself. With the pistol held close to his own body, well out of

Lance's reach, the gunman gave Lance a chance to take in the situation, no panic, one foot in place to stop the door being slammed, very professional.

"Come on in," Lance said. "You got some questions, I suppose. Where's your amigo?"

The cadaverous cop waited, and Lance looked out and saw the mean-looking one with the potbelly coming down the corridor from where presumably he had been standing guard.

Lance wasn't worried. He expected a little melodrama with Central American cops. And the mean one had caught him in an obvious lie about not knowing Joe and Bob. Lance was more concerned about what Mike Campbell was going to say than with this tropical Kojak and his wasted sidekick.

They came into the room and double-locked the door after them.

"No coffee?" Lance asked. "Let me order some sent up."

He picked the phone off the receiver but did not bother to dial because big-belly ripped the cord from the wall. They forced Lance to kneel by the bed and tied his wrists behind his back with the telephone cord.

"Sit on the bed. Here. People call me Turco. That is Adolfo. Your name?"

"Lance Hardwick."

"On your passport?"

"Miroslav Svoboda. I didn't get a chance yet to change it there, but I'm legally Lance Hardwick."

"Why are you in El Salvador, Senor Svoboda? That is not a norteamericano name. No one in the United States is named Miroslav. You are from eastern Europe?"

"No. My parents were. I was born in the United States."

Turco nodded significantly to Adolfo. "An eastern European and a Cuban. What does that tell you?"

"Marxists," Adolfo said sadly, as if he'd just discovered a fruit fly in an orange tree.

"That's what it sounds like to me too," Turco said.

Lance was a bit taken aback that they knew about Cesar Ordonez. But it stood to reason, he supposed, since they were all in the same hotel. Obviously these cops had been doing some kind of background check. He was glad he hadn't lied to them about the name on his passport.

"Why don't you leave me the address of your office, Senor Turco, and me and my friends will come around and see you this afternoon and straighten everything out?"

Turco shook his head.

What did he want? Money! That had to be it. But he had to be dignified about it. Give them anything. Mike would repay it if he could get rid of these two.

"Senor Turco, my wallet and identification"—he did not say money—"are in the back pocket of my pants lying on that chair. Unless I lost them last night, which is very possible. Maybe you found them? No? And that belt in my pants"—he'd spell it out for them—"that's a money belt. Why don't you take a look at it?"

Turco whacked him across the face with the back of his hand.

"Sorry," Lance said. "I didn't mean any offense. What the hell do you expect me to do with my hands tied behind my back except try to buy my way out?"

"*Talk* your way out," Turco answered.

"What do you want to hear?" Lance asked flippantly.

"Why you and your friends are here."

"We're on vacation," Lance said brightly.

Turco pulled the lapel of Lance's dressing gown to the side and, light as a feather, touched his right nipple with the glowing tip of his cigarette.

Lance screamed and rolled over on the bed.

The two Salvadorans waited until he had recovered and looked up at them.

"Release my hands," Lance pleaded.

"We're going to have to do something to quieten the noise of your screams," Turco told him.

Adolfo volunteered, "I think I can be of help."

"Very kind of you, Adolfo," Turco said. "You understand, don't you, Miroslav, that this will go very hard with you and that it will be very slow until you tell us what we want to know." He pulled a folded straight razor from his pants pocket as he was saying this, opened its blade and examined the light glinting on the vertical scratches left by the honing strap. "Of course you know what to expect. You have been trained to withstand any torture we could give you. Isn't that what they told you, Miroslav? Where? In Prague? Or did you train in Russia? You speak fair Spanish. My guess is you came to us via Cuba. No, don't say anything, Miroslav. It's much more important that you listen now. Very carefully. Are you ready?"

Lance watched Turco's eyes. He had eyes like those of a sadistic schoolteacher Lance remembered from when he was very young, who liked to play with his victim, let him believe he was going to let him off, before hitting him with something worse than even his victim had been prepared for.

"I'm listening," Lance said grimly. His chest hurt like a crazed hornet sting that wouldn't ease up.

"Good. This is the way I work, Miroslav. I do not start with the fingernails or the eyes. I go straight for the balls. Empty the testicular sacs. No trouble at all with this blade, Miroslav. Some bleeding and some pain, but nothing like what is to follow."

Turco ran the flattened blade down Lance's chest and sheared off some chest hairs. He effortlessly sliced through the dressing gown's belt, then continued down Lance's belly with the flattened blade.

Lance held his body rigid, and his eyes stared down at the gleaming sharp steel of the straight razor as it neared his genitals.

With a flick of the wrist, Turco lifted the blade off

Lance's belly and suddenly chopped its cutting edge down on his thigh. Lance felt only a sting as the honed metal parted his skin and saw his blood well up along the razor's length. It had missed his penis by little more than an inch.

Turco raised the blade slowly until it was before Lance's face. He let the blood drip from the razor's end.

"Tell me why you and your friends are here," Turco said softly. When Lance did not respond, Turco went on. "You will tell me. I know what I am saying. Adolfo and I have had much success in persuading men like you to give information. But you should not be thinking about us. You should be thinking about yourself. Because you will have to make up your mind very soon if you want to continue having balls hanging between your legs. I make no other promises, only that if you tell us what we want to know, I will not cut off your balls. On the other hand, I promise equally strongly that if you do not answer my question, you will feel this blade do its work."

Lance's pain diminished with increasing fear. The fact that Turco was taking such great care to explain himself carried a sinister ring of sincerity. Turco and Adolfo reminded him of a pair of surgeons—careful, patient, experienced . . . skilled professionals.

Turco nodded to Adolfo, who grabbed Lance's left ankle and sat on his right foot, forcing his legs apart. Turco grabbed Lance's balls in his left hand and touched the razor's edge to their roots.

"I'll talk! I'll talk!" Lance yelled.

"I haven't asked you the question yet," Turco said softly.

Lance felt the razor nick his scrotal sac.

"We're here to get Sally Poynings! The millionaire's daughter who joined the guerrillas!"

Lance felt the razor lift from his testicles.

"Who sent you?" Turco asked.

"Her father hired us."

Lance felt Turco release his balls.

Turco walked to the center of the room and put the razor on a table. He nodded to Adolfo, who allowed Lance to sit on the edge of the bed again. Lance saw he had confused Turco with his information. At Turco's bidding, Adolfo unbound Lance's wrists and then worked at connecting the phone lines again. He picked up the receiver, nodded and handed it to Turco. Lance smoked a cigarette and massaged his wrists. While Turco dialed, he took the opportunity to pull on his shirt and pants. He was already feeling better now that he was no longer trussed like a sacrificial victim. The leftist posters he had collected as souvenirs bulged in his back pocket—crudely printed graphics of fists clenched and of chains being snapped, along with bullshit about what the Clara Elizabeth Ramirez Metropolitan Commando would do to the capitalist pigs. Lance intended to pin them on a wall of his West Hollywood apartment as a joke. Turco would probably get the wrong idea if he saw them, so Lance let his shirt hang loose over his pants and hoped the posters would not be noticed.

"So there is a rich American woman with the leftists," Turco was saying over the phone. "No, colonel, I never heard a word about it till this norteamericano told me just now. No. No. He's not hurt. He can walk. Sure. I'll bring him right over. I know this could be big for all of us. Top secret."

He put down the receiver and walked up and down the room, deep in thought, anger on his face. In the end, he went to the door and beckoned for Lance and Adolfo to follow.

Adolfo prodded Lance occasionally with the little gun, which was now concealed inside a paper bag. Lance saw none of the others on the way down or in the hotel lobby.

Turco told him to drive, and got in beside him. Lance adjusted the safety belt as Adolfo got in the back seat. Turco jabbed his forefinger in the directions he wanted Lance to drive.

"So you come down here to show you are better than us," he said in a menacing voice.

"What do you mean?" Lance asked.

"You find the girl and bring her back and say we couldn't have done it."

"I don't know why he hired us instead of dealing with you," Lance said. "I don't even know why it has been kept quiet about the girl having gone with the rebs. I'm just a hired gun. But one thing I can tell you—I never heard talk about any of us being better than any of you people."

Turco was quiet again. Lance figured he was pissed off at not having been informed by his superiors about Sally. He had no way of knowing that Turco and Adolfo had murdered Bennett and thus could be said to have a vested interest in the case. In truth, Turco had just assumed that the girl went back to the United States after her lover's death. That she had not, and had joined the guerrillas instead, was of no great consequence to him; but that he had not been informed of it was. That might mean something. Then again, it might not.

Traffic was heavy and their progress was slow.

"How were you going to go about finding this girl?" Turco asked.

Lance was pleased to hear the note of hostility in Turco's voice replaced for the first time by something else. Curiosity. Lance had other worries in his head, now that he knew he was going to hang on to his balls. He had given away Campbell and the others. Blown the mission. In order to save himself. Any of the others would have done the same thing, he reasoned. But they hadn't. And he had. He didn't know how he could face Mad Mike on this. After being let live down the coke thing on the Chesapeake. He sure was fucking them over now.

"Well, I don't have the exact plans of what we intended to do," Lance told Turco as he followed his directions to a big building. "All I've seen is our weapons and the local team in the eastern end of the city."

"Could you find them again?"

"Sure. I know where the house is."

"Take us there now," Turco ordered.

"Like hell I will. I don't trust you two no farther than I could throw you. You was speaking to a colonel on the phone. You tell him to come along, and I'll drive you all there right away."

Turco pointed to an entranceway. Armed sentries walked up and down. "Pull in. Wait here. Adolfo, any trouble, shoot him."

"I would like to," Adolfo said from the back seat.

Turco was gone for about ten minutes, then returned with a uniformed officer, a small, self-important-looking man with a clipped mustache. The officer got in back with Adolfo while Turco held the car door open for him. Lance by now was half-amused at Turco's swings from violence to almost servile politeness and back again. Turco climbed in the front seat beside him and courteously introduced him as Lance Hardwick, rather than Miroslav Svoboda, to Lt. Col. Francisco Cerezo Ramirez of the Treasury Police.

"Direct me to the eastern outskirts of the city," Lance told Turco. "I'll know the location when I see it, but we may have to drive around a little while."

"All that matters is that you find this house," the colonel said from the back seat.

"Are you going to stop the mission, sir?" Lance asked.

"That will depend." The colonel paused before saying, "I am keeping an open mind. You told Turco that you are being paid to find this girl."

"Yes, sir."

"How much?"

"A hundred thou. Each of us team members gets that. I don't know what our leader's cut is."

A silence followed this. Lance could almost hear their minds calculating numbers.

"Which is you leader?" the colonel asked after a spell.

"Mike Campbell. He wasn't at the football stadium, so I don't know if Turco and Adolfo have seen him." Lance drove cheerfully now, handling the wheel expertly.

"Her father is paying all this money simply to get the girl back from the guerrillas?" the colonel asked next. "Nothing else?"

"Nothing else so far as I've been told, sir."

"Is Mr. Campbell a reasonable man?" Colonel Cerezo asked, this time in English. "Do you think he is the kind of man who . . . who negotiates with others to get what he wants?"

Lance also switched to English. "It's not his money, sir. What does he care?"

"Very well put, Mr. Hardwick."

The mood in the car became almost pleasant after this. Turco passed Lance a cigarette. The colonel gave him a hit on a silver pocket flask of rum and did not include his henchmen. Lance picked up speed as they roared along an empty road. The open spaces on both sides had been transformed into vast shantytowns. He saw a suitable place ahead where the high roadside curb dipped down for an opening to something that had never been built. He checked his safety belt and drove close, then swung his left front and rear wheels onto the low curb and accelerated hard. The car, a Peugeot, shot forward, and when its left front wheel hit the sudden rise in the curb at increasing speed, the car was pitched over onto its right front wheel and its back rose up. The Peugeot teetered on its right front wheel for an instant before flipping over onto its roof.

Lance had done this stunt a dozen times on movie and TV sets, but always with a strong safety harness, a helmet and a roll bar to prevent the car's roof from caving in and crushing him.

He braced himself against the steering wheel and prepared for the shock of impact that he would receive hanging upside down by his seat and shoulder belts. The noise of the roof scraping along the concrete road inches from his head was deafening; the wrenching force of the belts squeezed the wind from his body; his arms and legs hit hard, painful objects; his neck whiplashed; but he was all in one piece.

Turco was thrown against him, and Lance had to push him out of the way to find the ignition key and turn the engine off. He released his seat and shoulder belts and came down on his hands and knees on the car roof. There was a smell of burning, but no smoke. Adolfo's little automatic pistol with its big silencer lay in front of him and Lance picked it up.

The door on the driver's side was knocked out of shape and wouldn't open until he kicked it out. He crawled onto the concrete roadway and rose dizzily to his feet. One of the front wheels was still slowly revolving. A van was approaching in the distance. Only a few dogs and very small children stirred in the shantytowns on either side of the road.

Through an open back window, he saw one of them moving inside the upside-down car. It was Adolfo's back. Lance put a bullet in it, aiming for the spine but hitting a bit to the right. Adolfo squirmed, and Lance leaned inside, found Adolfo's head and sent a bullet into his brain. The silencer made the pistol sound like a burst of air from a high-pressure tire.

Turco was breathing but unconscious. Lance shot him between the eyes and Turco's mouth relaxed.

The colonel didn't seem to be breathing. Lance shot him in the left temple, just to be sure. So long as they had told no one else before leaving their headquarters, his betrayal of Mike Campbell and the others had died with these three.

Lance looked up the road from where he knelt beside the upended car. The van was nearing rapidly. He pulled the Clara Elizabeth Ramirez Metropolitan Commando posters from his back pocket, hurriedly unfolded three of them and stuffed one into each of the dead men's mouths.

Chapter 9

THE seven members of one cell of the Clara Elizabeth Ramirez Metropolitan Commando sat on wood boxes beneath the banana-leaf thatch of a shack in a barranca near the San Salvador football stadium, safe from the interference of outsiders in the densely populated squalor of the shantytown. As they often did, they were grumbling about having to take orders from a Cuban. They quieted down when one of the children who acted as lookout warned them of Paulo Esteban's approach.

The big Cuban shook hands all round and found himself a box to sit on. He bided his time before making his request and went out of his way to avoid giving the impression that he was the one now presiding over the meeting. But no one was fooled. Paulo's requests were in reality direct orders. The Commando members would have to have a very good reason before they could refuse him. This time they knew they had such a reason and were looking forward to saying no to him. They had no ideological differences with Esteban—they too were good communists—they were just sick of Cubans telling them what to do.

"What brings you here today, Paulo?" one of them finally asked.

"Comandante Clarinero has a raid set for tomorrow. As you know, the army has been boasting that they have wiped out his force by bombing his camp in the mountains. They even claim that Clarinero is dead. We want to show the people that not alone is he alive and well but is still operating at full strength. He will do this by staging a big raid. I will be there with him, and so I must leave in an hour for the mountains. We wondered if you would escort a BBC television team to the location of the attack so they can film it."

Several members shook their heads.

"We can't help you, Paulo."

"We're too busy."

"We have have more important things of our own to attend to."

The Cuban was used to this and did not let it faze him. This was the drawback with all these little semi-independent cells: although the cells increased security by each being sealed off and thus unable to betray other cells, their isolation promoted entrepreneurial tendencies, independence of authority and other evils among the members. Paulo had been trained to put up with such behavior at this stage of the revolution. It would all be very different after they were victorious. These squabbling Salvadorans would find out then who knew how to run things best. In the meantime they could be soothed with a little flattery.

"I understand how you freedom fighters have matters of great importance to attend to," the Cuban said. "Those of us in other groups are comforted to know that in moments of need we can turn to the Clara Elizabeth Ramirez Metropolitan Commando for assistance. We know we will not be refused. Or that if we are, it will be because of unavoidable circumstances."

Thus put on the defensive, the members were anxious to justify their refusal.

"We too have a revolutionary action to perform tomorrow."

"At the latest."

"It's more important than guarding a camera crew for that glamour boy, Comandante Clarinero."

Paulo smiled. "I admit that at times the comandante behaves like a clown, and it's true he is always too much in the limelight while men—and women—who achieve more than he does die unknown and unremembered. Yet the revolution needs him. We need him because foreign journalists know who he is, with his dopey mustache and silly bugle, his wealthy background and norteamericano education—he is one of the ruling class and they respect that and the fact that he has joined us against his own class. Everyone in El Salvador knows who he is; and so long as he lives on in freedom and carries on the fight, the government has to admit it lacks control. So even if you and I don't like the tunes he plays, we must still listen to his bugle."

Without exactly saying it, Paulo had indicated to them that he and they were in agreement, as comrades-in-arms, on all the major things. He coasted on that for the moment.

"You and I are full-time revolutionaries with little patience for the personal failings and weaknesses of others," Esteban went on. "But as mature people, we realize that we must work with others who lack our strength and commitment and that we must transcend both their weaknesses and our own in order to forward our noble cause—dictatorship by the working class. *We* will rule! Nationalist revolutions are only a stage in the struggle. And now, comrades, share with me, your fellow freedom fighter, your reason for not assisting the rest of us with the television crew."

"You read about the colonel and the two members of the Treasury Police we assassinated here in San Salvador?"

Paulo laughed delightedly. "Of course. Congratulations. I hadn't known it was this cell—"

"It wasn't. No one in the Metropolitan Commando did it."

"But your posters stuffed in their mouths—"

"Listen to our story. We had the two Treasury Police rats, but not their officer, on a hit list. We tried but could never trace them to their homes. They were torture experts and they both worked on Escandell death squads. We have been trying to kill them for months. We thought we might get a chance at the Ritz Continental, where they had guests at the hotel under surveillance. It didn't work out. Last we saw of the two was them leaving the hotel with a norteamericano. They and their colonel were killed about an hour later. Now listen to this. A van driver who is sympathetic to our cause but is not an active member came to us when he got off work, which was hours after the killings. He spoke with a member of another cell when he heard that the Metropolitan Commando had been credited with the assassinations. He had stopped at the scene of what he thought was a road accident—a car was upside down and a man stood beside it. The man held a gun in his face, a small automatic with a silencer, and demanded to be driven downtown. This man spoke Spanish but was definitely a norteamericano. The driver described him. He was the one that Ricardo here had seen leave the hotel with the two Treasury men. This norteamericano killed them, not us."

They were all pleased with the look on the Cuban's face. For once he had no quick and persuasive reply to what they told him.

"What do you intend doing?" Paulo asked.

"Kill this foreigner."

"Without finding out what he is up to?" Esteban asked.

"This is San Salvador, not the mountains or Usulutan province. We have no power here. How could we capture him alive? He is not worth such a big risk. We should kill him quick before he does something else."

Paulo nodded. "That certainly would be a reasonable

precaution. Have you any idea yourselves why he might have done this?''

Ricardo spoke. "To me he looks like a CIA agent. My guess is that the colonel and those two stepped on somebody's toes in the power structure and were ordered eliminated. If the CIA did it, there must be some United States involvement.''

"The colonel was not important?'' Paulo queried.

"No,'' Ricardo replied. "The two plainclothes agents were more dangerous to us than the officer. Cerezo Ramirez was his name—but nothing to do with Clara Elizabeth Ramirez.'' He grinned. "Suppose someone in the government wanted to get rid of them—perhaps they had discovered something about him—and the politician or army man got the CIA to kill them as a favor to him. The CIA decided to pick on us as a sure way to conceal their own involvement. What we must do is teach the CIA a lesson that they cannot play games with us. We must kill their agent. They will understand that.''

"I agree.'' Paulo smiled and shook hands with each of them. "I will get someone else to guide the television crew. I must hurry to the mountains. Good luck to you and your work for the revolutionary masses.''

After Paulo Esteban had gone, Ricardo said, "He's not such a bad guy after all.''

Lance Hardwick was pleased with himself. The leftist group that had made the posters was being blamed for the killings. They had denied it, but no one believed them. Campbell and the others would never learn now that he had betrayed them. Lance had felt a strong urge to boast of his exploit, to take at least Bob Murphy into his confidence, but he couldn't think of any way to explain his actions without admitting also that he had betrayed the team. And he had no intention of ever telling that to anyone. Even at the cost of not being able to brag about what he had done.

Lance had never killed before. He felt kind of sorry for the colonel, but he looked as if he had been killed in the car wreck anyhow—at least, he had looked dead when Lance put the bullet in his skull. The other two had only gotten what they had coming to them. He felt no remorse for having wasted them. Lance scratched his balls, glad they were still there.

"What's delaying Mike?" he asked Joe Nolan. "Why don't we get going and find this chick?"

"Mike is a planner," Joe told him. "He knows how to wait and hit at the right moment. But you found that out for yourself on the Chesapeake."

Lance laughed. "So we just have ourselves a good time while we can?"

"Yeah. I expect Mike will give us an alert before we pull out, but I don't know. Hell, we may be tromping around in this heat, loaded down with equipment, in two hours' time. I say have a good time while you can, kid. Bad times are sure to come."

Joe mopped the sweat from his forehead. It was 97 degrees, according to a lighted readout on an office building. Even when Joe did not move at all except for breathing, he still sweated like a pig. The drops of perspiration ran into his eyes and stung them. The evening and night were cool, and when Joe had his way, he spent all day in the air-conditioned hotel and hit the streets only after sundown.

But today Lance had persuaded him, against his better judgment, to take a walk about town. All of them were beginning to get bored and crazy. They hardly saw Mike or Cesar anymore, and had never once seen Andre since their arrival in San Salvador. They knew Mike and Cesar were combing the city, trying to buy hard information on Sally Poynings' whereabouts. So far Mike had found out she was with a group headed by Clarinero; that she had been thought killed in an aerial attack on his camp; that later she was reported as having been seen alive. Since Clarinero's group was thought to contain at least two hundred men and was now on the move, it could not be hit effectively by a small team of mercs. They would have to continue to hang loose and wait for the call.

Lance had said, "I can't spend another afternoon in this fucking hotel room or the lounge. Heat and sweat be damned, I'm going outside."

Joe had gone with him for lack of anything else to do. Harvey and Bob tailed along behind, only half mindful now of Campbell's regulation that they not form groups of more than two. They walked aimlessly and slowly along one of the downtown boulevards, in the swelter and noise of the ultramodern city: Lance and Joe in front, Bob and Harvey lagging behind.

None of them heard the noisy little motorbike mount the sidewalk some way behind them. The little machine wove in and out of the pedestrians, carrying two riders. The two members of the Clara Elizabeth Ramirez Metropolitan Commando targeted Lance and agreed to take out Joe along with him. Two dead CIA agents were even better than one. They sped on their machine, uncaring for other pedestrians now that they had zeroed in on the two they planned to snuff.

Pedestrians scampered out of the way of the noisy little bike. However, one pedestrian felt hot and belligerent and in no mood for jumping out of the way for anyone. When Bob Murphy heard the exhaust of the motorbike behind him on the sidewalk, he did not clear out of its way—only looked out of the corner of his eye and muttered a curse. The heat and humidity were one thing; assholes on a motorbike who thought they could make him jump for his life were something he was not going to take.

As the bike and its two riders came alongside Bob, with its left handlebar brushing against him, Bob chopped backward with his extended right arm. His arm caught the first rider across the throat and scraped him off the bike, along with the pillion rider behind him.

A submachine gun clattered to the sidewalk from beneath the guayabera of the first rider. Bob immediately recognized it as an M76, made by Smith & Wesson. Bob had seen it used by U.S. Navy SEAL teams in Vietnam and by various Special Forces and Ranger units. He reached down and picked up the gun before its owner recovered. But the pillion rider saw him reach for it.

The pillion rider had not lost his grip on his weapon, a .22 automatic, with which he had intended to blow Lance away as he had done Chips Stadnick and other enemies of proletarian freedom. He had fallen on his ass on the sidewalk as the bike went from beneath him, and he now aimed his pistol at Bob before the stocky Australian could grab the M76 submachine gun.

He must have forgotten about Harvey Waller. Or not seen him, because anyone who had seen Harvey wasn't likely to forget him. Waller never instinctively shrank from sudden violence; his eyes never blinked in shock; his body never stayed rooted to the spot. Instead, he was drawn to sudden and unexpected mayhem coldly and functionally, as a shark, detecting irregular pulses and the taint of blood in water, becomes alert, calculating, fast, stony-eyed.

Harvey threw himself against the side of the sitting man and deflected his shot at Bob. Harvey clutched at the .22 automatic in the man's right hand but couldn't reach it. Before his opponent could turn the pistol on him, Harvey twisted his hand into the man's face, his thumb found the cheekbone, then the hollow beneath the brow; from below and from its outer edge, he twisted his thumb behind the eyeball and gouged out the left eye.

The glistening eyeball dropped out of the red, empty socket and hung on a thick white thread of optic nerve and a half dozen ribbons of muscle. As the man screamed and twisted his head, his eyeball bounced against his cheek. He hardly noticed Harvey wrench the gun from his hand.

Harvey's cold frenzy was not sated. He touched the automatic to the bridge of the man's nose and squeezed the trigger. The man fell on his back on the sidewalk, and Harvey stared at the scorched hole he had drilled in the still face with the empty eye socket.

Then he twisted on the other rider, who was on his hands and knees fearfully watching Bob take possession of his submachine gun. Harvey tried to put a bullet in each of his eyes. He hated fear. He only *disliked* people's eyes . . . unless they contained fear. He missed with his first shot—it was at least two inches too high, and the bullet sank through the bone of the forehead. His second shot was fired as the head was jerked back from the impact of the first bullet, with the result that the point of entry was much too low, completely missing the eye and hitting the middle of the cheek.

"Get down fast!" Bob hissed.

They both hit the pavement and wriggled for cover. Bob had seen nothing—he was just responding to the situation as he had been trained.

Lance Hardwick and Joe Nolan had looked behind them when they heard the riderless motorbike scrape against a parked car and fall on its side, engine still kicking and rear wheel spinning. They didn't hear the sound of the shot that Harvey deflected, but they saw him attack the man and shoot his companion. Next, they saw Bob and Harvey flatten themselves on the pavement and crawl for cover a few milliseconds before a wave of automatic fire ripped over them from the palm trees and bushes on the center strip of the boulevard. Lance and Joe dived for cover themselves.

Bob Murphy gripped the M76 submachine gun by the barrel shroud with his left hand. His right hand set the selector switch on full auto and then retracted the cocking handle along its track into the cocked position. He fired a trial shot into the bushes, but lost three shots because the trigger was heavy and the gun's cyclic rate too high.

"Harvey, check if he had any spare magazines."

Harvey moved, crablike, back to the body and drew a

hail of fire from the bushes on the center strip. Bob pinpointed the source and delivered a short burst of 9 mm parabellum slugs. The bushes heaved, and a body pitched forward into the roadway and lay still.

One car accelerated past, but the other traffic in each direction had braked to a halt fifty yards or so short of the firing zone. The drivers left their cars and crouched behind them to see what was going on. Those caught in the choked traffic behind blew their horns in mounting frustration at the inexplicable holdup.

Pedestrians had melted away. A few stood in distant doorways, but the recently crowded sidewalks on both sides of the boulevard had emptied except for the combatants.

Harvey found one spare magazine for the M76 submachine gun, and on the second body he found two for his pistol. As soon as Bob saw he had a second magazine with another thirty-six shells, he strafed the bushes in the center strip of the boulevard. He dropped one gunman; but another, behind the trunk of a palm tree, escaped his fire, delivered a withering burst at him and retreated to the far sidewalk of the boulevard under cover of friendly fire.

Bob changed magazines. He yelled to Harvey, "I see three of them over there."

Harvey looked disgustedly at the low-caliber pistol in his hand. They heard Lance shout.

Lance went first, then Joe, zigzagging across the road to the center strip. They drew automatic fire from the three guns on the far sidewalk. Lance took an M76 from one of the men Bob had shot. He threw a spare magazine back across the road to Bob, then another. Joe got himself an M16 assault rifle from the other body.

The firefight raged across the boulevard. The mercs had the advantage now, holding the center strip as well as one half of the boulevard, effectively cutting off their three adversaries and pinning them down behind parked cars.

The leftists, realizing they now were in a losing position,

tried to move east from car to car in order to make a getaway.

"Let them go!" Bob shouted.

Neither Joe nor Lance heard him as their weapons rattled lead. Lance crippled one man by catching him in an ankle, and then finished him off with a burst to the chest before he could reach the shelter of a car.

"Let them go!" Bob yelled over and over till, finally, in a lull in the firing, they heard him. "Hold your fire! Let them go!"

The two survivors made off eastward along the far side of the boulevard, leaving their dead behind them.

"Follow me," Bob shouted. "Let's get the hell outta here! We can't afford to get arrested any more than they can!"

Joe had to pull Lance by the shoulder, and Harvey too was unwilling to leave, feeling cheated by not having had much of a part in the major firefight, owing to the small caliber of his pistol. The four men kept their weapons and ran from the area cleared by combat to mix in with the crowds of onlookers and stalled traffic. Before they could reach the crowds, armed members of various security forces suddenly swarmed out to meet them—National Police, Treasury Police, National Guard, Customs Police and some other uniforms they did not recognize. Enough automatic weapons were trained on them to chop them into goldfish food.

Bob Murphy threw his M76 to the ground and raised his hands. He looked at the others, but Joe and Lance had already been convinced by this Spanish armada and were dropping their guns. Only Harvey, with his useless short-range .22 automatic pistol, seemed unwilling to put down his gun. He finally let it fall.

"Thank you very much, Harvey," Bob breathed gratefully. "You just saved all our lives with that one small act of kindness."

"I ain't no fuckin' coward," Harvey muttered. "If I had a submachine gun, they'd never take me alive."

A Treasury Police sergeant yelled at them both in Spanish. Lance talked to him, and he did some yelling at Lance.

"I told him you don't speak the lingo," Lance explained to the others. "He said we're not to talk among ourselves. From now on he'll give me orders and you follow me."

Bob was about to say something witty, but changed his mind because of the look on the sergeant's face. They stood there silent and without moving while several members of the different security forces argued with each other. Meanwhile, the bodies lay untended and the traffic was still halted in both directions by police just standing in the roadway, doing nothing. They saw one driver, who kept impatiently honking his horn at them, led away in handcuffs. The members of the different security forces were becoming angrier at one another in their argument.

"They're fighting over who takes us prisoner," Lance explained in an undertone. "My bet is on the Treasury Police."

His bet won. They were escorted at gunpoint to a police van and pushed inside its steel doors. They sat on metal benches facing each other and waited, along with their guards.

One of the policemen pointed at two men being led to the van at gunpoint. "Your enemies," he told Lance.

The two men and more policemen climbed into the back of the van, and the doors were slammed behind them. The police all seemed to know the two prisoners they had brought in last and jeered at them in a seemingly friendly way, calling one by the name of "Ricardo." The two prisoners remained silent and sullen. No one said anything to the four mercs. After the van had traveled for about ten minutes, it slowed to a stop. The policemen opened the rear doors and pushed the two Salvadoran prisoners outside. The two men stayed where they were, one sitting in the roadway and the other standing next to the van doors and trying to get back in. One policeman booted him in the chest as the van moved forward.

Two of the cops in the van poked their M16s through the open rear doors and mowed down the two men from a distance of about ten yards. The van continued moving and the police shut the rear doors. The cop next to Lance said something.

Lance translated it for the others. "They were trying to escape."

Chapter 10

JOE Nolan sat on a wooden kitchen chair in an otherwise empty room, eight by ten, brown-yellow walls, tiled floor, light fixture behind a cage in a very high ceiling, no window, steel door, a peephole two-thirds of the way up the door. Silence.

He had stuck to his story. He was an American tourist. He knew the other three: they stayed at the same hotel. He had broken no law, only defended himself in a vicious attack. As an American citizen, he expected a quick release. No, he had no complaints to make about his treatment by the Treasury Police.

Joe had sat in a cell often enough before to know how to keep still and wait for events to take their course. He sure as hell was not looking for a way to attempt an escape.

As always when engaging the enemy, Comandante Clarinero had set up the six companies of his brigade as watertight units—two assault companies, one reinforcement, one communications, one watchdog and one supply. Normally the two assault companies carried out the mission, with the reinforcement company as a backup. The watchdog company sealed off access roads, set up antiaircraft defense, created diversionary tactics or whatever the circumstances demanded. Watchdog was often aided in this by the communications company, who also kept lines of supply and retreat open and generally did everything it was no one else's job to do. The supply company's responsibility was ammunition, weapons, drinking water, food and equipment. In a regular army the assault companies would be the elite group and attract the best fighting men, but this was not so in Clarinero's brigade, because with an army of irregulars fighting a guerrilla war, the focus of combat rarely occurred where it was planned. Any of the companies could find itself spearheading the attack or bearing the chief brunt of an assault. In fact, the supply company was regarded as being the most dangerous to be a member of, since it was less mobile than the others.

Paulo Esteban and two other Cuban advisors were with the communications company. They watched the air shimmer over the broad Lempa river in the heat of early afternoon. The twenty-eight Salvadorans in the company set about their tasks, keeping to the cover of the undergrowth at the river's edge. At this point the Lempa ran roughly north-to-south, from the border with Honduras into the Pacific, dividing off the eastern third of El Salvador from the rest of the country. Guerrilla strategy was to blow the bridges and keep them down, crippling the movements of government troops and sealing off the eastern provinces.

About a half mile downstream, army engineers worked on a barge and, aloft, in the twisted steel framework of the bridge's central span that the rebels had destroyed three months previously. Armored personnel carriers and dug-in gun and mortar emplacements guarded the approaches to the bridge on both banks.

The three Cubans trained their binoculars on the workers and soldiers at the bridge, and when they tired of that, they lowered their binoculars and watched the river water flow past and the Salvadoran guerrillas prepare their gear.

Comandante Clarinero stubbornly refused to allow them to take an active role or issue instructions during an operation. Their function was to observe and to offer constructive criticism and advice *after* the event. Both Cubans and Salvadorans recognized he limited Cuban power with this tactic, and the Salvadoran members of the brigade greatly enjoyed observing this order strictly. The Cubans' only revenge was to sit back and watch them going about something the wrong way and say nothing with superior smiles on their faces.

It can take only one inexperienced man to foul up an operation. The guerrillas usually had no shortage of inexperienced men, so they were used to things going wrong and rarely bet everything on any single thing happening. It wasn't the best system, but it worked.

The company's lieutenant went over things one last time. "We drop the first barrel in the water in"—he consulted his watch—"ninety-three seconds' time; the second barrel goes in when the first is about halfway to the bridge—I will give the signal; and the third barrel goes in immediately after the first barrel blows."

The Cubans smiled among themselves, especially about the ninety-three seconds. It didn't matter a damn about the exact time the barrel went into the water, since the river currents would control the time of its arrival at the bridge and they had no idea how fast the currents were. Anyway, Clarinero and the assault companies would wait till they heard the sound of the first blast before doing anything.

Two of the guerrillas dragged a barrel to the riverbank and, behind the cover of a tree, dropped it into the water. The barrel was an aluminum beer keg packed with TNT with a radio-activated detonator. Days ago, each barrel had been weighted and tested to float upright about four feet below the surface. The ten-foot whiplash antenna on each barrel was concealed in leafy tree branches.

The Cubans watched the barrel float away and followed the six feet of leafy branches that protruded above the water and that marked the keg's position as it was taken by currents into midstream.

"Keep an eye on that barrel," Paulo Esteban told the others. "Once you lose sight of it, it will be hard to pick up again at a distance."

"Let's not depend on our Salvadoran friends to keep track of it then," Manuel said.

"It looks very natural," Paulo said. "Just like a branch sticking up from a submerged log."

"Do you think they'll have nets protecting them?"

"Clarinero's men said not, for what that's worth."

The third Cuban said, "Manuel tells me that Clarinero knows nothing of the television crew."

"No, I thought it better not to tell him in case he would try to protect Miss America from them," Paulo said. "I organized an escort for the crew while I was in the city—it's a BBC camera crew here on special assignment from London. If we give them something worth watching, all the U.S. networks will use it too. Clarinero thinks this raid is being made to boost his image. He'd be very offended if he knew its real purpose is to show off the girl."

"The man's a fool," the third Cuban said. "Why do we tolerate him?"

Esteban smiled. "Because fools have their uses when you keep them in their place. Clarinero's use is to steer the people's nationalism toward our cause, and his place is out there dodging bullets with a reckless laugh."

Manuel snickered. "And the girl?"

"She's in love with him, you've seen that." Paulo snapped his fingers. "She'll do whatever he says. And he'll do what we tell him to."

"Why is the girl's presence being made public now?" Manuel asked.

"We can't trust the Salvadorans. If her father asks politely for her, they'd be quite likely to insist on sending her back. We have to polarize all concerned on her presence here if it's ever going to benefit us."

"Use an American against America?" Manuel queried.

Paulo slapped him on the shoulder. "Now you got it."

They watched the lieutenant and his men drop the second barrel into the river. It too floated concealed beneath the muddy water, with only its radio aerial sticking above the surface, camouflaged with leaves and branches. The men readied the third barrel, to be dumped in the water after the first one exploded.

The three Cubans moved higher on the bank to follow the course of the first barrel. It had to be detonated at just the right moment—too late, and the river currents would have carried it beneath and beyond the repair work on the bridge and it would be wasted. Distances were hard to judge across water.

"We'll wait till we see the aerial branches just about touching the barge," the lieutenant shouted up to them. The guerrilla sighted through his binoculars once again and then beckoned to one of his men to fetch the small radio transmitter that would send the signal to detonate the charge inside the barrel. The man stood next to the lieutenant, the whiplash antenna of the transmitter quivering above their heads.

Paulo Esteban followed the pitching leafy marker far downstream. It was almost at the black barge upon which a huge crane was lifting ironwork for the bridge. The barge was moored in midstream, and it seemed that the current of the main channel would bring the barrel very close to the barge, as they had hoped. Men ran about the deck of the barge as the crane raised its load of steel T-beams to the damaged span overhead. Tiny figures climbed about in the bridge's framework high above the water. Through Esteban's binoculars, the green leaves concealing the aerial seemed to be almost touching the upstream end of the barge.

Paulo had to check himself from calling out a command

to Clarinero's lieutenant, knowing that the Salvadoran would ignore it as a matter of principle, even if it meant missing the opportunity of blowing the bridge. The Cuban muttered under his breath and stared hard through his binoculars.

"Fire!" the lieutenant yelled to the man with the radio transmitter.

The man pressed the key to send the radio signal that would detonate the charge inside the barrel.

A few yards from him, the third barrel, not yet placed in the water, suddenly expanded into thousands of hot metal fragments in a scorching blast of yellowish orange light. The lieutenant and his men were lifted off the ground by the blast. Their flesh was torn from their bones, and their bodies thumped lifelessly back to earth, ripped, gouged, battered.

Paulo Esteban picked himself out of the dirt. He was bleeding from a cut on his neck, and another on his left arm. He could see that the two other Cubans had survived the explosion also, protected from the main force of the blast, as he had been, by an earth bank.

"They used the wrong radio to send the signal," Paulo shouted at the two Cubans, who crouched motionless with shock. "Help me find the right one before it's too late."

Esteban ran among the mutilated bodies of the Salvadorans, searching for the transmitter. He ignored everything except what he was looking for. He snatched up a shattered plastic box with a snapped aerial. He looked downriver toward the bridge and pressed the key.

One side of the long black barge rose on a surge of water. The barge might have righted itself again on the river had not the crane unbalanced it and caused it to tip over. The boom of the crane crashed down on the span of the bridge, crushing girders and metal supports and bringing the lot down into the water. Men fell from the ironwork like ants from tall grass.

The three Cubans watched the distant destruction in

silence, and then the sound came to them upriver seconds later, their ears still ringing from the first blast they had survived.

Paulo Esteban ignored the mangled Salvadorans all around him, wiped the blood from his neck and nodded his head in satisfaction.

Bob Murphy looked the Treasury Police officer in the eye. "I don't think I'm such a tough guy. Sure I'll talk if you torture me."

The officer spoke English. "It would be simpler, no, for you to tell me without the torture?"

"I'll tell you whatever you want to hear rather than be tortured. But first I got to find out what it is you want to hear."

"The truth."

Bob smiled patiently. "I've already told you that. The truth isn't what you want to hear. We both know that. Me and my friends were walking down the street and some crazies on a motorbike attacked us. We fought back. You know the rest. Now that's the truth. But that's plainly not enough for you. Tell me what you want me to say, and if it's not too extreme, maybe I'll say it. Of course I'll deny it when I get back to the States and say you tortured me. That might cost you a few million if I can get some congressmen to raise the issue."

The Treasury Police officer smirked. He climbed out of his chair, a bulky, stocky man like Murphy himself, stretched his arms and cracked the knuckles first in one hand and then the other. He reached for the phone on his desk, dialed a three-number extension and said a few words in rapid Spanish. He replaced the receiver and nodded to Bob.

"You come upstairs with me."

Upstairs. All Bob could think was that they usually took you to the basement for torture. Easier to soundproof against your screams. But this was Treasury Police headquarters in San Salvador. An occasional scream or two in this building would probably not even be noticed. He hadn't seen or heard of Nolan, Hardwick or Waller since they'd been separated on their arrival here. They might be dead already or dying at this very moment. For an instant he visualized their bodies hanging on meat hooks on a cinder-block wall. He followed the officer up an ornate curving staircase.

In a narrow room with a high ceiling, Bob sat on a wooden chair. A technician attached electrodes to his skin, plugged in the wires to a machine on a steel trolley and watched a dial needle.

"First I ask you simple questions we both know the answers to in order to see what your reactions are," the officer told him.

Bob had hardly been able to keep from laughing as soon as he saw the polygraph machine. He knew the simplest way to beat a lie detector every time—he had only to firmly clench his anal sphincter as each and every question was asked and answered. There wasn't a polygraph machine invented that could sort that out.

The town of Corralitos was proud of its bus service. The two buses ran from opposite ends of the town every half hour and usually passed each other in the square. They transported chickens, small pigs and all kinds of merchandise, as well as people. Everyone knew that so long as they could hear the clatter of the buses over the rough cobblestone streets of the town, everything was normal. People here lived in the danger zone between guerrillas and government soldiers, so that every little reassurance was noticed.

Those waiting for the buses found areas of shade from the burning heat of early afternoon. Few people were about in this, the hottest part of the day. After the heat peaked, people would emerge from their siestas, and the activities of the day would recommence. The buses were late. However, there was nothing very unusual about that, and those waiting either chatted or dozed in the shade.

One of Clarinero's assault companies filled one bus at its terminus, and the second assault company filled the other at the opposite end of town. They were waiting for the sound of the bridge explosion as their signal to start.

"There it is," Clarinero said with a smile, and the men in the crowded bus cheered as they heard the dull thump to the north of the town.

Clarinero used his M16 to poke the terrified bus driver in the roll of fat about his waist. The man put the bus in gear, and they set out toward the center of town. Clarinero sat next to Sally. He smiled happily at her and squeezed her hand.

"You promise no one's going to get hurt?" Sally asked again.

"I've already promised you that twenty times," he said. "I want you to see what we do with your own eyes."

"Then why do I need this?" she asked, holding out her M16 for him to take.

He pushed it back to her. "So that people will believe you. If you hold only a flyswatter and say you will harm no one, people will not be impressed. But if you hold an M16 and do not fire a shot, they will remember that."

At that moment they heard a second explosion.

"They shouldn't have done that."

"It's much too soon."

"They were supposed to space out the three blasts to create a continuing diversion."

"They fucked up."

Clarinero stood in the aisle of the lurching bus, faced back and raised his hands to quiet the men. He had to shout to make himself heard above the engine and the rattling of loose panels and windows.

They listened and were reassured.

It all sounded crazy to Sally, but, what the hell, she was

going along for the ride. She had come all this way to see something, and now, by God, she would see it.

"Here they come," one of the men behind them shouted.

A green army truck came thundering toward them on the narrow street. It and the bus squeezed by each other with inches to spare and without either driver slowing so much as 1 mph. A second military truck grazed the side of the bus farther down the street.

The guerrillas cheered the courage of their captive bus driver—who now seemed to be enjoying himself—and the stupidity of the government soldiers rushing out as reinforcements to the river bridge without noticing their enemy on the way in to take over the town in their absence. Three more army trucks passed them in the town square.

Even Sally laughed. "I never thought that what you said would really work. I guess you must really know what you are doing!"

Clarinero looked genuinely flattered at this compliment from her.

They met the other bus outside the barracks on the town square.

"Drive in," Clarinero ordered his driver.

The driver began to ease the front of the bus between two stone pillars, when an unarmed uniformed soldier tried to close the large wooden doors against it. The fender of the bus hit one of the doors.

"Idiot!" the soldier howled and shook his fist at the driver. "You scraped the paint on the door. When the captain sees this, I'm going to tell him who did it, you old fool!"

"Let us in or we'll wreck your door," Clarinero called.

The soldier peered carefully into the bus for the first time, looked horrified at all the armed men inside it and took to his heels. The guerrillas laughed, and the bus drove into the enclosed courtyard of the barracks, followed by the second one.

"No shooting!" Clarinero ordered his men as they poured from the front and rear exits to take cover.

This was when the BBC TV camera crew arrived in two taxis. They got nice shots of the fourteen government soldiers left to guard the barracks being sent home unharmed by the guerrillas, and of course they took all the footage they could get of the pretty blond guerrilla with the M16. Her identity was later supplied to them by a Cuban contact. Clarinero seized weapons and ammunition. Before he and his men retreated from the town, they blew up the barracks and set fire to a coffee warehouse—which pleased the cameramen.

As Clarinero had promised Sally, no one was hurt.

"I'm an American, and you filthy goddam yellabellies had better not try to paw me about!" Harvey Waller looked down at the Treasury cop he had just decked.

The man lay on the tiled floor of the windowless room into which they had locked Harvey at Treasury Police headquarters. The cop's lower lip was split and blood trickled down his chin.

"Get up before I boot ya in the kisser," Harvey snarled.

The cop jumped to his feet real quick and assumed a karate stance.

"I couldn't give a shit for that furrin' nancy-boy prancin' you go on with," Harvey told him and belted him in the left eye.

The policeman had raised his forearm to ward off the blow, as his training in the martial arts had taught him, but Harvey's big hammer fist came through all the same, made an arcade game out of his brain and crumpled him in a corner of the room.

As the cop lay there gasping and moaning, Harvey toed him in the belly, just to let him know he was getting irritated.

"Pity I still need you in working order," Harvey told

him, "or I could really have a little fun with you. On your feet, punk."

The policeman climbed unsteadily to his feet, no karate stance this time.

Harvey pointed. "You got the key to that door?"

"No key, senor."

"You got a gun?"

"No gun, senor."

"You telling me the truth, motherfucker? If I find one on you, I'll tear your head off your shoulders."

The cop's voice rose in anger. "If I had a gun, I would have killed you with it already!"

Harvey grinned. "I believe you."

The policeman was in his early twenties, big, burly, strong, had never had his ass whipped by someone he was supposed to be interrogating. He had been put on this American after the Yank had shown signs he was not the gentle type. The young cop had swaggered into the room and tried to push Harvey around. The rest was history.

"Come over here," Harvey said to him.

The Treasury cop warily obeyed, but ashamed also at being told what to do by a detainee.

Harvey grabbed him in a stranglehold and exerted pressure. The cop began to wheeze and croak for help. The door to the room was thrown open and a tear-gas canister flung in. The door slammed shut before Harvey could get to it.

The canister hissed gas into the room while Harvey banged on the door and offered to go quietly.

The cop joined him and pleaded in Spanish. He got a reply from the other side of the door.

"They say this is my punishment for letting you get the better of me. Next time I am to be more careful."

Harvey nodded. "You'll be a real mean mother when you grow up, kid."

The door was finally opened when both were nearly blinded and asphyxiated by the tear gas.

Harvey couldn't see to get at them as they beat him with

truncheons. When he fell, they kicked him with their heavy boots as he lay on the cool tiled floor of the corridor.

Mike Campbell pressed the elevator button for the sixth floor. It went no higher.

"That's strange," he said to Cesar Ordonez, "I was sure they said he was on the seventh floor."

When they got out on six, a guard with an Ingram submachine gun pointed to a steel door in a wall with a closed-circuit TV camera above it. "They'll open it when they see you."

The electrically operated steel door swung inward after a few moments, and they climbed a flight of stairs to the seventh floor.

"Mr. Murdoch will see you now," a pretty receptionist told them with a New York Puerto Rican accent.

Andrew Murdoch was tall, handsome and fit, every inch a Wall Street WASP with some Gary Hart–style charm. His handshake was firm, his palm dry, his teeth sparkling white. He was the first man Mike had seen wearing a business suit and tie in San Salvador.

"I've been on the phone to Dwight Poynings since you called me," he said to Mike. "Understandably, he's a bit upset that things are not working out smoothly down here. From my short phone conversation with you earlier today, Mr. Campbell, I understand that you wish information on your missing associates. I have made it clear to Poynings that information is all I can supply. I don't know what he told you I could do for you before you came to El Salvador. Certainly I had no knowledge he gave you my name."

"I understand," Mike said. "You are simply the only American businessman he knows who is a resident here. My four missing associates and I came here to investigate a major business opportunity for Poynings. I am not free to discuss the details, as I am sure you will appreciate."

Murdoch nodded. "Why not go to the American embassy?"

"That would be like phoning NBC. Poynings hates publicity."

"How long have they been missing?"

"Two days."

Murdoch shook his head. "That's not good. All the same, I doubt they'd murder four Americans after all the fuss that has been raised over previous American deaths. I think I can find out in a matter of hours where your friends are if they are still alive. If they are not, it will be more difficult. Care for a martini, gentlemen?"

Obviously Andrew Murdoch's move to the tropics had not changed his life-style in every detail. He expertly shook Bombay gin, a sprinkle of vermouth and ice.

Cesar nodded in Murdoch's direction and whispered to Mike, "CIA?"

Mike shrugged.

"I guess you fellows must think me a bit paranoid with the two armed guards at street level and another on the sixth floor, plus the limited access up here," Murdoch was saying. "By the way, there are even more security precautions which are less evident. This is a dangerous country in which to be, but you wouldn't believe how good it is for business. If Salvador's central bank would only free up more foreign exchange, there'd be no limit to entrepreneurial opportunity here."

"That the only reason you're here?" Cesar asked with a sarcastic edge to his voice.

It was lost on Murdoch. "You bet. Sure I got to hide out up here and I can't put the name of my company on the door. I used to have a place down the street a few years ago, a big ground-floor space with plate-glass windows, the company logo, a canopy, the lot—till the damn guerrillas threw bombs inside it. The place was a total loss. Four of my staff were killed, but I escaped with some cuts and bruises. Just lucky, I guess. Now I have to live behind high walls, and armed guards, travel to here from my home in a garkmobile—''

"A what?" Mike asked.

"Garkmobile. After 'oligarchy'—members of the ruling families usually ride in Jeep Cherokee vans with armor plating and bulletproof windows. They buy them in Miami and fit them out here with armor at a cost of forty or fifty grand. It was a legit tax deduction for me with the IRS. They questioned it, and you should have seen the look on that IRS inspector's face—it was at their Church Street office in New York, they haul me in every year, the bastards—you should have seen the look on his face when I claimed submachine guns and bulletproof vests and everything as a business expense. Most people who use that kind of equipment in their work don't pay taxes!"

Lance was terrified they'd inject him with scopolamine or some other truth serum and find out he was the one who had wasted the colonel, Turco and Adolfo. For that, he knew they'd dissect his nervous system, ganglion by ganglion, from his living and feeling tissue with no anesthetic. Or worse.

He remembered the name of a book he had looked at by an Argentine who had run into trouble with the military dictators there, *Cell Without a Number, Prisoner Without a Name*. That was how he was beginning to feel already— after only two days. . . . And they hadn't even beaten him yet! The electric cattle prod had yet to come.

He was doing fine and sticking with his story of being an innocent tourist. Only now and then it would strike— the fear that they would drug him and that he would admit he had killed three of them. Not *one* but *three* of the Treasury Police. He tried to imagine what they would do to him.

Mike Campbell had decided to abort the mission and do what he could to obtain the release of the four men, even if it meant admitting why they had come to El Salvador. He was hanging on to his one last hope—Andrew Murdoch, a business friend of Poynings' who might or might not be a U.S. government agent of some kind. If Murdoch drew a blank, Mike would waste no more time—and he realized he had wasted enough already, dragging his ass around the city searching for them every place he could think of, trying not to arouse curiosity or draw attention to himself.

Mike jumped when the phone rang in his hotel room, and he was annoyed because Cesar grinned at his nervous reaction. Mercs don't expect their mission leader to start nervously when a phone rings!

It was Andrew Murdoch.

"Campbell, I don't know whether to tell you to run for the hills or take a limo to the presidential palace. In any case, it's probably too late for you to do anything now. First, the good news. Your four men are all in Treasury Police custody here in the city. All four are alive and unharmed."

"They're okay," Mike told Cesar and began breathing easier. "Thanks, Murdoch, I owe you for this. What's the bad news?"

"Poynings has gone off his rocker."

"In what way?" Mike asked guardedly.

"A British TV unit shot film of his daughter taking part in a guerrilla raid on the town of Corralitos, northeast of here, on the Rio Lempa. Apparently they flew their film or videotape overnight to London, showed it on TV there—Britain is five hours ahead of Eastern Standard Time—so the East Coast U.S. stations had it in time for their evening news same day, which is today."

Mike glanced at his watch and said into the phone, "Boston is one hour ahead of San Salvador. It's eight here, so this happened two hours ago on the seven o'clock news?"

"Right." Murdoch's voice was crisp. "All three networks carried it. Poynings was forced to allow his own stations to carry scenes of his daughter running about with an automatic rifle. You can imagine the knot that tied him in." Murdoch's voice trailed off as if he were stifling a laugh.

"What did he do?" Mike asked.

"He went on the air, claimed the Nicaraguans were trying to blackmail him, denounced the State Department and claimed that he himself was a good American, that his daughter was having a nervous breakdown or was drugged. It was all highly emotional."

"Did he say anything about us?" Mike asked, knowing it was useless now for him to try to conceal anything from Murdoch.

"No. Nothing. All this certainly answers some questions I had on my mind as to why you were here." Murdoch paused to give Mike a chance to say something. When he was greeted by silence, he went on. "My advice to you is to go see someone in the military here, tell him what you are doing and ask his help. Now that this story is out about Poynings' daughter, the military should be pleased to help you if you promise to give them the credit for anything you manage to achieve."

Nolan, Waller, Hardwick and Murphy were dropped off at their hotel by the Treasury Police and given an hour to shave, shower and change their clothes. Mike and Cesar would accompany them to see the general. Mike summoned Andre Verdoux, seeing no point in leaving him out of things now. Either they were in clover or being kicked out. There wasn't much Mike could do about it, one way or the other.

Mike learned for the first time why the four had been detained. He pumped their Treasury Police driver for more information on the way to the general's.

"Everyone calls him 'the general,'" the Treasury man said. "Maybe his family and close friends call him by his first name, Victor. You don't hear people talking about him by his last name like they do of others. He's always 'the general.' And everyone knows which general is meant. If one officer tells another 'The general says he wants this,' the second officer might wonder whether the general had really said it or whether the first officer would dare put words in the general's mouth he hadn't said. He might wonder, but in the end the second officer would do whatever it was the general was supposed to want rather than risk the consequences of crossing him. That's how powerful he is.''

"He's an Escandell," Mike said. "Isn't that one of the oligarchical families?"

"It's not one of the biggest or richest families, but its members are very powerful. The Escandells are not big landowners like some of the old aristocrats. Their power is in the armed forces and security forces. So he is not a snob. The general is a man of the people. We all like him, and he looks out for us.''

Mike was surprised at the casual English and unguarded attitude of this young officer. He had apparently decided he was among friends and could speak off the record.

Mike sounded him out on this. "Did the general say anything about us?"

"He said you were like family to him."

Mike exchanged a glance with Andre. "Like family?"

"Yes," the officer said. "Your men killed those members of the Clara Elizabeth Ramirez Metropolitan Commando. That was the guerrilla group which killed his brother-in-law, Colonel Cerezo Ramirez, and two other members of the Treasury Police. The general says you avenged his brother-in-law's death and that his family is grateful."

Lance felt his stomach tighten. He was sorry now he had not told Mike Campbell everything that happened. Mike would have looked out for him and steered a safe course. Lance felt that anytime now something was going to go badly wrong and he would be exposed. The general sounded like the last person he should be near when and if this happened. Lance tried to roll down a window of the Cherokee van to get a breath of night air, but the inch-thick Plexiglas was sealed in place.

They pulled off the highway into a residential suburb that was mostly winding roads between high stone walls, many of them floodlit, with armed guards standing with glowing cigarette tips in the dark outside the heavy wooden doors or inside the strongly barred gates.

They received a visual check from four uniformed Treasury policemen before a massive wood door in a high wall was opened to admit their vehicle.

"Is this the general's home?" Andre asked when he saw the lighted picture windows of an ultramodern luxury house beyond a swimming pool with underwater illumination.

The driver laughed. "He lives in a mansion. This is only the place he built for his mistress."

At the door, Victor Escandell greeted them like long-lost friends. Bald, going to flab, but still a very domineering presence, he shook their hands and slapped their shoulders. He spoke only in Spanish, and the officer who had been their driver translated as much as he could for them, since the general didn't pause much to give him a chance to catch up. The general explained that he understood English well and that they should speak it to him—it was just that in conversation he never had the time to search for the English words he needed. He felt more relaxed using an interpreter.

"My good friends, avengers of the wrong that has been done to my sister," he told them on the doorsteps, hands outstretched as if he were addressing a political rally, "welcome to my country, make yourself at home in this house, enjoy yourselves tonight, for we have work to do together in the days ahead."

As they followed the general inside the house, listening to his praise for them for having killed the Metropolitan Commando members, Lance started to get that sinking feeling in his stomach again. He couldn't help thinking how Hollywood would handle the scene where he announced in a loud voice to everybody, "It wasn't the leftists who killed those men. I am the one who killed your brother-in-law." If he actually did say it, Mike would probably think he was stoned again.

A dozen women stood about inside the house in sexy, low-cut dresses. They all had black hair and flashing dark eyes, and were a little tipsy from the drinks a uniformed soldier served them from a tray. Another man in uniform mixed drinks behind a table covered with a huge white cloth. Bottles of rum and other drinks, bowls of fruit and neat rows of upturned empty glasses stood on this table. Another table held an array of food dishes.

The general introduced Maria to them, a tall, placid-looking woman getting a little heavy on the beam.

"Maria is the general's friend," their officer driver turned interpreter added in English.

It was clear he meant that Maria was off limits to them. None of the other ladies were introduced, and no introductions were needed. They had ways of making themselves understood.

One spoke English. She said she was Rosita and acted as a go-between and explainer for the others. The officer who had driven them apparently considered this chore beneath his dignity and spent his time chatting with another man there. He beckoned Mike over and introduced the man as Major Rafael Chavarria, who commanded a "hunter battalion"—troops trained by the U.S. Army to root out guerrillas. Mike could see that this meeting was not accidental, and in a little while the general joined them.

Bob Murphy also joined the men in conversation, after he persuaded one of the ladies to release her hold on his dick. Compared to these Latin lovelies, Eunice back in Vermont was about as attractive as a barn door. Yet, he would be loyal to her. It wasn't always easy, but to him it was important.

The others had no such conflict of interest. As they consumed increasing volumes of the smoothly blended rum-and-fruit drinks, the women grew ever more beautiful and more desirable in their eyes.

Someone put on tapes. Lance, Cesar and Andre, good dancers and able to speak Spanish, took their pick of the women. Joe and Harvey shuffled about as best they could to the complicated Latin rhythms.

After a while Rosita announced in English, "I'm bored. You know what I do when I'm bored? I take off my clothes."

She took off her clothes. Not all of them right away, but piece by piece in time to the music.

Then two of the women, who had been dancing with each other for want of a man, started peeling off their dresses. Stark naked, they touched bare nipples as they danced with each other, then bare bellies, then really got involved up close with each other.

Most of the other women had partially or completely disrobed. But not Maria, the general's woman. She went and sat in a corner by herself, fully clothed, sipping on a big drink served to her on a tray by the uniformed soldier.

Lance, his shirt off, was writing the word *salud* in lipstick across the belly of a tall girl with a gorgeous body who wore nothing but high heels. He sent her to belly dance for Mike Campbell, the general, Bob Murphy and the Salvadoran officers—in the hope she could distract them from their serious talk.

Chapter 11

CAMPBELL looked down at the riddled bodies of the three government soldiers their companions brought in. He looked up at the wooded slopes outside the town.

"Let's go after those bastards," he said to Major Rafael Chavarria.

"We'll call in planes at dawn tomorrow and see if we can pin them down," the major said evasively.

"Dammit, we know where they are now," Mike exploded. "Sitting up on that hill laughing at you."

"It would be a disaster for me to go in after them," the major explained coldly. "My losses would be too high to be acceptable."

Mike understood the officer's thinking. The major was not a coward, he was a career military man. As such, he always had to make himself look good, regardless of the outcome of the battle or campaign. Even if he succeeded in wiping out this pocket of guerrillas at the cost of high casualties to his men, back at military headquarters the casualties would be remembered rather than his victory. Nowadays, no officer, unless he was some kind of military genius at a time of full-scale war, could live with the reputation of using his men as cannon fodder. His own soldiers might frag him or, as had happened in El Salvador, switch sides by joining the guerrillas.

"You have any objection if my team goes after them?" Mike asked.

The major waved his hand at the wooded hills. "Be my guest."

Mike walked toward the mercs, who were in a huddle apart from the regular soldiers. Mike and they wore regular Salvadoran army combat fatigues and carried U.S.-supplied weapons. Each man had an M16 assault rifle and Colt semiautomatic pistol, plus a unique Central American addition—a razor-sharp machete in a long leather scabbard.

"I ain't messing with this thing," Bob Murphy said, clumsily handling his machete. "You seen the way the local people use these things? They'd chop us to pieces."

"Not me they won't," Harvey Waller said, happily swinging the tempered blade in wild arcs all about him.

Lance Hardwick was inclined to agree with Bob's assessment. "I saw this woman in the town this morning—she was no more than twenty, a real beauty, and she had this kid of maybe three or four along with her. She was hunkered down and had the kid's hand splayed on a tree stump, cutting the kid's fingernails with this humongous machete, chop, chop, chop, and not gentle, either—really bringing the blade down. That sweet-looking lady could serve one of us up as a fillet with a couple of turns of her wrist—you included, Harvey."

"Been a lot of people thought they could do that to me," Harvey growled. "I'm still lookin' for the ones that got away alive."

Lance was about to kid Harvey until he saw that he was perfectly serious. Lance let it go.

In spite of what they said, all the men brought their machetes with them. In addition, Mike found an old M79 grenade launcher in good condition and buckled on a belt of 40 mm grenade cartridges. The M79 added five pounds to his load, not counting ammunition, but Mike liked the weapon enough to put up with that, in spite of its being rendered almost obsolete by the grenade launchers included on many modern combat rifles. He just liked the feel of the wood stock and wide-bore short barrel, the way it handled like a squat old-fashioned shotgun that breaks open when the locking latch is pushed all the way to the right. He peered through the barrel to make sure it was clean, and inserted a grenade cartridge until the rim of the case contacted the extractor. He snapped the weapon shut and pushed the slide-type safety catch found on regular side-by-side shotguns.

General Victor Escandell had assigned Chavarria and his hunter battalion to work with Mike's team in going after Comandante Clarinero and Sally Poynings. It was obviously Clarinero whom the general wanted. He was openly using Mike as both a goad and free unofficial advisor to Chavarria.

The general had known a surprising amount about Mad Mike Campbell, and at the party he had laid it on thick to the major about how cunning and ruthless this American mercenary was known to be. Then he turned to Mike and told him, in the major's hearing, that if Mike had any complaints or that if anything stood in the way of his progress, he had only to contact him or one of his brothers to have things straightened out. With a generous smile, the general informed Major Chavarria that Campbell was a godsend, that Mike would nail Clarinero for him and rescue the girl, leaving all the glory to the Salvadoran army. The major began to look more cheerful when he heard that.

"There's one thing I want you to clearly understand, Senor Campbell." The general's voice boomed above the noise of the music and raucous laughter of the women. "Our price for helping you is Clarinero's head." He chuckled as he watched the naked woman in high heels tease them with her dance. "On a plate."

Mike and the team left the town at a steady run in a single line, with Joe Nolan at point. They had no battle plan—only that they were not going to let the guerrillas that had seized the town escape unscathed. After slaughtering the town's garrison of twelve soldiers, the guerrillas had executed its mayor and another leading citizen before robbing and burning its bank. They were part of Commandante Clarinero's fighting force, but none of the townspeople had seen either the comandante or a blond girl with them. Chavarria's battalion and the merc team had arrived in trucks. Retaking the town had cost the lives of three of Chavarria's men. So far as they could tell, there had been no rebel casualties. Now the guerrillas had melted back into the forested mountains as quickly as they had appeared.

Mike and the others felt a need to make contact with their adversaries. Once they had engaged them in a firefight, they would have their feet wet, so to speak. They were all a bit frustrated by their wait in San Salvador.

"Calm them down," Andre cautioned Mike as they trotted along. "Everyone's too eager. Someone's going to get killed."

Mike acknowledged his mistake with a smile. "I'm as bad as the rest of them. Thanks, Andre, it's good to have you along." He shouted up the line to Joe Nolan at point. "What's this, the Kentucky Derby? Slow down. You're going to get your ass handed to you if you don't go careful."

Like Mike himself, Joe didn't need to be told twice when he was going about something the wrong way. He slowed his pace and grew more watchful, using hand signals to control the men behind him.

They were moving through small fields in the uplands beyond the edge of the town. Fields had been cleared some distance up the slope, and it was evergreen forest the rest of the way. They had seen the guerrillas, perhaps fifty to sixty in number, retreat this way. The path the rebels had taken into the dark trees was broad and well used. Even though the rebels had moved out of town fast as the government troops advanced, Joe, as he went, scanned for trip wires and antipersonnel mines they might have had time to set.

Once in the trees, the sinister stillness and darkness of the woods made every one of them more cautious, no matter how eager they were to draw first blood.

Mike moved up along the line to number three position, so he would be able to see what was happening and give orders while things were still breaking. He didn't like going in blind into the forest after the rebels any more than the Salvadoran major did, but Mike and his men didn't have time to dance around on the edge of things.

They made their way along the winding path through the tall, bare lower trunks of the evergreens, each like a telephone pole with an umbrella of leaves at the top. The "Christmas tree" smell was pleasant, the turf was soft and springy beneath their feet and they enjoyed the coolness and respite from the broiling sun. They kept up a fast clip in spite of their watchfulness and fear of booby traps, leaving twenty feet between each man in case they got raked by automatic fire. Their week on the Chesapeake had made them all fit, and living it up in San Salvador hadn't softened them too much.

Joe Nolan crouched, and held up a hand for them to stop. One by one, the men dived for cover and lay ready with their weapons. Joe beckoned Mike forward to join him.

"Listen," he said when Mike crept up alongside him.

Mike heard nothing.

Joe shook his head after a minute. "I could've sworn I heard something."

"We'll wait," Mike said.

They stayed put and listened in the forest stillness.

A guffaw. They both heard it. Directly ahead, on the path they were traveling.

Mike turned about and signaled to the others to hold their

positions. Then he nodded to Joe, who crept forward with Mike two paces behind him. Joe slowed at a twist in the trail and peered around a massive trunk. He pulled his head back fast and gesticulated to Mike.

"How many?" Mike whispered.

Joe peeked again. "Four. All together."

"Can you take them?"

"I'll try."

"I'll be right behind you," Mike guaranteed.

They both checked, for maybe the twentieth time, that their M16s were switched to full automatic.

Joe nodded to Mike.

As Joe stepped forward from behind the tree trunk to confront the four guerrillas, Mike kept by his side. The rebels sat on their backpacks in the middle of the trail, talking and smoking with their rifles across their knees.

With a rapid zigzag of his rifle barrel, Joe toppled all four of them in a single burst of fire, using only about half of the thirty-round magazine. Mike didn't fire a shot. They both waited and watched for a moment.

"I'll go back for the others," Mike said.

He had them drag the four bodies away from the path into the trees and slung a hand-held radio transmitter after them.

Mike said to Joe, "They'll be alerted by the lack of radio response if they didn't hear your burst of fire. Keep up a fast pace from here on. I'll be right behind you."

Mike lost no time in moving them out. If they were going to lose the element of surprise, perhaps speed would make up for it.

If any of them had ever doubted the value of what they had done every day on Assateague Island, running endless mile after mile up and down the beach, they found out its benefit now. The going was all uphill, and the higher they climbed, the steeper it became. The path tacked from side to side up the mountain like a sailboat against the wind.

Joe Nolan spun about, wildly gestured for them to take

cover and dived into some thick prickly bushes. Moments later, a platoon of twelve men came down the trail in single file, spaced apart, rifles at the ready. The mercs, hardly breathing where they lay hidden only a few yards away on both sides of the trail, listened to each of the guerrillas pass: his footfalls on the litter of the forest floor, the way each of them brushed against the branch of a bush, one man's belch, another's sniffle. Each one of the mercs had wondered for a panic-stricken instant if he had forgotten to conceal some part of himself or his equipment, leaving a foreign object visible in the bushes upon which a guerrilla's eye might chance to fall. But there was nothing for the guerrillas to see, and they continued downhill along the trail.

Mike waited a couple of minutes before he stood and hissed to the others, "They've gone back to see what happened to the rearguard. We gotta move forward fast now and hit the main group while we can. Remember, from this point on we got to watch our ass with that platoon behind us."

Joe hit the trail even faster than before. The others wound along behind him, confident in Mike Campbell's leadership—all except Mike, who wished he knew what the hell to expect and had some contingency plans, or even a plan, he could rely on. Sometimes a soldier had to jump in with both feet, and at such times it was better to act than worry.

After a steep climb, they came to the top of the wooded hill. The trail bore to the right, following the highest ground, which had only a thin cover of trees. Huge slabs of rock jutted from the soft cover of vegetation. Joe motioned that he was going ahead alone to reconnoiter.

He came back in a few minutes. "They've left another four guards on the trail to cover their rear. These ones are a lot more alert than the first four."

"They've probably heard that the others are missing," Mike said. "But they'll think it's just a foul-up unless that platoon finds the bodies. Any sign of the main group of guerrillas?''

"I didn't hear anything. But they can't be far ahead of us.''

Mike slung his M16 on his back and drew his machete. He pointed its blade at Nolan, Murphy and Waller. They drew theirs.

"No shooting" was all he said.

They watched the four guerrillas from the cover of bushes.

Mike whispered, "We could never get closer than this without them spotting us. I'm going to draw them to us. Ready?'' He looked them over quickly, then shouted to the four guerrillas, "Compañeros! Aqui!''

The rebels looked startled and stood undecided.

"Aqui!'' Mike shouted again, invisible in the bushes.

They came running, assault rifles at the ready.

Mike popped up right next to one, using his motion to deliver a short, sharp chop with the machete. The steel blade buried itself in the guerrilla's skull with a whack— the same sound it had made on the unripe coconuts Mike had practiced on. He had to put one foot on the lifeless man's shoulder in order to yank the blade out of the splintered bone.

To his right, he saw Joe Nolan deliver a series of chops to his struggling, groaning victim on the ground. The man clutched at the blade of the machete with his bare hands till their flesh was cut to ribbons from the bones. Joe dug at him with the long blade till he lay still.

Harvey stood over his dead rebel, who was sliced open across the chest, and the merc smiled like a family butcher over a showpiece of prime ribs.

Bob Murphy missed with his first swing at his guerrilla. The man saw the blade descending on him and pulled back. The terrorist took another backward step as Bob's brawn followed through on his swing. The rebel directed the barrel of his M16 at Bob's gut and went to squeeze the trigger.

Before his brain managed to send the message to his trigger finger, Harvey gave him a sideways cut to the upper arm that severed the nerve.

The guerrilla stood there shocked, as in a still from a movie, while Harvey moved next to him, jaws working frantically on a wad of gum. Harvey held his machete in a two-handed grip, with the blade balanced on his left shoulder, and he took a mighty swipe that made the blade scream through the air.

He cut the guerrilla's head clean from his shoulders.

Harvey looked after the head as it flew through the air and disappeared into some bushes. He grinned his sick grin and said to the others, "If this was Fenway Park, that would have been a home run."

Lance, Cesar and Andre tried not to blanch as they saw their four comrades return smeared in blood and carrying dripping machetes.

Elated now, with a manic smile Harvey smeared blood with his hand onto Lance's clean fatigues and yelled at him, "Come on in! It's warm! It only seems cold when you're standing out there!"

Lance gagged.

"Enough!" Mike barked and faced Harvey down.

"Crazy fucker," Bob Murphy muttered at Harvey in Lance's defense.

Harvey retorted, "That's not what you were saying a few minutes ago when I saved your bacon."

Bob nodded. "That's true, Harvey. But calm down now."

"You be calm, Murphy," Harvey sneered. "I'll save your ass while you look cool."

Mike let them talk themselves out and mutter curses for a while, then he led all of them deliberately slow past the four hacked-up corpses and beyond. That brought everyone back to reality, especially the fact that they were in unknown territory again, that they were no longer king of the hill and could easily end looking just like the four recently deceased on the trail behind them.

"The main group of rebels has got to be near," Mike said. "As soon as we see them, take cover in a line at right angles to this path. I want ten feet at least between each man."

He nodded to Joe Nolan to take the lead again. Mike followed in number two position after telling Andre to cover their rear.

At one bend in the path that was easy to recognize, Andre hung back to lay a trip wire. He attached the wire to a rectangular polystyrene Claymore antipersonnel mine which he had placed out of sight next to the path. Then he removed the safety pin and covered the mine with forest litter. When Andre caught up with the others, he passed the word along about the location of the trip wire. That was the trouble with a mine—it could cause as much damage to the side that carelessly laid it as to the enemy. It was impersonal about whom it killed.

The main body of guerrillas were eating C rations in a forest clearing when Mike and the team came upon them. The mercs were immediately spotted by lookouts and had to dive to the ground to avoid being raked by automatic fire. The bullets ripped through the leaves of the undergrowth and smacked off tree trunks. The twenty-five or thirty men dropped their spoons and cans and grabbed their M16s, AK-47s, M2s and Mini-14s.

Campbell slipped the safety on his M79 grenade launcher, sighted quickly and shot a grenade cartridge into the main body of guerrillas.

The explosion tore limbs and flesh from those nearest it, hit others with fragments, knocked down more with the force of its blast and frightened the wits out of the rest—long enough for the merc team to shower them with automatic fire from their M16s. The rebels dropped like flies. Then Mike followed through with a second cartridge shell. But by this time the surviving guerrillas had spread out, and the grenade only took out some on the left flank.

The hostile force had broken up into pockets of resistance behind good cover and were returning fire now with threatening accuracy.

"Take cover!" Mike yelled at Hardwick and Waller, who were standing out front, feet apart, blazing away as though they were at the O.K. Corral.

They obeyed, fortunately for themselves, because a withering hail of fire was now directed at them by the surviving guerrillas, who had gotten over their initial shock. The rebels were contained in four pockets, and they were coordinating their attacks. They still outnumbered the mercs by more than two to one—and the question now was, Who had got whom pinned down?

Mike had an answer to that question. His M79. Using the graduated leaf rear sight, he sent in grenade after grenade until he flushed each pocket of guerrillas from cover. When they realized they were being systematically wiped out, the guerrillas tried a desperate charge. The survivors now barely outnumbered the mercs, and they came at them with the ferocity of cornered rats.

Mike kicked off with his M16, and his bullets curled one of the guerrillas in on himself like a worm wriggling on a hook.

Another of his bullets entered a rebel's chest, the entry wound only a pinpoint of blood on the man's combat fatigues. But when he slowly turned around as he fell, Mike saw that the exit wound in his back was big enough to stick his fist in.

They kept coming at the mercs, so crazed with last-ditch terror they couldn't shoot straight and hardly knew what they were doing.

The mercs blew them apart with close-up automatic fire. The last two still on their feet got hit with so many bullets from so many M16s, their bodies swayed and leaked from the multiple punctures caused by the high-velocity 5.56 mm projectiles.

Mike checked on the carnage to make sure all had been hit. He had learned the hard way that he could never assume a man was finished fighting just because he was lying down. But all these men were dead.

The mercs took this time to check their weapons and magazine supply.

Mike walked over to them and pointed. "We have some friends back along the trail I'd like you to meet. Andre will lead the way."

The leader of the guerrilla platoon couldn't be positive that this was the place he had seen the four-man rearguard placed, until one of his men found blood drops on some leaves. The blood was fresh, still liquid on the rebel's fingers. The leader was about to radio back when they heard the shooting.

"They must have used a different trail to bypass us," he shouted to his men. "Let's take them from the rear! On the double!"

The shooting uphill from them continued, along with grenade explosions, as they ran along the path to their friends' aid. They had been farther off than they first thought, and the shooting stopped before they even got close. They had no idea who had gotten the upper hand, but they were coming anyhow. They did not slow their pace, rushing uphill along the winding path, fast as they could go with heavy boots, rifles and backpacks.

As they ran, they almost trod on the hacked-up corpses of the second rearguard. Although these men had all seen combat before, this sight—involving comrades they had seen alive such a short time ago—was enough to quench their revolutionary fervor. But their leader urged them forward, promising that vengeance would be theirs; and in a moment they were charging along the trail after him to slaughter their enemies.

The rebel leader's leg caught in the trip wire so hard he fell over it, and the Claymore blew before he hit the ground. Its C4 explosive projected seven hundred steel balls in a 60-degree array in the direction they were coming from. Lethal to about forty-five yards, the steel balls missed some members of the platoon who were sheltered by the bodies of others.

Those nearest were chopped to pulp and died instantly. Those farther back were less fortunate and began to die noisily and painfully from their mortal wounds. Two were injured only in the legs; one was hit in the left arm; and two were completely untouched and stood there with their mouths hanging open in horrified amazement.

The mercs took them clean away with a burst of M16 automatic fire at gut level. Harvey ran in gleefully with his Colt pistol to finish off any still moving.

Chapter 12

THERE was no doubt about who was giving orders now to Major Rafael Chavarria's hunter battalion. It was Mad Mike Campbell. He and his team had arrived back in camp the previous evening just as the cooks were about to serve food. The major and the other officers had already left to dine at the town's single restaurant. Mike kicked over pots of stew and vegetables, overturned trestle tables and benches, knocked a sergeant out cold who tried to stand up to him, waved his M16 in the faces of three companies of soldiers and told them they had some work to do before they ate. He loaded them into the trucks, stopped outside the restaurant in town and, regardless of rank, packed the protesting officers into the trucks with the men. They were unloaded at the base of the wooded slope and ordered to climb the path to collect the weapons, ammunition, boots and other equipment from the rebels the mercs had killed. Neither Mike nor any of his team said one boastful word. They let the results speak for themselves.

On the way back to camp, the trucks dropped off the officers at the restaurant, while Mike and his team returned to the camp to eat with the men. Although the soldiers had grumbled and cursed until they had seen the dead guerrillas, by the time they got back to the camp with the captured weapons, their morale was high and they had a new leader. Campbell was giving orders now.

Later that night, one of the battalion's radio operators came to Mike's tent to tell him he had just heard rebel field radios on the air. One nearby transmitter had just sent details about the Americans present, had described the guerrilla defeat and had said the Americans had come to capture a blond woman they believed Clarinero was holding.

"Damn," Mike grumbled, "I wonder how they got hold of that."

"They have spies and infiltrators everywhere, sir," the radio operator said.

Mike crawled back into his tent to get a few hours' sleep beneath a mildewed blanket on stony soil.

In the predawn darkness, Campbell and the major pored over a map by the light of a propane lamp. The major had gotten over his rage at Mike's actions when he had received, the previous night, a personal congratulatory radio message from the general that credited him with the head count of dead rebels. This was one tide the major was willing to float with. This morning he remembered that the general had once described Campbell as a "godsend," and he now saw the wisdom of that description. So far as the major was now concerned, Mike had only to say the word; and if the major could deliver, Mike would get it.

"The C-130s should be taking off about now," the major said.

"How many did you get?"

"Two."

That would be fine. These American-piloted planes were effective in spotting insurgent positions. The major and his officers all agreed that Clarinero and the rest of his forces would not be far away. Although the comandante was known to split up his men, and often attacked several places simultaneously, the various groups never strayed very far from one another.

On two previous occasions, government troops had cut off and liquidated an arm of Clarinero's forces. Both times, Clarinero's main force had counterattacked from nearby and wreaked bloody vengeance on the recently victorious government soldiers.

Mike had demanded that the major call in reconnaissance planes. They would be hearing from them in the next hour if they came as promised.

"If they come," the major repeated from time to time for Mike's benefit.

"If they don't, you're going to have to radio the general to find out why they didn't," Mike warned him finally.

The major looked more upset about this possibility than he had ever done about fighting guerrillas.

Mike laughed and poked the major in the ribs. "Don't worry. Soon as we get the girl and finish Clarinero, we'll take off home and leave you in peace."

"God willing," the major said with a watery smile.

The soldiers had breakfasted and were ready to move out on the trucks; the sun was burning the mist from the tops of the evergreens in the foothills; and there was still no word from the planes.

"So maybe we gave you some bad advice at times," Paulo Esteban conceded to Comandante Clarinero.

"Putting our revolutionary funds into Mexican pesos instead of the hated Yanqui dollars certainly turned out to be bad advice, Paulo," Clarinero said. "The devaluation of the Mexican peso did our movement more harm than all the Salvadoran government hunter battalions put together. I think you Cubans should pass on to us some more of all that money the Russians give you."

"I tell you they don't give us much money," Paulo said exasperatedly. "Who the hell wants rubles? What can you buy with rubles? They give us credit. Credit for what? Russian goods, of course."

"Which are no damn good."

"Which are no damn good," Paulo agreed. "But that's beside the point. Look, you need five million Yanqui dollars to keep going, right? You have five million sitting outside in the sun not a hundred yards away."

"She's got blond hair and a big mouth," Manuel put in.

"You're talking about ransom?" Clarinero asked, clearly annoyed.

"Of course," Paulo answered.

"She comes to us as a sympathetic observer," Clarinero said, "and you want me to behave like a common criminal toward her?"

"It's all justified because it forwards our aims, helps the revolution," Esteban said smoothly.

"I'm not one of your communist-party goons, Esteban. Leave her out of this. If I have to, I'll raid some of the big banks in the provincial capitals."

"And lose a lot of men," Manuel pointed out.

"All to save that peach-fuzz blonde for yourself?" Pablo insinuated. "Seems to me you're putting your own creature comforts ahead of the military aims we hold in common regardless of our political views, Clarinero."

"She's a friend," the comandante said evenly. "I don't turn against a friend because I can gain some advantage from it."

"I think she's more than a friend," Manuel jeered.

"Are you trying to claim you're not fucking her?" Paulo asked directly.

"None of that is your business," Clarinero said abruptly. "I am in command here. She will not be held for ransom, and I will not hand her over to anyone else, either."

"You've been told that these American mercenaries are here to capture her and that they have the support of the general," Paulo said, trying to bring back their argument to a conversational tone. "Last evening you lost almost sixty men to them, more than a quarter of your fighting force. The girl isn't safe with you anymore, comandante. We will take her to a more secure environment.''

"I suppose you mean Nicaragua," the comandante sneered.

Esteban did not reply. He looked out the tent flap at the last wraiths of mist lifting from the trees in the dawn sunshine.

"I think she should be sent out aboard the supply plane," Paulo said. "Shouldn't be long now."

Clarinero jumped to his feet, eyes blazing. "No!"

Up to this point it had been just an argument. The comandante could always ignore the recommendations of his Cuban advisors. They could criticize him later to the FMLN ruling body, but who cared? There would be some new crisis by then that would make this look like an unimportant side issue. And once a man had his own armed force out in the hills, he was fully answerable to no ruling body. But this was different. . . . Now they were threatening him.

The comandante had set up camp overnight in the trees next to the flat grassy area in the valley bottom where the ammo supply plane was scheduled to land at daybreak. It was an old American DC-3, said to have been used by Somoza to drop barrels of gasoline, after he had run out of bombs, on the Nicaraguan capital during the overthrow of his dictatorship. This prop plane suddenly turned the Cubans' demands from an annoyance into a real threat. No one was going to take Sally from him!

The comandante calmed himself, sat down again and ran his finger down the list of needed supplies he would give the pilot for his next run. Let Esteban think he had put the matter out of his mind. He knew what he must do. When that plane landed, he would take Sally with him to meet it. The Cubans would never dare argue with him in front of his men. His men were loyal to him and would tear Esteban and Manuel apart with their bare hands if he told them to. For one wild moment, he thought of forcing the two Cubans to leave on the plane—but then he realized that this could jeopardize his future supplies from Nicaragua, which were, after all, arranged by the Cubans. He would have to live with their continuing presence in his camp, but he would keep them in their place.

"I am depressed at the loss of all those good men," the comandante said. "But I have taken big losses before and rebuilt my strike force. It's the waste of human life that makes me very sad."

Esteban had his pat Marxist-Leninist explanations for all that, and he ran through some of them for the comandante. Then the three men heard the engines of the prop plane coming in for its landing—in this kind of operation, a plane wasted no time in circling. It came in and got out again without ever turning off its engines.

"We should go," the comandante said, about to stand.

Manuel put his finger on one item in the list of supplies. "Look here."

Clarinero looked.

Esteban caught him behind the left ear with the side of his heavy revolver, and the comandante slumped to the floor of the tent.

Esteban stepped outside the tent and called, "Sally!" He waved to her to come and stepped back inside the tent.

Manuel was emptying a bottle of ether over a face towel.

"There's damn all we can do unless we can get a fix on their location," Mike was explaining to Andre when a radio operator came at a run to the major's tent.

"The planes have seen them, sir! About a hundred and fifty men moving across the next valley, but away from us. They saw the planes, and one fired a SAM-7 missile but missed by a mile. I checked with HQ and they say we have no troops in that area, sir. So it must be the guerrillas. I have the map coordinates here."

The major marked the position of the enemy column on his field map, dismissed the radio operator and slumped dispiritedly in his camp chair.

"They're inaccessible," he complained.

"Crap," Mike said. "If they can go in there, so can you."

"What about our supply lines?"

"Fuck your supply lines. Make sure every man is carrying a three-day ration of fresh water, his rifle and lots of ammo. Those are all the supplies they'll need, and the sooner they wipe out these guerrillas, the sooner they'll be back here at the camp kitchen."

"There's going to be trouble among the men," the major said morosely.

"Tell them that I'm just waiting to make an example of the first man who crosses me," Mike said grimly. "Tell them I'm a pal of the general's, and that so far as the general is concerned, I can put any one of them on a spit and cook him."

The major nodded appreciatively. "They'll believe that, all right."

Campbell stopped in the shade of a massive evergreen, looked at his compass and checked the map. "I think we're right here." He pointed out the spot for the major. "What do you think?"

The major had no opinion. He had the unwilling, sulky look of a child being taken somewhere against his will.

"I agree," André Verdoux volunteered. "There's that range there on our left, so that if we follow this stream it will take us between these two hills and we'll end up in that valley west of this one where Clarinero's men were spotted. Only trouble is, they were heading north. Where will they be now?"

"I'm guessing they'll circle back to the west," Mike said, "and we'll find them in this valley."

"Why?"

"Because they'll be suspicious of the way we pulled

out of town so quickly and they'll suspect a trap," Mike said. "Why would we just go away and leave the town almost unguarded. So they'll hang around here until they get hard information on our whereabouts before attacking the town again. I think I'm right in saying, major, am I not, that normally your troops would have occupied that town until you had made sure the guerrillas' main force had left the area."

"That's right," the officer said shortly.

Mike had loaded nearly everyone aboard the trucks and pulled out of camp without a word as to where they were going. Andre, by this time, had borrowed a field radio and they had monitored outgoing messages to the guerrillas from their spies in the town. But this time their spies had nothing to tell them except that Chavarria's battalion and the norteamericanos had gone somewhere.

Mike was depending on these messages being enough to halt Clarinero's northward march. Well outside view from the town, he had ordered the trucks to pull into the hills. Then he had marched the soldiers and his mercs up and down hills and through forests until he reached where he was now. It occurred to Mike that he was going to look very foolish if Clarinero had not risen to the bait and had either kept on marching north or gone back immediately to recapture the town. But no military leader can refuse to act on his hunches for fear of looking foolish. So Mike told himself.

Two-thirds of Chavarria's hunter battalion had been trained in Panama by U.S. Army sergeants. The battalion consisted of eighty-seven men plus seven mercs against Clarinero's 140 or 150. What Chavarria's side lacked in numbers, it more than made up for in training. The guerrillas would have the edge on them in dedication and desperation, which in this case were pretty much the same thing; that made Mike anxious to put the fear of God into the soldiers dealing with him. Neither side had any advantage in weapons. The comandante and his men would have the advantage in knowing the terrain; but against that,

Mike and Chavarria would have the advantage of surprise—
they hoped. Chavarria's fit of sulks suited Mike's plans
exactly, since it left him in total control.

"Ordonez, Murphy, Waller—no, you stay here, Harvey—
Nolan, you three select two men apiece from our Salvadoran
buddies here and move out as scouting parties," Campbell
said. "That means you don't engage their forces, you
come back to us instead. And look out for a bimbo with
blond hair."

As Ordonez, Murphy and Nolan picked their men and
prepared to move forward along the stream bed, Harvey
Waller resentfully asked, "Why did you change your mind
about sending me?"

"Because if you had laid eyes on any of them, Harvey,
you couldn't resist the chance to blast them."

"True enough," Waller grunted and stopped bitching.
He wasn't going to tell Mike how he had spent weeks
hunting down that commie prof in Harvard and how he had
waited for just the right moment.

All three scouting parties came back several times as the
battalion advanced, but each time they had nothing to
report. When they had moved into the valley itself, keeping to the wooded cover of one slope, it was not long
before all three scouting parties appeared almost simultaneously with news of armed guerrillas directly ahead in
the scrubby evergreens. They could not approach nearer
because the guerrillas had placed outlying patrols of three
and four men.

Mike said, "Clarinero will stay put here till he gets a
radio message on our whereabouts, and then he'll decide
how to act."

"It could be he knows we're here," Andre suggested
quietly, "and that he's ready for a showdown."

"That's what he'll get," Mike said without hesitation.

Campbell gathered his team about him.

"Okay, men, let's not forget our primary objective.
We're *not* here to fight rebels. We're here to pick up a rich

man's daughter, alive and unhurt. Remember that. If anything happens to her, our mission has failed. Objective number two is to take out Comandante Clarinero. We promised the general that, but it's only number two.''

"I came here to kill Cuban communists," Cesar said in a sour voice.

"All right. Objective number three, help Cesar fumigate some Cuban bugs. But first, the girl. Don't fuck up on that. Which means we can't launch a frontal attack. Waller and Hardwick, you come with me. We're going in to get the girl. Rest of you, stay here and keep these soldiers quiet, even if you have to strangle them to do it. If you hear shooting, drive them on ahead of you—stampede them in. Let's go.''

A little way on, Mike stopped, and they fixed bayonets to their M16s. Then they moved cautiously forward till they saw a guerrilla patrol moving among the bushes ahead of them. The patrol had three men, and though they lay in wait for it, it veered off in another direction. A bit farther on, they heard another patrol—this time of five men, smoking and talking. Mike shook his head and they kept out of sight till the patrol had passed.

Mike held up his hand for them to stop at a narrow, well-beaten path, probably a deer trail. They hid behind some trees and waited.

They heard feet shuffling through the dry forest litter and then saw forms moving some distance away: three men, coming along the path. Lance and Harvey looked at Mike. He nodded, holding up one finger to Lance, two to Harvey and pointing three at himself. They nodded.

They scrunched down low as they could get behind the leaves of the low bushes, taking a last look at the steel bayonet at the end of the barrel but not daring to move to make sure it was still attached tightly. Each one fixed on his prey, ignoring the others.

Lance tried to control his breathing, keep it regular and easy—he felt he was gasping for breath like a fish out of water. His heart was pounding. His goddam pulse was pounding! In his left wrist. His palms were sweating. He clutched his M16, which felt greasy and slippery in his grip. His nose was running. The back of his neck itched. They were still coming along the path. His right eye was watering. He would probably fuck up, and Mike would kill him if this kamikaze guerrilla, who had probably been fighting since he was eight years old, didn't first rip him to bits. . . .

Lance Hardwick sprang up to meet the first man, who was ambling watchfully, M16 slung on his right shoulder, right hand resting on the weapon. Holding his rifle sideways, Lance delivered an upward thrust of the flattened bayonet blade to the man's midriff, so that the steel slipped easily through the ribs, like a knife between the slats of a venetian blind.

Lance felt him struggle, skewered on the bayonet, a bit like a big fish tugging on a fishing rod. Then the contorted, writhing body slipped in its agony off the blade and curled up on the ground, making horrible groaning noises, with blood streaming out of the wound onto the man's wrists and over his bare arms.

Lance vomited.

Harvey Waller did things in style. He hit the second man with the tip of the bayonet a few inches above his pecker, drove the blade in and lifted up, raising the guerrilla off the ground like an oldtime farmer pitching hay. The bayonet cut up through the man's belly, and his entrails spilled out. Harvey set him back on his feet and jerked the blade from his body. The rebel staggered about on the path, trying with both hands to keep his innards from falling out, not succeeding, and stepping and slipping on his own guts and looking down in anguished horror at his empty, eviscerated body cavity and at the throbbing tubes and entrails on the forest floor. He fell facedown in his own digestive tracts and did not move again.

Harvey looked pleased with himself.

Mike Campbell held his bayonet point to the neck of the third man. The guerrilla looked back at Mike with pride and hatred in his eyes, and did not flinch at the death of the first man. It was Harvey's disemboweling of the second man that broke him. By the time that was over, his hands and legs were trembling so badly he could not have used his rifle even if he had not had a length of sharpened steel at his throat. A smell of shit wafted through the air, and then he also pissed in his pants, leaking out over his combat boots.

Mike nudged him with the bayonet in his Adam's apple. He said in Spanish, "You have a wife and children?"

"Si."

"You want to see them again?"

"Si."

"You know who we are?"

"The norteamericanos come to kidnap Sally Poynings."

"Is she here?"

"She left by plane at daybreak."

Lance spoke in English. "The bastard is lying, Mike."

"Maybe," Mike answered him, then said in Spanish to the guerrilla, "Where is Comandante Clarinero?"

The guerrilla looked at Mike with fear-distended eyes, his chin raised high by the pressure of the bayonet tip. "Directly ahead of you, about eight hundred meters."

"Do you have Cubans here?"

"Two. Paulo and Manuel. They left with the girl."

"Where to?"

"I don't know."

"What's your wife's name?"

"Inez."

"I'm going to take a chance on you," Mike told him, removing the bayonet from his neck. "You got government troops that way. You got Clarinero that way."

"I go this way," the rebel said, pointing up one valley slope, "and may God bless you, senor."

"My regards to Inez."

The man shucked off his rifle and ammo belt and ran up the hill so fast that even Harvey Waller half-smiled as he said to Mike, ''If I risked letting a man go like that, you'd curse me out for being a weak-brained pansy.''

Mike laughed. ''No fear of you ever letting mercy lead you astray, Harvey.''

As the mortar crews dug into the ground with shovels and set the baseplate, Campbell went from crew to crew, checking on their work. He found fault with them all. The square, flat, pressed-steel baseplate of the M2 light mortar had a toothed spade under its rear edge that, if sunk properly, took a firm bite into the ground and anchored the firing tube.

''You're going to be firing over our heads as we attack,'' Mike yelled at one crew in Spanish. ''You expect me to do that while you fire with a loose baseplate? You have no accuracy when a mortar has a loose baseplate. You could bring your shells down on my head. And you assholes better make sure you kill me, because any of you that scores a near miss on me is going to wish he had been stillborn.''

The mortar crews went back to work to get their weapons set up properly. Each crew got the baseplate level and immovable in the earth and set up the short, smooth-bore tube and its bipod with single-spike collars. They hand-cranked the elevating gear. Mike reckoned the comandante's main position was fourteen hundred meters away, which was well within the 1850-meter range of the M2. One man stood by each tube, ready to muzzle-load the 60 mm high-explosive shells.

When Mike was satisfied, he nodded to Major Chavarria to give the order for his men to advance. The major himself stayed behind to supervise the mortar crews.

As the mercs moved forward through the forest with the Salvadoran regular soldiers, Mike gave his team their instructions. ''This country's civil war is not our business.

Our business is to find that damn girl. Clarinero knows where she is, which means we have to find Clarinero.''

The mortars opened up behind them, and the shells whistled over their heads and exploded in the forest ahead of them.

Between the explosions, Mike shouted in Spanish, ''When the barrage stops, go in fast. Overrun them.''

The soldiers looked less than enthusiastic about this idea. Mike had been pushing them around since dawn, force-marching them in the hills, and now he was pushing them into contact with the enemy—something they liked to avoid as much as possible. But they dared not stand up to him, because they were afraid of him and the mercs. Also, they knew he was a friend of the general. That meant he could do anything to them and get away with it. Fighting the guerrillas would be the easier way out—but they didn't have to look happy about it.

The mortar barrage stopped, and the officers and sergeants urged the men forward.

''Move it!'' Mike roared in Spanish. In English he said to the mercs, who kept to the rear, ''You hold back till we locate the comandante.''

As the government soldiers met little resistance and saw that their mortar attack had scattered and confused the enemy, they needed no further encouragement. Now they went in for the kill on their own account. Blackened areas with toppled trees and uprooted soil marked the points of impact of the mortar shells. A few rebel bodies lay about, and the soldiers finished off those who were wounded, but not many of the rebels had died in the mortar attack. The guerrillas were retreating in disorder through the trees ahead of the soldiers. They hardly even paused to fire back at their pursuers. The government soldiers forged on after them, firing from the hip as they went, shooting the rebels in the back and trampling on their bodies as they passed over them.

''Comandante Miguel!''

Mike had heard the regular soldiers call him this. He and his team ran down to where a group of soldiers were spraying wounded guerrillas with bullets. A sergeant, highly excited, pointed down at a man lying on his back. The man wore fancy handmade leather riding boots and sported Pancho Villa mustaches.

"It's Clarinero," the sergeant said. "We got him!"

First Mike examined the man's wounds. His eyes were bright and feverish, and he seemed weak already from loss of blood, which was thick and sloppy as mud on the left side of his fatigues. A big mortar fragment seemed to have entered his chest cavity, and he had a bullet wound in the left shoulder.

"Can you speak?" Mike asked in Spanish.

The wounded man answered in English. "Sally is gone."

"I know," Mike replied, switching to English also. "As you see, comandante, my men are not fighting yours. We are here only for Sally Poynings."

"I understand."

"Where is she?"

The comandante's face became contorted, and Mike guessed that this was not from the pain of his physical wounds so much as from what he saw as his own disgrace. "The Cubans took her to Nicaragua in a plane this morning. They want money for her, but I wouldn't agree, so they tricked me and took her by force."

"Where in Nicaragua?"

"I don't know."

"You've got to help us find her. You won't be conscious much longer. You know you're dying, don't you?"

"Yes."

"Tell me anything you know to help me find Sally," Mike said urgently.

"I don't know anything." Clarinero's voice was growing weaker.

Mike helped him to some water from his canteen. "Tell

me something. Anything. Paulo and Manuel were the Cubans' names, isn't that right?''

"Paulo Esteban.''

"Esteban!'' Cesar Ordonez blurted out. "I know who that low bastard is.''

Clarinero smiled sadly. "Sally warned me about him. I thought I could always handle him.'' His look became intense. "Maybe he will return with the others. Yes. Listen to this. In four days, on Friday morning, five Cubans will infiltrate from Honduras into El Salvador through the Sombra Oscura—Esteban may be with them. He is the one who will betray our revolution to Moscow. He took Sally away.'' His hand reached out and clutched Mike's arm. "Sally—you must tell her . . . tell her that I loved her.''

The grasp of his fingers relaxed on Mike's arm and the feverish light faded from Clarinero's eyes. His mouth hung open beneath his Pancho Villa mustaches.

Comandante Clarinero was not the first legendary man Mike had seen die. He knew they die in much the same way as any other man.

Chapter 13

"CHAVARRIA is only an errand boy for the Escandells—but you wait and see, he will outrank the rest of us," Major Sepulveda told Mike as they bounced along in a Salvadoran army Jeep. "Chavarria took officers' training with me in Georgia, and we've both been in Panama. You Americans gave up on him in both places. But he's got the right connections, and the Escandells know he is loyal to them no matter what. And that's more important in the Salvadoran army than being a good soldier. Which I am! Which is why the general sent me with you on this mission instead of Chavarria."

"I told the general I didn't want Chavarria," Mike put in.

"I don't blame you. But this won't be a help to me. The Escandells don't trust me. I speak my mind and I don't give a damn who likes it or who doesn't." He laughed. "Last time I offended someone, I spent six months as military attaché at our Buenos Aires embassy."

The major spoke no English, and Mike had to concentrate in order to follow his rapid, colloquial Spanish. After Clarinero's death, Mike and the team had been greeted as heroes in San Salvador by General Victor Escandell—there had been another big party for them at his girl friend's house. But Mike felt depressed. He was further than ever from completing his mission. It was one thing to go after Sally Poynings in El Salvador, but it was quite another to go into Nicaragua after her. The contras were fighting the Sandinista communists on Nicaragua's north and south borders, but inside the country it would be his team of mercs against everyone else. Perhaps they would strike it lucky with these Cubans coming in through the Sombra Oscura, which Mike had learned was a mountain pass. The general had put Major Sepulveda on this assignment, with Mike and the team along as observers, and had explained to the major Mike's demand that the infiltrators be taken alive. The major did not strike Mike as the type who took many live prisoners.

Campbell needed the Cubans taken alive if he was going to gather information on Sally's whereabouts from them. The rest of the team felt no better about things than Mike did, except for Cesar Ordonez, who was finally getting to go after some Cuban communists!

"These are the bastards I've been waiting to come up against," Cesar said fiercely. "These are the ones who gave my country to Russia, who took everything my family had. I'll get them for it."

The others nodded vaguely, bored by now of Cesar's preoccupations.

"That Paulo Esteban," Cesar went on, "he's the one I have to kill with my own hands. He was specially picked by Castro to stir up trouble in other places."

The Jeep carrying Major Sepulveda and Mike Campbell was followed by two trucks. They turned off the two-lane highway and traveled along a narrow, twisting country road into the foothills. The occasional car or truck they met had to find a place to get off the road to let the military vehicles by, even if it meant reversing some distance before them. There was no argument about who had the right of way on the narrow road.

They finally pulled off this road onto a series of stony lanes at the base of a high range of mountains. The Jeep's driver never hesitated at forks or turnoffs, seming to know the way well. They piled out of the vehicles in a sheltered hollow on a hillside, and the soldiers pulled camouflage netting over the two trucks and the Jeep, parked close together. They cut off leafy branches and stuck them upright in the netting. Mike admired the quiet professionalism of these troops. In a matter of minutes they had concealed all three vehicles so that they were almost impossible to spot from elsewhere at ground level—a much more difficult task than concealing them from the air alone. Soldiers crawled beneath the vehicles with what Mike recognized as car bombs.

The major showed him the three triggering devices before he handed them to the men to arm the bombs.

"You see where the mercury runs along this tube and forms a couducting link between the two electrical contacts?" the major asked, jogging the device steadily as it would be if it were attached to a truck over a stony road. "There's a two-minute delay after the contact is made, to give all the vehicles a chance to trigger their mechanisms if the guerrillas hot-wire them and drive away. We don't want the first explosion to act as a warning."

"Those bombs don't seem hard to disarm," Mike observed.

"You're right. We have to keep them that way, since we usually have to disarm them ourselves. But you'll see, we'll string tripwires around the Jeep and trucks and attach the wires to antipersonnel fragmentation mines. When the guerrillas discover the mines and disarm them, they never look any further." The major laughed. "Joke is, they often don't even see the tripwires left for them to notice and they blow themselves up with the mines."

"Don't you lose a lot of trucks?" Mike asked.

"Yes, but there's nothing I can do about it," the major said. "If I leave a few men to guard them, they may be slaughtered by thirty or forty guerrillas and the trucks taken anyway. No, I may lose a lot of vehicles, but I've had damn few successfully stolen from me. I'll kill those rebels any way I can, with trucks or with guns."

"What if some innocent campesino is just curious and decides to take a look?"

Major Sepulveda grinned crookedly. "There's no such thing as an innocent campesino."

Having spent the night in the freezing mountain air with nothing but a bellyful of cold C rations and a worn military blanket, Mike and his men had ever-increasing respect for Sepulveda and his soldiers. They heard no bitching at any time, and the two sergeants had the twenty-two men in place at the Sombra Oscura before dawn broke.

Mike watched the steep-sided mountain pass in the faint gray light of early day and shivered. Whatever he had expected in Central America, he had not foreseen he would suffer from cold!

The major crouched beside Mike and said, "You see now why they like to come through this pass? They can see clear through it to the other side, and so can't be ambushed inside it. Once they get through the pass and beyond the point where we are now, they can spread out anywhere in the trees and we could never catch them. In order to arrive here at daybreak, when they come through, we have to spend the entire night on the mountainside. It would be worth it if we knew for sure that someone or something important was coming through, but they might not use this pass again for another two weeks. They have a choice of twenty others almost as good. So it's only when we have inside information that we stake out particular passes. Half the time nothing happens even then."

"My men and I have enough food and water to spend

another three days up here," Mike said, "now that you've shown us the Sombra Oscura."

"Maybe you won't have to wait longer than today," the major said. "When Cubans say they will come, they always do."

The sky by now was a light gold color, and the pass, deep within its high walls, was in a chill gray shadow. The place got its name, the major said, because the sun never shone in it.

In spite of the shadows and the sparse light of daybreak, they immediately saw the five figures when they appeared at the other end of the pass. The five stood and watched for a moment and then they began to come forward.

"OK, Cesar," Mike said. "Do your stuff. Be careful, and good luck."

"Five of these red traitors for the meat grinder," Cesar growled and winked at Mike. He stood and walked out to meet the oncoming men.

They stopped when they saw him.

Cesar waved.

One of the five continued to walk forward. He stopped warily within shouting distance of Cesar.

"Comandante Clarinero sent me to meet you," Cesar bellowed down the pass, and his voice echoed off its high walls.

"Radio Venceremos says the comandante is dead," the infiltrator shouted back.

"He is. I was with him when he died. I have important messages for you. Is Paulo Esteban with you?"

"No."

"Too bad," Cesar cried. "One of you will have to go back with this information to Paulo. Do you know where to find him?"

"Yes."

"Good. Then come. It's not good to stay here in the open."

The infiltrator still had his doubts. "You are Cuban?"

"From Gibara."

"I'm from Baracoa," the infiltrator said.

"That's just down the coast," Cesar shouted. "Perhaps we share some friends!"

The prospect of hometown gossip overcame the infiltrator's last lingering caution, and he waved to the others to follow him. He and Cesar were still shaking hands and laughing when the others joined them.

The five Cuban infiltrators no longer clutched their Kalashnikovs watchfully. One admired Cesar's M16 so much that Cesar exchanged weapons with him. They were impressed by the way Cesar sauntered along as if he owned the place. They were highly pleased at their good fortune in meeting another Cuban. None of the five particularly cared for Salvadorans anyway.

When the government soldiers sprang out at them, Cesar managed to push three of the Cubans off balance. The soldiers were fast enough to grab all five before they could use their rifles.

"Nice work," Mike complimented the major.

"With your assistance," the officer insisted modestly.

Some of the military blankets they had slept in were now draped across boughs and saplings to form a cloth wall about seven feet high and fifteen long. Four of the Cubans sat on the ground on one side of it, their thumbs tied together behind their backs. From the other side of the blanket wall, the fifth Cuban screamed rendingly, howled, sobbed, talked, whimpered, then screamed horribly again.

Most of the government soldiers sat about indifferently, smoking and warming themselves in the early morning sunshine, not bothering to watch what was happening and not bothering either to move away so they wouldn't have to see it.

Harvey Waller looked on with a smile on his face, not missing a thing.

Cesar Ordonez went for a walk by himself.

Lance Hardwick looked and then ran to Mike, gray-faced. "Jesus, Mike, you gotta stop them. They're skinning the poor bastard alive with boiling water and razor blades. He's trying to tell them everything he knows and he can't stop them."

"Go take a walk, kid," Mike told him in Spanish with a steely look on his face.

Lance began to argue, but Andre Verdoux, who realized that Mike was taking this attitude and speaking in Spanish for the benefit of the four Cubans, led Lance away half-forcibly.

Mike pointed at the Cuban who had spoken first with Cesar. "You said you knew where Paulo Esteban was."

"So you are the gringos after Senorita Sally," the man said scornfully. "She does not want to go back with you, and you will never catch her."

"You're next behind that blanket—after they finish with your friend."

The man looked as if he had just swallowed something that was now doing unpleasant things inside his stomach. "If I tell you what I know, they would still torture me."

Mike shook his head. "Before I came here, I thought I might have to offer a reward." He pulled a manila envelope from a pocket of his fatigues and held the papers it contained before the face of the Cuban—a one-way airline ticket from San Salvador to Mexico City and a Costa Rican passport, both in the name of Federico Gomez.

A burst of squeals, almost like those of a pig, rose form the other side of the blanket; then a hoarse voice pleading for mercy, offering anything, *anything*; then the words dissolved into screams and howls.

"That doesn't look much like me," the Cuban said of the passport photo.

"You've been ill since it was taken. Look, we'll put you on board that plane and wait till it takes off. You can see here that the general has guaranteed your safe conduct.

Once you're in Mexico City, just identify yourself as a Cuban and your embassy will fetch you."

The Cuban was hanging in tough, in spite of the sounds of brutality on the other side of the blanket. "I'll tell you what you want to know, but only if you stop the torture and free the others along with me."

Mike shook his head sadly. "I tried to stop this torture before it started, but I found that instructions had been issued without my knowledge. The most I am allowed is to make this deal with one of you."

"You must free my comrades!" the man insisted.

"You're not in a position to make conditions—"

Mike was interrupted by hideous yells and then more screams.

"*I'll* tell you what you want to know," one of the other Cubans said, looking terrified. "Only he and I know where Esteban is. Give *me* the ticket!"

"Senorita Sally is with Esteban in a training camp for Salvadoran guerrillas about fifteen kilometers south of the Honduran border," the Cuban that Mike had originally approached blurted out, making sure he was the one to be credited with the information. "The place does not have a name. The camp is a clearing in a mountain valley. I can show it to you on a map."

There was silence now from behind the wall of blankets. A soldier came out to where the four Cubans sat on the ground. He was stripped to the waist and had smears of blood on his arms. Grabbing one of the Cubans by the hair, he hauled him to his feet and dragged him stumbling to the other side of the blankets.

Mike untied the thumbs of his Cuban collaborator, which made one of the sergeants fetch Major Sepulveda. By the time the Cuban had marked Mike's map and given him directions, the man newly taken behind the blankets had started screaming in agony.

"We've found what we need to know," Mike told the major. "Stop the torture."

"Remember when the general told you that you were coming here only as an observer?" the major asked. "This is what he meant by that. We have our own way of doing things down here, so don't interfere." He called over to one of his soldiers, "Drive Senor Campbell and his men, along with this Cuban, to Ilopango airport. The Cuban has a safe conduct out of the country." He spoke coldly and quickly, and looked in Mike's eyes impassively as a bloodcurdling howl rose from behind the blanket. Shaking Mike's hand, he said, "I hope you find the girl. If I can help, just let me know."

Mike sent Harvey to gather the team and walked down the path with the soldier and the Cuban.

"Mike," the major called after him with a smile on his face, "don't forget to disarm the booby traps on your truck."

The shouts and screams of the Cuban being tortured followed them down the mountain path till they turned into a valley and were out of earshot.

Campbell sat in the front of the truck with the Salvadoran soldier. The others sat in the back of the truck, facing each other on wooden benches that ran along both sides. Ordonez sat directly opposite the Cuban.

"You smirk at me one more time, you'll never get on that plane alive," Cesar warned the infiltrator.

"I didn't smirk at you," the man said. "I didn't even look at you. You're just searching for an excuse to break the agreement we made, so you can kill me. Isn't it enough for you to have already caused the deaths of four of your countrymen?

"What the fuck are you saying?" Harvey demanded to know, and whacked the Cuban across the mouth with the back of his hand. "You speak English here, understand?"

The Cuban cowered from him and held his arm before his face. "I no understand you," he said in English.

"That's better," Harvey said approvingly. "I knew you

could speak English if you tried. Just keep talking so we can all understand what you say. I'm tired of listening to goddam Spanish. Half the people in New York speak it and everyone down here. What's wrong with English? They all know English, only they pretend not to.'' He turned to the Cuban again. ''If you'd talked English all the time instead of Spanish, you wouldn't have ended up a goddam stupid commie. Am I right, Andre? Don't you feel different since you started talking English instead of French?''

''Very different, Harvey,'' Andre said wryly.

Harvey looked satisfied and let his features relax again and his head to nod in motion to the moving truck over the rough road.

A little later, without warning, Cesar lunged at the Cuban, knocked him off the bench onto the floor of the truck and then sat on him, strangling him.

Andre jumped Cesar and yelled at Bob to help him. ''We follow Mike's orders,'' Andre shouted, and continued to wrestle with Cesar but could not tear his hands from the Cuban's throat.

Bob reckoned that what Andre said about obeying Mike's orders was true—although he otherwise had no objections to Cesar strangling the Cuban—so he lumbered over and effortlessly swept Cesar's fingers from around the man's throat. After that Bob placed his squat bulky body on the bench between the two Cubans and listened to Cesar grind his teeth in frustration.

Chapter 14

THE UH-1H helicopter, crammed with the mercs and their weapons, flew above the scrubby landscape toward the Honduran border. After they had put the Cuban aboard the flight to Mexico City as promised, Mike wanted to waste no time in getting to the Salvadoran training camp inside Nicaragua. The longer they waited, Mike reasoned, the less chance they would have of finding Sally there. General Victor Escandell had wanted to give them a third party at his girl friend's house to celebrate the deaths of the four Cubans, but Mike asked instead for a helicopter and clearance for it to land in Honduras. No problem.

"While Andre and I make the weapons pickup," Mike told the others, "you guys had better get in some R and R in the next couple of hours. We move out today."

He and Andre picked up the weapons at what would have been a middle-income suburban house in the U.S. except for the fifteen-foot wall surrounding it, the steel-plated door entering the compound and the closed-circuit video cameras. As always with a Cuthbert Colquitt deal, the goods were in order. Mike and Andre started to load them into the Cherokee van borrowed from the general.

The two teenage sons of the house's owner helped them. They refused the money Mike offered when they were finished, but eagerly accepted two green track suits with blue lettering: MURRAY HILL TRACK AND ROAD CLUB—unused leftovers from their training days on the Chesapeake.

As Mike drove away, he said, "It seems like a year ago since you had us running up and down the beach on Assateague Island."

"We're all beginning to feel a little frustrated," Andre acknowledged.

Their heavily laden Huey chopper took some rifle and small-arms fire in the mountains near the border, but suffered only one direct hit, which punctured a neat hole in a metal plate high in the fuselage. The pilot knew his stuff, and with only a little searching around, found the Honduran military camp they were looking for and touched down on a landing site at its perimeter.

They were met by twenty-five men in combat fatigues with M16s slung on their shoulders.

"I know these are 'bad guy' contras," Andre said, "but even so, I thought they might look a little more pleased to see us."

"I suspected we might have difficulties," Mike said and nothing more.

The "bad guy" contras were so called to distinguish them from the "good guy" contras led by Eden Pastora on Nicaragua's southern border. Both contra forces fought the Sandinista communists of Nicaragua, but Pastora's group had been part of the revolution and grew disenchanted only after the hard-line Marxists took over. Many of the "bad guys" on the northern border had been in the dictator Somoza's dreaded National Guard. Both contra groups were armed and financed by the CIA. Mike had his worries about what the spooks at Langley, Virginia, might have to say about his mission. According to the media, with the CIA in Nicaragua anything went—so long as it was against the Sandinista Marxists. Mike had a shrewd notion that the CIA might not be willing to extend these open-season rules to him, yet he had no choice but to enter Nicaragua through territory held by the "bad guys." This large, heavily armed welcoming committee was not a reassuring sight.

One of them was a Cuban, and he and Cesar Ordonez apparently knew each other from anti-Castro campaigns. Mike spotted that the Cuban was urgently telling Cesar something amid all their greetings and laughter.

In a minute, Cesar drifted by Mike and said to him in an undertone, "Once they get us inside the camp, they have orders to disarm us and detain us until further notice. The orders are from Washington. My friend says that if we head due south through this scrubland for about two kilometers, we'll be in Sandinista territory after we cross a small river."

"Good work, Cesar," Mike said. "Do what I do. Pass the word along."

"Do what Mike does."

"Do what Mike does."

Mike stopped and held his stomach. He unbuckled his belt and headed for the bushes.

The sight of each of the gringos being hit with Montezuma's revenge so soon after arriving on the chopper cracked up the contras. They had all heard that the gringos spent half their time squatting on toilets or behind bushes when they came to the tropics. Even so, it was funny as hell to see them all struck like this at the same time.

It took the contras a couple of minutes to tell and listen to some jokes on this general subject. Then they got anxious when there was no sign of anyone's returning from the bushes. They looked for the squatting gringos, found they had been conned and gave chase.

When Mike heard the hue and cry raised behind them, he called to the team, "We got them beat. Just keep up this pace, watch where you step and keep together."

The slope down to the river was gentle, and running through the scrubland was not difficult. The thorns were long and sharp, but in scattered clumps that were easy to avoid. However, their combat boots left a clear trail in the reddish sandy soil.

They kept up the pace, and the voices behind them grew no nearer, although they did not drop away in the distance, either. Quite suddenly, they found themselves on the river bank.

"Little river!" Harvey said. "This is a fucking torrent!"

It was true. Although the distance was hardly thirty feet from bank to bank, the river raged in violent foam, and its racing waters had a hollow, dull roar. They could not hear now how close their pursuers were, but they could not be very far. The mercs would have to find a way to cross this river.

Upstream a little way, a narrow fallen tree trunk stretched across the river. It looked rotten two-thirds of the way across, and it was hard to imagine the wood bearing the weight of Bob Murphy or Harvey Waller. They had no rope.

"Let me try," Lance volunteered. "I'm lightest, and I'm a strong swimmer."

Mike nodded.

Lance stepped out along the tree trunk above the roaring currents, crossing fast. The trunk gave way beneath his weight, snapped in two and plunged him into the racing torrents.

Lance disappeared for a moment beneath the swirling waters and then stood up in the middle of the river. The water came to a little above his knees.

Their fatigues hung soaked with sweat from their bodies, but despite the afternoon's heat, they made good progress through a series of foothills. They met no patrols, although the paths through the scrubland looked well-traveled and some of the wider ones had tire tracks. Every once in a while, they had to pass through cultivated tracts, mostly corn. They were seen and ignored.

"They figure we're contras," Mike said, "and hope we'll leave them alone if they leave us alone."

This seemed to work out all right. Nobody was looking for trouble. The mercs kept clear of villages, and those houses they passed close by seemed too primitive to be linked by radio to the armed forces.

Lance shook his head. "I'd heard that everyone in Nicaragua had their own Kalashnikov. These people are too poor to own even a steel shovel." They had just passed two men digging in a field with shovels carved from solid pieces of wood. "This place makes El Salvador look like Beverly Hills."

"Pity we didn't do something about it before the communists did," Mike said. "It may be too late now. But I don't want you to forget—we're not here to set wrong right. We're here to find Sally Poynings—kidnap the silly bitch if we have to. Then I'm going home."

They were crossing a group of fields, keeping an eye on a bunch of men working some distance away who hadn't seen them yet. They were fired upon from the opposite direction. The shooting was wild, but it was automatic fire. A lone man stood in a field on higher ground, aiming at them again.

Andre whipped his FN-FAL Paratroop battle rifle to his right shoulder and squeezed off a single shot. The rifleman crumpled.

Now the distant men in the fields were running. Through his binoculars, Mike saw them pick up assault rifles.

"A people's militia," he said. "Lance, you're going to meet some of those just-plain-folks with their own Kalashnikovs that you were talking about. Eleven of them."

The workers came charging across the fields to cut them off.

"What the hell do they think they're doing?" Andre asked.

"I think they expect us to run for our lives," Mike answered.

When the militiamen saw that the seven armed men continued on their route regardless of their advance, they slowed and did some talking among themselves. Both sides were well within range of each other, but there was no more shooting yet.

"If they got any sense," Mike said, "they'll go back to work and forget about us."

But the militiamen didn't. Although they chickened out on a direct assault on the mercs, they now tagged along behind, no doubt hoping to raise the alarm when given the opportunity or waiting for a chance to pick the intruders off one by one without having to risk a firefight.

"I can't allow this," Mike muttered to no one in particular.

They were walking alongside a patch of thorny brush, and Mike, fast as a shadow, slipped around the other side of it. The mercs moved onward as if nothing happened, staying bunched together so that one of their number would not be missed. Mike crouched on the sandy soil behind the thick brush and pulled a British 36 defensive hand grenade from his belt. He had found the cast-iron pineapple among the team's weapons at the pickup point. It might have been put there by mistake, but more likely it had been added for good luck—arms dealers had their superstitions, too.

Mike found himself a hollow in the ground, since this grenade created a bit of a problem—it weighed about a pound and a quarter, and its throwing range was only about ten yards, yet its range of fragmentation varied from twenty-five yards on soft ground to about two hundred fifty yards on a hard surface. In other words, if the man who threw the grenade with its four-second delay didn't find protection within that time, he'd get his ass blown off. And it was a sturdy little British machine that delivered the goods.

Mike pulled the safety pin and held down the safety lever. The red crosses painted at the top of the pineapple pattern signified this was a high-explosive model.

He heard footsteps on the other side of the thorn scrub. He waited till they were directly opposite him, lobbed the 36 hand grenade over the top of the scrub and threw himself into the hollow.

It seemed as if the grenade blew in even less than four seconds. Its fragments of hot metal tore their way through the thorn scrub, showering him with twigs. Mike sat up in the hollow and emptied the forty rounds in the magazine of his Uzi submachine gun. He fired in short bursts through the thorns where he thought any survivors of the blast might be standing.

Two of the team used their battle rifles and then stopped. Choking dust and smoke filled the air. Mike could barely hear sounds because of his ringing ears. He figured it was safe for him to get up and walk around the thorn thicket to take a look.

It wasn't a pretty sight. Half of them were still alive. Jagged fragments of cast iron, traveling outward in all directions from the grenade blast, had torn through their body tissues. These fragments had not entered the flesh in neat holes as streamlined bullets did, but gouged their way in, turning end over end as they seared and broke apart muscle and bone, until the body itself absorbed all their impact and they came to rest deep in the tissues, or they exited from the body on the other side, leaving a gaping hole even larger than the entrance wound.

A few had been hit by bullets also—those who had not immediately fallen or who perhaps had escaped the deadlier grenade fragments.

They were all beyond help. Mike could do nothing for them without getting into major commitments. He did not feel good about killing these people—after all, they were farmers defending their home soil. It was not their fault that their government interfered in the affairs of other countries. However, it was their misfortune.

Mike turned to walk away and catch up with the team. He felt a sharp pain in his upper left arm and heard a shot. He looked and saw his sleeve ripped and the cloth absorbing blood. He spun about, and another bullet whined past his right ear. Almost at his feet, one of the dying militiamen, with a huge blotch of bright scarlet blood on his shirtfront, lay on his back and aimed a .32 revolver at him with a wavering hand.

Mike jumped away, and another bullet missed him. The Nicaraguan followed Mike with his eyes, still lying on his back, unable to sit up. Mike ran around behind his head, making it necessary for the nearly immobilized militiaman to lean back his head and see him upside down. Even so, the Nicaraguan brought the revolver alongside his face to try for another shot.

A flat red rock about a foot across lay near Mike's feet. His left arm hurt like hell, but he stooped and picked up the rock with both hands, raised it above his head and slammed it down into the face and searching eyes of the militiaman.

Sally had been pleased at first to be given a wood hut all to herself, until she found out why. Most of the wood buildings in the compound were dormitories, one for women and the others for men. The small huts were occupied by guerrilla officers and by Cuban trainers. Other than sleeping, everything else was done outdoors. Or almost everything else . . .

Paulo Esteban stood in the open door of her hut, looking in at her. As usual, Manuel tagged along behind him like a faithful dog. Esteban had seen her coming from the women's showers. There was no lock on her door, not even a bolt, to keep him out. There was no one to whom she could complain. She was not a Salvadoran guerrilla. She was not under the protection of any of the guerrilla officers here—

none of them had known Clarinero personally (she still did not believe what Radio Venceremos said about Clarinero's being dead, even though it was the rebels' own radio station). All that anyone knew in this Salvadoran guerrilla training camp, somewhere in Nicaragua, was that she had come with Paulo and Manuel. Therefore she was "their woman." Some things hadn't changed much with the glorious revolution. Esteban's woman. Somewhere in Nicaragua. Oh yes, she was finding the real truth for which Bennett and she had searched. And she was glad there was no video camera to record it.

Esteban enjoyed tormenting her. Here was a gringa who understood his taunts in Spanish. So few did.

"What did the little rich girl learn today about the real world?" he asked from the doorway as Manuel snickered behind him.

Sally sat on the edge of her folding camp bed, brushing her long blond hair. She said, "Get out of here!"

He and Manuel came in and closed the door after them.

"I asked you a question," Paulo said in a menacing voice.

"Then I'll give you an answer!" Sally shouted, waving her hairbrush at him. "The little rich girl, as you call her, learned that the real world is back in Boston, not down here where one set of fools brainwash another set of fools to do someone else's bidding!"

Paulo walked across and shook her by the shoulders. "You're going to have to change what you say if you ever want to see Boston again. Before we let you go home, we will already have released a whole series of videotapes of you praising what we are doing in El Salvador and Nicaragua, and your father will be compelled to show them on his television stations. The sooner you agree to begin making these tapes, the sooner you'll see Boston again."

"You'll have to brainwash me first!"

"There's no brainwashing here, Sally," he said, his

Chapter 15

THE worst heat of the day had passed by the time Mike Campbell and the team got to the area where they believed the Salvadoran training camp to be. Except there was no sign of it in the forested valley where it was supposed to be.

"This map is not in high detail," Mike said, pointing to the chart the Cuban had marked for him and comparing it to a more highly detailed military chart. "It could be this next valley over."

"Or the Cuban could have been lying," Lance commented.

Mike smiled. "I've noticed you think people lie under pressure, Lance, even when they're bargaining for their lives. But I tell you that when you have someone with his back to the wall and he suddenly sounds as if he's started to tell the truth, you can usually rely on it. I've been fooled by some good liars in my time, but never by a guy sweating out what he thinks may be his last hour on earth. A lot of men choose the path of virtue when they see that truth can buy their freedom and another lie can hang them. They take no more chances. Let's look at that next valley before we mouth off our worries."

They moved out, and Bob Murphy said to Lance, "Mike had to put you down that time. He's telling you something he's learned himself. See how he didn't get all wound up when things weren't where they're supposed to be. That's what makes him a top man to lead a mission. He doesn't expect things to work out easy. He even gets suspicious when things work out like they're supposed to. Even now, if that camp isn't in the next valley, I bet he has two or three more plans swimming around in his head."

The Aussie was giving Mike more credit than he deserved. Mike had slapped Lance down—as he would any man who made negative, defeatist comments as a matter of habit during a mission without backing them up with constructive alternatives. Mike had no other plans if they could not locate this camp, and he didn't need a rookie like Lance to remind him they were invading Nicaragua on the word of a Cuban communist.

The training camp was in the next valley, halfway up the side of the far slope. The sun had begun to set and the light wasn't great; but through his binoculars Mike made out more than a hundred figures moving about inside the compound, and sentries on the perimeter, but no wire or guardhouses.

He handed the binoculars to Lance. "Keep watching. See if they come and go any old way or if they avoid certain areas that might be mine fields."

Mike's left arm throbbed painfully. Andre had cleaned and dressed the wound, which was an angry red furrow channeled out of his flesh by the militiaman's bullet. The wound did not interfere with his arm movements; and so long as it did not become badly infected, it would heal into just another memento on his body of battles past and almost forgotten.

They ate C rations, and were ready to move down into the valley at dusk. Mike figured it would take them about an hour to walk to the camp's location, so he left just about that much dying light to make the trip. He wanted to arrive at the camp in darkness. From all they could learn, the compound seemed nothing more than a collection of wood huts in a forest clearing. There were no fortifications, no attempt had been made to conceal the camp from the air, and people down there seemed to wander in and out at will. But there were guards. Presumably there would be an arsenal. And it had more than a hundred occupants, men and women. The mercs could learn nothing more from this distance and in the fading daylight.

Mike briefed them on his general plan: "We go down unseen, spot the girl in the camp, take her with minimum fuss, march through the night toward the Honduran border and cross at dawn. Okay?"

None of them were so simpleminded as to believe things would actually happen this way. But not even Lance said anything. After all, Mike had told him earlier that the training camp would be in the next valley, and it was. Even he could not argue with success.

They became lost for a while on the way down the valley and up its other side, and finally got their direction right by the numerous oil lamps being lit in the camp itself. The looming shapes of the trees against the lighter sky made it reasonably easy for them to find their way through the woods in the gathering darkness. Occasionally a thorn bush made itself known to one of the team, and the rest were warned off by the whispered curses of its discoverer as he freed his legs from it.

"They don't seem to have a generator," Mike said. "Each of these oil lamps illuminates only a very small area, which will be good for us. We should be able to see Sally easily enough if she walks close to any of the lamps. One bad thing may be that with only lamps for illumination, they probably turn in very early—so we don't have much time to find her tonight. No more talk from now on. No cigarettes or lights. And try to walk more quietly—they don't have nocturnal forest elephants in Central America."

They did the best they could, but in the darkness it was

impossible to move silently through undergrowth and over dead branches.

A voice called out to them in Spanish: "Who's there?"

Mike nudged Cesar, the only native Spanish speaker, to reply.

"We're the new training unit," Cesar called back in a broad Cuban accent. "Our truck broke down and we got lost trying to take a shortcut."

This explanation was greeted by laughter, then the reply, "And *you've* come to train *us*!"

As footsteps approached, they all ducked down and hoped they wouldn't be seen. Cesar walked toward the man and they shook hands.

"Where are the others?" the Salvadoran sentry asked.

"Roberto," Cesar called, and Bob Murphy lumbered up to the Salvadoran.

When the sentry put out his hand, Bob grabbed it, pulled him forward off balance, and chopped him twice with the side of his right hand. The others heard a bone snap and a sigh of expelled air. They left the crumpled sentry on the forest floor behind them.

"You can't expect all of them to be that dumb," Mike whispered warningly.

By now it was pitch-dark. The camp, with scores of lighted oil lamps swinging to and fro in the slight breeze in the otherwise dark valley, looked a little like a large ship on a night sea. They made their way slowly and as quietly as they could, climbing to the slope directly above the camp.

When Joe Nolan walked nose-first into a gun muzzle, he knew it was a Kalashnikov by the full hood over the front sight. From about ten paces to the right, a flashlight flickered on his face for an instant. Then all was dark again. The muzzle of the assault rifle was now pressed in earnest just below his right eye. Joe Nolan was no Cuban, Salvadoran or Nicaraguan—that much anyone could tell, even in a momentary flashlight beam.

Joe couldn't speak Spanish, but even if he did, he could not for the life of him think of something plausible to say.

It was Cesar Ordonez who spoke, from the darkness behind Joe. "Very good, compañeros. I had sworn we would be able to infiltrate among you without being noticed—from what I saw of the camp awhile back. It looked like a very loosely run place. You surprised me, I admit that. I am one of your new Cuban instructors. This norteamericano speaks no Spanish. He is an explosives expert and is one of us."

The gun barrel did not budge from Nolan's cheekbone.

"Being cautious, eh?" Cesar went on in Spanish in his strongest Cuban accent. "You have a right to be. We cannot be too vigilant for the revolution, no? Well, I have my papers here and other documents." Cesar fluttered them in the dark.

Campbell smiled grimly at Cesar's ploy to get the second man with the flashlight to reveal his exact whereabouts and to take his hand off his trigger to operate the flashlight.

It worked.

The flashlight beam sprang out at the papers in Cesar's left hand, and the muzzle of the Kalashnikov was withdrawn a few inches.

That was all Joe Nolan needed. He knocked aside the rifle barrel with his right hand, which gripped a U.S. Marine Corps combat knife. Nolan could see the man's face by flashlight, and he drove the knuckles of his left fist into the man's mouth and hung onto his lower jaw, with his fingers between his teeth, to keep him quiet. On Nolan's first thrust with the combat knife, the Salvadoran dropped the Kalashnikov unfired. He tried to fend off Nolan with his arms and fists, but, in a frenzy, the merc stabbed at everything that came his way, severing two of the man's fingers before finishing him off with blind thrusts to the body.

Nolan's left hand was bitten across the knuckles from

voice turning gentle. "All we ask is that you see the truth as it really is."

Paulo stroked her breasts. She brushed his hand away. He immediately replaced it, stroking her more aggressively than before.

She tried to stand, but he pressed her down into a sitting position again on the camp bed.

"No!"

His hands crept inside her shirt.

"Paulo, I said no!"

He peeled the shirt from her shoulders. She was not wearing a bra. He stroked her breasts and fondled her nipples, and in spite of herself she felt them grow erect.

"I'll scream," she threatened.

"If you do, I'll have to gag you, Sally. Remember last time, how you nearly choked."

She protested only weakly as he pulled first her fatigues and then her panties off her legs.

"But not him." She pointed at Manuel.

She was bargaining now.

"Manuel is a revolutionary, Sally. He deserves everyone's gratitude. And he's my friend."

He pulled her to her feet and made her stand there naked, facing him.

Manuel came behind her, unzipping his pants.

Paulo caught her by the shoulders and forced her to bend over.

"No, no, not like that!" she whimpered as Manuel forced himself into her from behind.

Esteban unzipped himself and pushed her upright again. He entered her brutally. The two men pounded into her, and she sobbed and pleaded with them to stop hurting her, her voice half-stifled as she was pressed between their bodies.

the man's upper teeth, and on the palm from the lower teeth. But at least the guy died without making a sound, and that was what counted now.

As Harvey Waller saw Joe brush aside the Salvadoran's rifle muzzle from his face, he went for the one with the flashlight. Harvey had been using a stave, twice as long and twice as thick as a baseball bat, to feel his way in the dark. He brought the stave down with all his strength and poleaxed the Salvadoran who had the light. He kept thumping the man's body with the length of timber, raising the stave high above his head and bringing it down in mighty strokes that made a sound as if they were hitting a wet burlap bag. As the others moved out, before joining them Harvey took his time about enjoying one last tremendous whack with the stave.

Campbell looked through the Star-Tron night-vision system at the camp beneath them. The optical device consisted of a hand-held tube, which could also be mounted like a telescopic sight on a weapon, with a cameralike lens on one end and a binocular-style eyepiece at the other. The lens focused all the available light onto an intensifier tube, and the tube amplified the light to give an image with maximum contrast. The device could work at levels that seemed pitch-dark to the unaided eye, utilizing starlight and other forms of illumination available at night. All the oil lamps made it child's play for the device, and Mike could plainly see the features of the people in the camp beneath him, even of those outside the pools of light made by the lamps. He watched in vain for a blonde. It occurred to Mike that Sally's hair might have been dyed black by this time in order to make her less noticeable. He remembered her features from the photos he had studied, and no woman he had seen so far looked even remotely like her. Mike took the Star-Tron from his eye.

"That near bunkhouse is for women only," he whispered to the others. "That's where she's got to be. Bob and

Lance, sneak down behind the farthest of the four men's bunkhouses, steal a few oil lamps, pour the fuel on the back wall of that farthest bunkhouse, light it and get back here fast as you can without being seen. I'm betting on all the women in their bunkhouse rushing out to help quench the fire, except Sally. She must be disillusioned by now, unless she's gone totally commie. Who knows? Main thing is, Lance and Bob, make it look like an accident. Chuck away the lamps so that no one will know right away what started the fire. That will give us a little extra time to get away if all goes well; and it won't blow everything if things don't work out right away. Any questions? No? Okay then, good luck.''

Murphy and Hardwick crept stealthily into the dark. It never ceased to surprise Mike how silently Murphy's bulky body could move.

Campbell handed the Star-Tron to Andre Verdoux. "You take charge while Cesar and I go to the women's bunkhouse. Keep scanning the compound. If you see Sally somewhere else and think she can be grabbed, send Joe and Harvey after her. We all rendezvous here with you. Watch your back for roving sentries.''

Mike stayed where he was for the moment, and in a little while they saw a wide orange tongue of flame lick up the back wall of the farthest bunkhouse. The wooden buildings in the clearing were military style—built of plywood and two-by-fours, with pitch-coated roofs—rather than being peasant-style structures of bamboo with banana-leaf thatch. But the wall burned just as well. Except that nobody noticed it.

They heard muffled shouts from inside the burning bunkhouse. The flames had by now taken hold on one corner of the tarred roof, as well as having spread along the back wall. Men emerged from the bunkhouse door. They shouted. Others gathered. They started running back and forth.

Mike held Cesar back. "Give 'em time.''

The flames on the roof far outshone the feeble lanterns, and they could see large numbers of men and women passing buckets, basins and cans and throwing water on the flames.

Bob and Lance returned and gave the thumbs-up to Mike and Cesar as they moved out.

The women's bunkhouse had emptied as Mike had predicted. Using the Star-Tron, Andre had not been able to spot Sally anywhere in the moving throngs, and Mike considered that no one had a sharper eye for ladies than Andre.

This end of the camp seemed deserted, but Mike and Cesar proceeded warily. A fire like this would be a tipoff to a really experienced man that the rest of the camp was worth keeping tabs on. Mike considered that the really amazing thing about obvious diversions was how often they worked.

Mike held up a hand, and Cesar stopped. He had seen something. Just a slight movement up ahead. In the darkness next to one of the small wood huts. Mike had seen only a shadow. Maybe only a flicker caused by an oil lamp. Maybe nothing. . . . Then, by the light of the distant flames, both he and Cesar saw a man come toward them. He had an automatic rifle slung on his right shoulder and was padding around watchfully. This was one man who had not been fooled by the fire. He hadn't seen them yet. Maybe he just sensed something. . . .

He stood at the corner of an unlit hut. Silent. They could hear the shouts of the firefighters, and every now and then they could see the face of their adversary in an orange glow of flame.

An oil lamp was suddenly hung outside a hut not far away, and they heard footsteps running in the direction of the blaze. The man scowled at the light for illuminating his position and temporarily spoiling his night vision.

Mike held an eight-pointed throwing star before his face by its central disk. He flicked it backhand so the points rotated rapidly from top to bottom as it whirled through the air toward the lone man's head.

The star embedded itself in his temple above his left eye, with a sound like splitting wood.

Mike and Cesar rushed to the women's bunkhouse. It was empty. They wandered out again, at a loss what to do next.

About a hundred yards off, a door of a lighted hut swung open and a man came out, buckling his belt.

"It's a fire!" he yelled back into the hut through the open door. "A bunkhouse is on fire!"

"He's Cuban," Cesar hissed.

A big burly man came to the lighted doorway and looked across the compound at the flames. Then he turned his head to speak to someone inside the hut, and they could see his face.

"Paulo Esteban!" Cesar practically exploded.

Mike had to hold him forcibly back. "Are you sure?" he whispered.

"I've seen fifty photos of that bastard," Cesar whispered back. "It's him!"

"Let him go." Mike dug his fingers hard into Cesar's shoulder, and when that didn't work, Mike nudged him in the ribs with the muzzle of his Uzi. "First we find the girl."

Cesar was reluctant to hold back, but he knew he was up against Mad Mike and that crossing him now would be a very risky bet. So Cesar controlled himself. Though the likes of Esteban was what he had come for. Not for money, and certainly not for the fool girl.

The two Cubans ran past them on their way to the fire.

"Keep watch," Mike said and ran toward the hut.

Uzi ready, he cautiously peered into the open doorway of the lighted hut. A very sad looking, very pretty blond girl sat naked on the edge of a camp bed. She looked at him, frightened.

Mike said, "Sally Poynings, I presume."

Chapter 16

"HOLY shit!" Lance said. "I don't believe what my eyes are seeing!"

Lance Hardwick's eyes were seeing a naked blonde running hand in hand by lamplight with Mike Campbell across the compound, as if they were gamboling in some nudist movie—only, of course, Mike had on his fatigues and boots and guns, which kind of spoiled the effect or maybe increased it. Anyway, Lance decided, it looked weird.

Mike and the girl disappeared out of the lighted area, and soon after Lance heard them approach. He could feel her naked presence close by and wondered what she would do if he reached out and touched her warm skin.

"Here are your clothes and sneakers," Mike said to her. "Get them on quick. Andre, you take her and everyone else back the way we came. I have some business here."

Mike spoke in a rapid, impersonal voice, signifying he wanted no arguments. That didn't impress Bob Murphy.

"Where's Cesar?" Bob asked.

"He found some Cubans in the camp, deserted us and went after them," Mike said matter-of-factly. "He was

241

with me, so it's my job to go get him back. Now move out." He pulled out his compass and waited for Andre to do the same. They consulted the luminous dials. "Take a bearing north-northeast and stay with it as best you can. If I don't catch up with you, Andre, keep going. Cross that border by dawn."

"I'll stay with Mike," Bob told Andre.

"I agree," Andre said, for once with a note of friendliness for Bob in his voice.

"I got no time to argue," Mike snapped. "Rest of you, move out. Now! Move it!"

He had no need to keep his voice lowered anymore, because of the pandemonium in the camp below them. Sparks from the burning bunkhouse had set fire to the roof of the next bunkhouse. The firefighters had abandoned the first building to the flames and sought now to save the second.

Mike and Bob descended the slope and made their way through the deserted part of the camp to approach the firefighters from behind.

Mike whispered to Bob, " 'Preciate you coming along. My guess is that Cesar has already made the approach we are taking. He'll watch and wait till he gets a crack at Esteban—none of the other Cubans will distract him from that. He'll shoot, and then run for it."

"Jeopardizing our whole getaway," Bob whispered back. "Why not leave him behind and go on with the others?"

Mike did not answer right off, looking in the pools of light and the shadows. "Cesar has done a lot for all of us up till this happened. I'm not sure we'd have made it this far without him. It was my mistake. I should have foreseen that the chance to nail Esteban would prove too tempting for him at close quarters. He would have been okay if I'd left him back with Andre and took someone else with me to get the girl."

"So you blame yourself?"

Mike shrugged. "What's goes wrong is always the leader's fault."

Paulo Esteban had Manuel put men on the bunkhouse roofs to extinguish sparks and sent others to quench grass fires. When Esteban ascertained that everything was fully under control, he turned to leave, and for an instant, by the light of an oil lamp by the corner of one bunkhouse, he saw a face he recognized.

It was not the face of someone he was acquainted with. It was a face he had seen before somewhere. After a moment's thought, he had it.

"Manuel!" he called urgently, hauling out his revolver. "I've just seen someone up this way. I'd swear I know him from that pamphlet of photos of Miami Cubans active against us. The fire"—it suddenly occurred to him—"it's a diversion! Quick! Back to the girl!"

As they ran, Paulo came across three Salvadorans with Kalashnikovs and he ordered them along, too.

Cesar Ordonez stalked them. He knew he had been seen by Esteban and spotted as a stranger. Esteban had been too far off for Cesar to kill him at that time. Then Esteban had thought to check on the girl—Cesar knew where he was going and why. Cesar had to get Esteban now, or Mike and the others might not get away. Cesar cared nothing for his own safety. If he could kill an international communist provocateur of Esteban's status, his own life would be worth sacrificing. Mike Campbell had his priorities, and Cesar knew he might be fouling up things for him; but the importance of Cesar's own priorities outweighed those of Mike, which were only to rescue a spoiled rich bitch who, had she been poor and from an unknown family, would readily have been abandoned to pay for her mistakes. Cesar said to himself that he would never have broken off from Mike's mission and endangered it for the sake of an ordinary Cuban communist. But Paulo Esteban was too big a fish to let slip through his nets. No matter what the consequences, Cesar had to kill him. He was duty-bound. For a proud and free Cuba once again.

Esteban and his fellow Cuban now had three men with Kalashnikovs along with them, but that was not going to save Esteban. Cesar was dedicated to kill only one man here; the rest were immaterial. He personally was going to rid the world of Paulo Esteban.

Cesar ran from shadow to shadow, staying out of the circles of feeble light given off by the oil lamps. Esteban was easy to tell from the others, since he was a foot taller and twice as broad across the shoulders. Cesar knew he was headed for the small wooden hut where Mike and he had found the girl. Cesar ran at full speed and got to a place where he thought he would have a clear shot at Esteban as he passed through an area lit by three lamps. He checked that the selector switch of his Uzi was on full automatic. He could hear them coming.

The other Cuban was first through the lighted area. Cesar held his fire. He would get that one later. Then the three with Kalashnikovs. But not Paulo Esteban.

Cesar heard a sound immediately behind him.

"Don't turn around," an amused Cuban voice said in his ear.

Cesar felt the barrel of a gun pressed into the back of his neck.

"Keep still," the Cuban told him.

Cesar clutched his Uzi, finger on its trigger, wondering if he whirled about would he get off a burst of fire and catch Esteban with a fatal bullet, in spite of the almost certain bullet in his own neck. It would be worth it.

"She's gone! Gone!" Manuel was shouting at the small wood hut.

"I thought so," Esteban said calmly in Cesar's ear. "But taking her wasn't enough for you, was it? You had to come after me also. You know who I am. Paulo Esteban. I know your face."

"Cesar Ordonez."

"Of course. Forgive me, I should have remembered. There are people in Havana who would give their eyeteeth to spend a few hours with you, alive and talkative, Cesar. You would be a big prize for me to deliver in ordinary times. But unfortunately, losing Sally Poynings would hurt my reputation more than capturing you would build it. So I am forced to offer a deal. You for her."

The gun barrel pressed harder into the back of Cesar's neck.

"Do you expect me to believe you would keep your side of a bargain?" Cesar asked, trying to distract him.

The gun barrel eased for a moment.

Cesar spun around, finger already pressing on the Uzi's trigger. The submachine gun spat bullets. Esteban fired, shattering Cesar's spinal column with a .45 slug.

The instant the bullet sheared through Cesar's spinal cord, his trigger finger relaxed.

Esteban was faced for a moment by the staggering man, already dead and the Uzi in his hands, the Uzi that had coughed its last slug only inches from his arm and which was now pointing directly at his chest—but silent. Cesar toppled in a heap over the Uzi, still in his lifeless hands.

Campbell and Murphy heard the distinctive rattle of the Uzi's fire. They ran to where the sound came from and found Cesar's body.

Mike covered the dead merc's face with the bush hat lying next to him. Cesar's Uzi was gone.

"Let's get that bastard Esteban," Mike ground out savagely.

"We should go, Mike," Bob cautioned. "We should catch up to the others."

Mike saw the wisdom of this advice, but he found it impossible to control his rage and his desire to avenge his dead friend. Mike had now forgotten how Cesar had endangered everyone on the mission by taking off on his own. To Mike, Cesar was one of his men lost. Who deserved to be avenged.

"Mike, we got to move out fast," Bob pleaded. "All hell is breaking loose around here."

Campbell's mind snapped to attention. He felt he must have slipped into some kind of reverie. The alarm had been raised. The camp's occupants were rushing for their weapons. There was no question now of trying to hunt down Esteban.

Mike held the dead man's hands in his own for a moment and then placed them folded on his chest. "Good-bye, old friend."

He and Bob ran from shadow to shadow, heading for the spot where Andre and the others had set out from.

"There they go!" a voice shouted.

"Two of them!" another called.

Mike stopped in his tracks. "We'll have to head another way," he said to Bob. "We can't put them on Andre's trail."

But as they cut across to the opposite side of the compound, they were seen again, this time before they had gotten close to the perimeter. Bullets whistled over their heads and zinged off the sides of wood huts. Not far ahead of them, three men ran into an area of lamplight and were cut down in error by friendly fire.

When the Salvadorans and Cubans saw their mistake, they became more disorganized than ever. Groups of them ran this way and that, shouting and sometimes shooting at one another. In the confusion, Mike and Bob made it nearly all the way to the perimeter before they ran into serious fire.

Six or seven armed men were directly between them and the forest at the edge of the camp. Perhaps fifty, sixty or even more were chasing them from behind.

"We're goin' through!" Mike yelled at Bob. "Fast!"

They came out of the darkness at the guerrillas in front of them, both men using their Uzis. The Uzi was perfect for night-fighting, since all a man had to do to change the magazine was find one hand with the other. The magazine slipped up inside the gun's pistol grip, so precious seconds were not lost in fumbling in the dark, seconds that could cost a man his life.

The two advanced, their Uzis stuttering flaming messages of death. They overran the first guerrilla in their path. Their second victim's Kalashnikov jammed; and while Mike sprayed him with 9 mm pesticide, Bob removed the left half of a third guerrilla's skull with a concentrated burst of fire.

Campbell and Murphy were too busy exterminating to notice the bullets zipping past them from behind. Then one terrorist in front of them caught them by surprise. They hadn't seen him hide, and he popped up a few yards before them in an area of lamplight, about to spray the pair of them with his submachine gun (Mike remembered thinking it was a Sterling because the magazine feed was at a right angle on one side) when a bullet from behind, meant for Campbell's back, caught the terrorist with the Sterling between the eyes and dropped him at their feet.

After that, nothing could stop them. Bob literally overran one of their adversaries, perhaps never even striking him with a bullet, only walking him into the dirt with his combat boots, giving him a farewell step in the face that would certainly involve him in major dental work if he survived. Mike just rousted them as he would bobwhites out of long grass, and bagged three of them on a single magazine.

They slowed when they reached the cover of the forest, and Mike led Bob in a tight half-circle around the clearing to Andre's departure point, almost exactly in the opposite direction than they had been last seen running.

The Salvadorans and Cubans were sending heavy fire and now mortar shells deep into the forest at the point they had seen the two enter it. The dry undergrowth and trees had started to blaze.

Bob said to Mike, "The assholes have started a forest fire. Maybe they'll burn their whole fucking camp down."

Mike was consulting the luminous dial of his compass to get a heading of north-northeast. He said, "It couldn't happen to nicer people."

Andre kept Sally close by him, with Nolan and Waller in front and Hardwick in the rear. They were making good progress through the forest, considering it was night. Andre was pleased and surprised that Sally could rough it well enough—he had expected her to be a drag on them by being physically unable for hardship and by being mentally unsuited to anything but her own impulses. He had expected a pampered, spoiled brat. Instead, he found her to be a silent and determined survivor who realized she was clutching at some last straws.

As a woman, she was a mystery to Andre. He thought that he had reached the age where he was quite willing to leave many of these young women to men younger than he. The woman he understood still liked a man to hold a door open for her, light her cigarette, inhale her perfume. . . . Girls like Sally didn't smoke, didn't wear perfume and were likely to hold the door open for him and insist on paying a restaurant bill. Definitely not his style.

After twenty minutes of rough climbing, they heard shooting back at the camp. Everyone stopped. They could see clearly across the dark valley to where flames were still consuming the bunkhouse.

Andre said, "Mike's orders are to keep moving."

As they trudged onward, the firing back at the camp continued, ending with explosions of mortar shells and new fires in the forest near the edge of the clearing.

"Keep moving," Andre ordered. "Mike will catch up."

They marched hard up the side of the valley for more than an hour and reached its rim before Andre called for a five-minute rest. The lighted clearing on the far side of the valley was being engulfed all along one side by a huge forest fire, and many of the wood buildings were also aflame.

"I hope the bastards fry," were the first words any of them heard Sally speak.

They all laughed at the ferocity in the pretty girl's voice, and she laughed too. The ice between them was broken.

"Thanks for coming to get me," she told them as they set out again. North-northeast. The Honduran border was about fifteen kilometers away.

They kept moving through the night, stopping for five or ten minutes' rest every hour. They usually ate something, to help them keep warm, every time they stopped. The chill mountain night air made them glad to move on again after each rest, if only to warm themselves. Andre checked his compass frequently, but did not fool himself that he was traveling in anything like a straight line. The most he could hope for was to stay in one general direction. Both he and Mike had known from the start the low probability of Mike's ever catching up and joining them, even if all went well. But they could realistically hope that they would both cross the Honduran border not far from each other and at more or less the same time—all going well.

Andre understood Mike's directive to him. His responsibility now was to deliver the girl, come what may. To Andre, this was a triumph. He had been the one Mike was most reluctant to take along on the mission, yet when it came to handing over the leadership, Mike had passed it to him. Without any palaver. It was just "Here, Andre, take over." It sure as hell made one thing clear to everybody— Andre Verdoux was not yet over the hill!

"Fucker thinks he's Charles de Gaulle," Joe Nolan complained to Harvey Waller so that Andre could overhear.

Harvey laughed. They both liked Verdoux. Harvey said, "Naw, Andre's nose is too big."

Andre's Gallic pride shrugged off all such sniveling complaints from the lower orders. Cortez, in his time and perhaps over this same ground, forged onward with no greater resolution than Andre Verdoux.

Because of the uphill-and-downhill going, changes of routes, rests, easy stretches alternating endlessly with hard going, no one had any idea of how far they had traveled as dawn broke.

"We might already be in Honduras," Lance suggested.

That was possible, but no one believed it was going to be that easy.

"We can't be far off," Andre said, "but I'm not able to recognize anything from yesterday."

"We've come a different way," Joe agreed.

None of them mentioned what their muscles and bones and all the fibers in their bodies were screaming—lie down and sleep! At this time, twenty-four hours previously, they had been watching the mountain pass for the five Cubans after a night on the freezing slope. And from there they had hit the whiskey and whores in San Salvador for a few hours, then by chopper to the contras on this border—and it had been nonstop after that. Was the end yet in sight?

As daylight spread, they heard choppers.

"They're coming from the south," Harvey said. "From inside Nicaragua."

"Putting down men between us and the border," Joe added.

"They can't have seen us," Andre said.

"They must have," Lance put in.

Sally said nothing.

"Somebody must have sighted us not far back and called them in," Andre decided. "They've come down right in our path. Joe, scout around and tell us what you see."

A lot of men have enough courage to make good scouts, but not many have enough mother wit to know when to withdraw. Joe Nolan had both.

Joe was not gone long. "Shit, they seen us all right! And they're coming right this way! Those four choppers put in at least fifty men, and it looks to me like there's many more behind them. My guess is we got a solid wall of Nicaraguan regulars between us and the border. But meantime, we got those fifty jokers coming this way!''

Andre had to decide. There was no point in going back the way they had come, since they had already been spotted coming this way and would be seen again or attacked this time. They couldn't veer to left or right of the oncoming column and continue northward to the border since soldiers were sealing it off.

Andre told them hurriedly, ''We've come from the southwest, so now let's bounce to the southeast; and when we shake these troops, bounce back to the border farther east.''

Andre knew it was hopeless. They were an almost exhausted force up against fresh troops with superior numbers, mobility and surveillance. The only thing Andre could do was keep moving and hope for the best. He was feeling the frustration of fighting against unknown odds, and the thought flashed through his mind—maybe, after all, he was over the hill!

What if Mike had been right? What if he no longer had the nerve? They could never outrun these fifty men. Let the Hardwick kid go with the girl. And Nolan with them. He'd ask Waller to stay behind with him. Waller was no good; he'd be no loss to anyone. He and Andre would stay behind and hold the pass while the other three gained time to try for the border again farther east.

''Harvey, you want to make a stand with me and let the others go on?''

Waller didn't look happy. ''I suppose you're right, Frenchie. Better some of us go under than all.''

Andre stopped at a place with big rocks and some tree trunks where he and Harvey could hold out for a while.

''Keep going,'' he ordered the others. ''We'll catch up. Nolan, take over.''

The Nicaraguans were cautious. They came forward two

and three men at a time, covered by the others. This slowed them down considerably, so apparently they had a lot of respect for their enemy.

"I guess word has spread about us," Harvey said proudly. "You want me to take out a few of these pussyfooters?"

"No, let them burn up time and give the others and the girl a head start," Andre said.

But in spite of their caution, the Nicaraguans were advancing faster than it had first appeared.

"Okay, Harvey, blast away."

Both men used their FN-FAL Paratroop battle rifles to pick off individuals as they advanced. They hit five men and brought the forward advance to a halt. If left to themselves, none of the Nicaraguan soldiers would have risked showing himself again—but as always, there were an officer and sergeants present to make sure that things were not left to the men themselves to decide.

Andre and Harvey heard the officer shout and curse in Spanish. Finally one soldier obeyed him and jumped up and zigzagged forward toward the cover of a rock. Harvey nailed him with a single bullet and left him kicking in the dust. The officer cursed and shouted some more. Then all at once seven or eight men ran forward. Harvey got one of them. Then another seven or eight ran forward. Then more. And their advance was underway again, faster than before, in spite of the losses they were taking.

Both mercs whirled to meet what they thought was a surprise onslaught on their right flank; then they heard Lance shouting to them. All three had come back!

"They've cut us off that way," Joe informed Andre, squatting down and getting off a beautiful shot that sent a Nicaraguan to join his forefathers, clutching his head.

There was no time for talk. They had to beat back this attack before they could try anything else. Sally blasted away with Lance's Uzi and whooped like a cheerleader at a college game when she brought down two soldiers in her first wild swing with the submachine gun. Of course, she swung it around too far and almost shot Andre as well, which caused him to appeal directly to God in French.

Their added firepower bogged down their attackers again, who had now taken heavy casualties.

"They're going to get tricky on us now, Andre," Harvey warned. "They'll try us on the sides or circle round the back."

"Or call in air support," Joe suggest ominously, which made Andre glance involuntarily over their heads.

"Pull back," the Frenchman said, "but slowly. First you three. Harvey and I will follow."

Campbell and Murphy had almost come up against the Nicaraguan regulars sealing off the border, but managed to retreat without being seen. They were making their way parallel to the border when they heard shooting not far away. They guessed who was involved.

"Well, at least we've found them," Mike said. "I was afraid we two might get across safely and leave them behind—and it doesn't do for the leader to get home and leave some of his men behind him."

"You don't have to worry about that now," Bob said sarcastically. "We're all neck-deep in shit together."

The serene way in which Campbell reacted to major threats was one of the few things about him which needled Bob.

They came upon the others as they retreated before the Nicaraguans. Neither side had yet seen the two of them. Bob untied a small sack from Mike's backpack and handed it to him. Mike hurriedly untied the neck and showed its contents to Bob. The sack was filled with tiny grenades. These were the specialties Cuthbert Colquitt had promised Mike—the smallest hand grenades in the world.

Each of the olive drab metal globes, with painted letters "NWM" for its Dutch manufacturer and "V40-HE" for its model and high explosives designation, was only 1¾ inches in diameter, with a half-inch fixture on top to hold the safety pin, safety lever and striker. The V40 weighed only three and a half ounces, about half the weight of the next lightest fragmentation grenade, which meant they did not have to be lobbed like heavy grenades but could be thrown like stones.

"Cover me!" Mike yelled to Bob.

Mike's left arm throbbed with pain from the flesh wound he had taken, but that was no bother to a right-handed pitcher. He pulled the pin, and the lever released after he had chucked the grenade as hard as he could. The steel case of the V40 fragmented explosively four seconds later among the Nicaraguan regulars. The composition B explosive blew the four or five hundred steel fragments in all directions. The flying pieces were lethal within a range of five yards of the explosion, and inflicted terrible injuries on those within a twenty-five yard radius.

Mike found he could hurl the little grenades about twice as far as he could a normal grenade, and he kept a steady hail of the miniature steel globes of death descending on the Nicaraguans. Bob covered him with his Belgian FN-FAL, and then Andre and Harvey also as soon as they copped on to what was happening.

The Nicaraguan officer shouted, cursed, appealed to the patriotism of his men . . . but since most of the soldiers had already been cut by the tiny, hot razor fragments, this time it was going to take more than words to make them move any farther forward. Each time a V40 landed and exploded among them, one or more would roar, stagger to his feet and lurch about, holding on to some part of his body.

Instead of pulling back his men and regrouping them, their officer tried to redirect their attack on the sources of the grenades. This left them open to cross fire from Andre and Harvey, whose accurate FN-FALs began to take a heavy toll.

Mike flung one V40 that flushed four Nicaraguans at

once; and each, badly hit, performed individual variations on a grotesque dance of death, fingers plucking frantically at the burning steel hornets tormenting their flesh.

After that, no one did any more shouting, and the surviving Nicaraguan regulars ran for their lives.

Chapter 17

THEY kept heading south. Behind them, choppers ranged back and forth searching for them. But none came this far into the interior, assuming reasonably enough that the team would still be in the border area.

The sun rose higher and higher until it was almost directly above them and beating down on them with the glare and heat of a furnace. Mike called a halt in a stand of trees by a dried-up stream bed.

"I'll take the first hour's watch," he said. "The rest of you sleep. I figure we must be nine or ten miles in from the border by now, assuming we were less than a mile from it when we met the Nicaraguans. Get some shut-eye."

He didn't have to tell them again. Mike propped himself in a sitting position at the base of a tree, his FN across his knees. He was in the shade, and the mosquitoes and other insects were no worse here than anywhere else, which meant they were pretty plentiful. Best way Mike knew how to ignore insect bites was to worry about bullets puncturing your skin. Bullets made a man think more kindly of mosquitoes. . . .

He mopped the sweat from his face and looked about

the rough highland country. So long as they could hide out here away from populated areas and away from the border, they would be fairly safe. But their C rations were running low. If they had adequate rations, one option would be to hold out for a week where they were and wait for the excitement at the border to die down before attempting another crossing. He had to think of something bold, something the Nicaraguans would not expect. Maybe he'd be able to think better after he'd had a little sleep.

They took turns at watch, and in the cooler later afternoon, they woke up one by one. Helicopters were still ranging back and forth a few miles to the north.

Mike was refreshed. "I have a trivia question for you," he told the others. "Which American state is Nicaragua slightly larger than?"

They looked at him oddly and said nothing.

"Wisconsin," Mike answered his own question. "So it's not as if we'll be crossing Texas. Know why those choppers are north of us and not over our heads? Because it's inconceivable to the Nicaraguans that we would have come this far in from the border. It would be totally beyond their belief if we cut through their country from north to south and crossed the southern border instead of the one we are near now."

This was met by another silence. Apparently not only Nicaraguans would find the idea incredible.

"They've sealed the northern border against us in this area," Mike went on. "We could cut across the mountains to the east and try for a crossing over there, but we don't have food for a wilderness trip; we don't have equipment or clothing for high mountains; the 'bad guy' contras don't seem too sympathetic toward us; and it's what the Nicaraguans will expect us to do. It's only a couple of hundred miles to the southern border with Costa Rica." Mike looked around once more. He saw no more enthusiasm this time than the last, and he was done explaining. "All right, we move out." He led the way.

No one still said anything. They had been so near and yet so far. Freedom was still only ten miles or so one way, and they were headed in the other. What did Mike want? To be congratulated?

As dusk came on, Mike ordered them to camp for the night. He sent Bob and Joe out to bag whatever they could for the cook pot—which of course they did not possess. Andre and he went to forage for edible herbs—anything to save their C rations, which Mike had forbidden them to open. Bob shot a young deer, and they roasted pieces of it over an open fire. A hot meal was worth the risk of the fire being spotted, everyone agreed. The meat was tough as vinyl, but no one complained and they ate it along with strange-looking green leaves, which Mike swore were edible, and with obscene-looking funguses which Andre claimed were a delicacy.

Everyone felt better after a bellyful of warm food. They kept the fire going till they were ready to sleep, and then decided they would keep it going all night for warmth. They had gotten over their disappointment at not getting into Honduras, and Mike knew that after a night's rest and more hot venison in the morning, he would have a fighting squad on his hands again.

Lance made a pass at Sally and got put down.

The railroad wasn't on any of Mike's maps. The way the weeds grew up around the single pair of rails, it looked disused at first glance—but the tops of the rails were scratched and shining from the recent passage of wheels. It wasn't the kind of place where they would wait in hope of a passing train, but since the rails ran south, they followed them as the easiest path. There would be a greatly increased chance of running into Nicaraguans along the railroad line, but anything was better than breaking through scrub and thorny undergrowth, uphill and down.

The rails twisted in curves sharper than any of them had

thought trains could maneuver. They had walked alongside the rails for more than two hours when they thought they heard something. They were constantly watchful as they walked, but this sound was not coming from the scrubland on either side or from the air—the humming they all plainly heard was originating from the steel rails beside them. A train was coming!

An old steam locomotive appeared, heading south at an unhurried walking pace. It pulled four battered passenger cars that had no glass in their windows. Mike nodded, and the six mercs and Sally ran alongside the last car and boarded it. The car was half-filled with campesinos, many of whom had huge cloth bundles or baskets of vegetables. Chickens squawked in wicker and wire cages, and some hung upside down by their bound feet from hooks beneath the baggage racks, flapping their wings occasionally and stretching their necks to peer about. A pig grunted somewhere down the car.

When the mercs sat in two facing bench seats, their rifles, submachine guns and backpacks awkwardly jutting out and getting in the way, the campesinos already there hurriedly vacated their seats and went elsewhere down the car with their bundles. Those in the facing seats on the opposite side of the central aisle followed suit. Mike put a finger to his lips. No one was to say anything.

They waited for some more reactions, weapons ready if needed, but immediately the torpor of the rail journey returned to the car and they soon found themselves idly looking through the paneless windows at the rough hill country crawling by as the train negotiated sharp curves, the steel wheels at times squealing on the steel rails. A portable radio blared melancholy airs sung by men with guitars.

Lance overheard someone talking about them, using the words "ruso" and "sovietico." While the wheels were squealing, he told the others, "They think we're Russians or from one of the Iron Curtain countries."

"Good," Mike said. "Then they'll leave us alone. Don't let them hear you talk English."

He sorted among Salvadoran and Honduran bills from his backpack till he found Nicaraguan currency. He passed out money to each of them and returned to his maps, which did not recognize the existence of this railroad.

"I think this train has to pass through Matagalpa," Mike said under cover of the noise. "At least, it's a destination to tell the ticket collector. From Matagalpa we can continue down the eastern edge of Lake Nicaragua to the Costa Rican border. The lake is about a hundred miles long, so we'll be halfway there when we reach its northern tip."

Everyone nodded as if they had faith in what he said. The music stopped on the portable radio, and a newscast mentioned a volcanic eruption and people being evacuated from the area, right after which the train made a turn and a huge cloud of coal smoke came in the car's windows, which made everybody laugh. The newscast mentioned the efforts of the gallant revolutionary militias against the contras in the pay of the United States, and warned citizens of the dangers of certain capitalist "elements" that lurked within the state. This did not seem to be a reference to Sally Poynings or the mercs.

"Maybe they think we made it across the border," Joe said.

"The western press would have let them know that by now," Mike said. "No, I bet they're still searching for us all along the border area. Once they got the border sealed, then they could do aerial reconnaissance and ground sweeps. I bet that right now they're combing every square inch up there."

No ticket collector came by. They saw that other people jumped aboard the slow-moving train and that others got off—some riding for only a half mile or so, and some even jumping on for a few words of greeting and leaving again after a hundred yards. There seemed to be no stations or towns of any kind in sight of the railroad, yet there were plenty of people about now that they had descended from the higher hills and traveled farther south. Many of the dwellings they saw had ancient stone walls with fresh thatch or corrugated steel roofs. Children climbed aboard the cars to sell food, beer, fruit, nuts and even toys and souvenirs. The team bought large quantities of all kinds of food with the money Mike had given them, not caring if they were being cheated. But even these children, anxious to sell them things, would not smile at them. Being a Russian here was obviously not winning any popularity contest with the common people.

Two armed militiamen occasionally walked the length of the train. They were dressed in khaki, and their only weapons were two old heavy bolt-action rifles. The first time they appeared, Mike only barely managed to prevent Harvey from mowing them down with his Uzi. The two militiamen saluted the mercs, who saluted them back. Mike smiled, but they did not return his smile. After that, the two Nicaraguans studiously ignored them.

As things settled, Lance's mind turned to other concerns. He had expected Sally to be a giggling, chatty airhead; and instead he found her to be even more beautiful than he had expected, but silent, withdrawn and sad. He noticed how upset she became when she heard about Cesar's death, blaming herself for it, even though Mike explained to her that Cesar had got himself killed chasing Cubans *instead* of rescuing her. Lance understood that her recent experiences had shaken her up a little bit, but that was nothing a handsome stud like him couldn't put right. She got pissed off at him when he tried to explain this to her, and went to sit next to Mike. She changed the dressing on Mike's arm and made eyes at Mike in a way Lance was sure she intended just to make him jealous.

Joe, Harvey and Bob sat quiet and watchful, not missing a thing, their eyes roving to and fro, their hands resting very casually on their weapons. This was enemy territory. No one was going to take them by surprise.

Sally and Mike chatted and laughed while Lance fumed. Andre sat back and enjoyed it, as he always did when an older man beat out a younger one for the affections of a lady.

The mercs spent a tense half hour in the station at Matagalpa and were relieved when the train pulled out of the large market town. A ticket collector appeared and asked Mike if they wanted to go all the way to Managua. He said yes, and bought seven tickets, although the Nicaraguan capital was the last place on earth he wanted to be.

The radio still kept them informed. As yet, there was no mention of Sally or the team, but they did learn that the volcano was becoming increasingly active and that the entire area around it had been evacuated because of the danger of showers of hot cinders. A man in the seat back of Mike was telling someone they would be able to see the volcano from the train in a couple of hours.

Mike found the volcano on his map, and he and Andre estimated the area cleared of people and circled it with a ballpoint pen.

It was mid-afternoon when they finally saw the volcano. A long ridge of high volcanic cones, some with their tips missing, stretched off into the distance. The top half of one cone was hidden by a huge cloud of black smoke that drifted miles eastward into a widening tail. Mike waited till the train was at its closest approach to the mountain, by which point interest among the other passengers had long since waned. Volcanic eruptions and earthquakes were common happenings in Nicaragua. So too, apparently, were armed Russians on a train. The people may not like any of them, but they had to live with them.

Mike jerked his thumb out the window. Time to go.

*   *   *

El Salvador looked like the Garden of Eden in comparison with this part of Nicaragua. It was less populated here than in El Salvador, but the poverty was much greater. The hillside villages were picturesque in spite of their harsh primitiveness, or perhaps because of it; their ancient thick-walled churches half-tumbled by earthquake shocks, open sewers on cobblestone streets, revolutionary slogans painted on sagging walls. "No passaran!" was scrawled everywhere— meaning "They shall not come through!" and referring to the U.S. Marines, who apparently were expected any minute.

They were seriously challenged only once, by a small, spectacled man in a blue shirt who was with an armed civil defense committee patrolling a village they were circumnavigating. The man shouted something at them. When they did not reply, he repeated it.

"Sounds like Russian," Mike said.

"Let me handle it," Lance offered. He shouted something in a foreign language across the field to the man, and he responded in that language enthusiastically and began to come to meet them.

"He speaks Czech, Mike," Lance said. "I can handle it, but what about all of you?"

"Go to meet him before he reaches us," Mike said. "Tell him we're in a hurry. Say we're geologists."

"I don't know the Czech word for that. My mother spoke to me in Czech all the time, but she never once mentioned geology."

Lance met the man midway, talked with him for a few minutes and then hurried back.

"I told him we were Czech agricultural experts here to gauge the volcano damage so our government could send aid. As soon as he heard the word 'aid,' he told us we could go where we liked so far as he was concerned but that we'll need a clearance from the army up ahead to enter the danger zone."

Lance showed Mike a travel permit the man had given him. From this point on, when they ran into various armed civilian patrols, Lance did the talking in Czech with some Spanish words thrown in and displayed their travel permit. A lot of Czech and almost no Spanish seemed the best formula. As in every communist country, a certain percentage of the population was employed in running surveillance on the rest, and there seemed to be armed cadres of the dedicated all over the place to prod those who were less enthusiastic about their socialist paradise. These cadres were the big shots locally, but they always backed off in respectful awe when Lance spouted Czech at them. Maybe they thought it was Russian.

The mercs began noticing people on the hill paths driving burros loaded with pots and bedding, obviously refugees from the evacuated area. As the mercs neared the base of the smoke-shrouded mountain, they were passed by army trucks filled with people and their belongings. At this altitude, the ground was open—or at most covered with low evergreens—so that there was no way they could hope to sneak through the army checkpoints they saw ahead.

"Just keep walking," Mike said. "We'll aim for the midpoint between the two checkpoints."

As they walked through, they heard shouts. Finally, a Russian-built imitation Jeep bounced across the rough ground toward them. Lance stopped to meet it while the others walked on. He rejoined them shortly, and the vehicle returned to the checkpoint, but Lance seemed less than contented.

"I gave him the bit about Czech government aid and I think he understood me, though he spoke only Spanish. But he's one of these pushy young going-somewhere-in-a-hurry officer types. He said he would have to radio in to HQ to get verification on us. I told him not to bother; that we'd been approved and could not be delayed. I bet the little fartface radios in all the same and finds out no one has ever heard about us Czechs out here. Better not let them see us quicken our pace, guys."

Mike said nothing. They were now well uphill of the army checkpoints.

"What I can't understand," Sally said, "is why they don't put out an all-points bulletin or whatever you call it."

"Then they'd have to admit you were· in Nicaragua," Andre said.

Mike plodded uphill silently. The light was noticeably darkening as they climbed up under the cloud of smoke which had appeared black from a distance, but which they could now see comprised all sorts of olive, green, yellow and even purple coiling smoke as well as black and brown.

"You wouldn't live ten seconds trying to breathe that smoke," Andre said loudly for Mike's benefit as they climbed nearer to the dense cloud.

The smoke rolled down the slope high above them and then lifted off to hover over their heads. Mike kept climbing in a steady, preoccupied way.

They heard a volley of shots from downhill.

"Don't look back," Mike said. "Just keep going like you haven't heard a thing."

Another volley of shots.

"They're still only shooting in the air," Andre said, with a hint in his voice that they might not continue to do so.

"Keep going," Mike said. "That officer has probably made a radio call, like Lance said he would, but he can't be sure yet who the hell we are. And he doesn't want seven dead Czechs on his hands because somebody at HQ goofed and forgot to mention they were here. He'll be up to talk with us again. When he comes, I want you to drive, Joe."

"What?" Nolan asked.

"You heard me," Mike snapped.

Sure enough, a half minute later they heard the imitation Jeep laboring up the slope after them.

"Talk to him, Lance," Mike said. "Get him away from the vehicle."

Lance led the zealous officer away from the Soviet Jeep and launched into fluent Czech expostulations, with occasional Spanish phrases thrown in to further mystify him. Apart from the driver, two Nicaraguan regulars remained in the vehicle and covered the team with a Soviet PK machine gun. These two would be hard to fool.

Lance was smiling and shaking hands with the officer, who seemed a bit confused and unhappy. Lance shouted at the three Nicaraguans still in the Jeep and gestured at them to get out. They looked at their officer, who nodded his head uncertainly. Lance spoke volubly to Mike and the team in what they assumed was Czech and gestured for them to get in the vehicle. Harvey settled in behind the machine gun. As Joe Nolan drove away, Lance looked back and waved to the Nicaraguans.

Manuel had never seen Paulo in such a rage. Manuel was often afraid of Paulo, even when he was in his sunniest moods, so that now with Paulo's face gray from exhaustion, his eyes bloodshot, his huge frame trembling with fury, Manuel sent a quick prayer to the Virgin that he was not the one who was at fault.

Esteban stubbed a forefinger on the map spread before him. "What do you see there?"

Manuel looked. "Mountains? Ah, that volcano which became active, where they evacuated those people."

"What would you say to seven armed Czechs in that area?" Esteban asked.

"Czechs? I don't think so. You're sure they're not Russians?"

"Czechs."

"I don't think so," Manuel repeated, trying not to cause offense.

"What if I told you that one of the seven was a blond female?"

Manuel's jaw dropped.

Esteban went on, "What if I also told you that an officer

of the Nicaraguan army lent them a vehicle and a PK machine gun?"

"Santa Maria."

When they woke at dawn, they all felt queasy from the noxious fumes they had been breathing ever since arriving at the volcano. While daylight held, they had driven south around the volcanic cone at a level higher than its base. They used the meager shelter of the Soviet Jeep in which to sleep—except for Harvey, who claimed it would be an easier and quicker death to be caught in the open by a shower of hot cinders from the crater above them. Although the earth trembled periodically throughout the night, there was no fire and brimstone—only headaches from the fumes in the air, as if they had drunk and smoked too much.

The coiling smoke cloud still hung above them like an enormous thunderhead about to release a deluge, and the early morning daylight had that eerie brightness often associated with an approaching thunderstorm. The mountain slope was bare and exposed except for scraggy grass. There were no hiding places here, not even cover from attack. They understood now why Mike was keeping them higher up the slope than they thought healthy—that black cloud was their protection from the air.

But the cloud was not low enough to prevent choppers from coming in and searching for them. They heard their engines and then saw them before they were sighted themselves. A gunship tried a flyover from their rear. If the barren ground gave them no protection, it also made sneak attacks on them impossible. Harvey lay on the floor of the Jeep, and his machine gun spattered 7.62 mm bullets at the oncoming chopper. Its glass cowling shattered, and the pilot took the craft nose-up into the smoke to avoid the PK's bullets.

The chopper came down into visibility again a few

hundred yards downhill from them. Its door gunner scraped paint off the Jeep's hood as he raked them with fire.

Harvey returned fire from the bouncing vehicle, and they saw the door gunner fall back into the chopper's interior and his machine gun swing loose on its mount.

Waller's Russian gun had a 250-round square belt box and a cyclic rate of 650 rpm. He gave the chopper everything the PK had to give. The helicopter skewed sideways like a horse hit hard with a whip, and then kind of shuddered and sounded like a broken-down truck, till suddenly it dipped its nose and bit the dust.

They saw the chopper lie on the ground for a half second before it was consumed in a great fiery ball, which made Harvey whisper "Goddam" in awestruck admiration, like a connoisseur of beauty before a perfect work of art.

Two other helicopters made a wide swing around them, well out of the PK's range, which Harvey figured at about one thousand yards. The choppers came down about a mile ahead of the mercs but could not touch down safely on the steep mountain slope. Instead, each chopper rested one skid on the uphill side, with the second skid hovering in thin air, and unloaded airborne assault troops. The two choppers lifted off as the soldiers spread quickly up and down the slope to intercept the approaching vehicle.

Once they came in range, Harvey fired a machine-gun burst over Joe's head as he drove the Jeep, and four or five of the Nicaraguans went down like ninepins.

After that, the Nicaraguan assault troops lay in the grass and waited, invisible. Joe Nolan slowed and waited for Mike's instructions.

"Stop," Mike said.

Mike decided to make a vertical downhill run from where they were and then continue cutting around the base of the mountain. This would add a lot of miles to their journey and open them up to who knew what kind of troubles away from the smoke cloud's protection and out of the crater's danger zone.

Mike was just about to tell Joe to make the downhill turn when he saw the assault troops ahead jump to their feet and start running downhill. Some of them dropped their rifles; others looked fearfully behind them.

"Push on!" Mike yelled to Joe, who threw the fake Jeep into gear and lurched forward.

They were making good speed across the bumpy, grassy terrain, and the Nicaraguans were too busy running from whatever ailed them to intercept the mercs, when Joe saw, directly ahead of the Jeep, a long ribbon of moving gray stuff that steamed like cooked oatmeal.

"Lava!" Mike shouted.

Joe turned the steering wheel, brought the Jeep sharply about and drove alongside the moving lava. They saw now that this was just one of many fast-moving fingers of a more slowly moving broad front of molten rock descending the mountainside. They saw too what had terrified the Nicaraguan airborne assault troops, who were still hoofing it downhill before them. The fingers of lava, moving at the rate of a fast walk, broke without warning into rapidly moving rivulets that rejoined each other farther downhill, leaving islands of grass cut off by the lava channels.

One soldier found himself cut off on a diamond-shaped island maybe fifteen feet long. He ran its length and, in a spectacularly long jump, successfully cleared a rivulet of molten rock at its narrowest point.

Mike told Joe, "We won't go down any farther than we have to. Drive across through this shit."

"We've used up nearly all our reserve gas anyway," Joe said philosophically and swung the vehicle toward a lava stream and tried accelerating across.

The four tires blew on contact, and the rubber was cooked off the wheel rims in seconds. It took two minutes to cross the fifty-foot-wide lava stream less than six inches deep.

Halfway across, Joe called back, "Harvey, get out and push."

Back on the grass on the other side of the lava stream, running on the rims was slow and laborious.

"I can see two more streams ahead at this level," Mike said, standing up. "Then we can chuck the Jeep and head for Lake Nicaragua."

They could now see its blue vastness in the distance.

When they saw that some of the Nicaraguan forces had stopped running before the lava, they grew wary, thinking they had turned to fire on them. Then they saw that these men, about eight in all, had been trapped on a grass island among braided rivulets of lava. As the Jeep slowly plowed its way through a second lava stream, sometimes spinning its wheels as if in mud and threatening to stall in midstream, they had plenty of time to see how the Nicaraguans were faring.

Although both sides were within easy firing range of each other, all thought of hostilities had ceased. The competition of man against nature had for the moment become stronger than that of man against man. The mercs would even have helped the marooned soldiers, had they been able to do so without endangering themselves.

At first it seemed as if the eight soldiers had only to outwait the lava flow on their island and then escape when the flow waned and the molten rock hardened. However, it soon became evident that a major volume of the central mass of lava was flowing their way, and the channels of moving gray matter were visibly swelling and thickening—and their island shrinking.

The eight men changed from helping one another to crowding one another on their increasingly small patch of solid ground amid lava streamlets too wide to leap. Then the two weakest were pushed off by the others.

As the two fell full-length into the molten rock, they seemed to die instantly—like lobsters dropped into boiling water. The others watched horrified as their flesh was consumed and the white knobs of their yellow bones pushed through, as the corpses were dragged over the ground by the creeping shallow tide.

A lava stream was pinched into a strait at one point, too wide for a man to clear with a single leap. One soldier prepared to jump, clearly hoping to save himself by sacrificing the foot he would have to place in the lava for his second leap. On the other side lay a much larger island than their own—with higher ground where a man would almost certainly be safe from the lava flow if he could reach it.

The soldier jumped, pushing off with his right foot and landing on his left more than ankle deep in lava, three-quarters of the way across the channel. His left foot was no more than a second in the melted rock, and then he leaped again and made it to safety on the far side.

All that remained of his left foot was the gleaming white bones, like those of a well-cleaned skeleton.

By the time the Jeep had negotiated the lava flow, crossed a stretch of grassy land and entered the last flow in their path, there was only one man left on the original and still-diminishing island. He had pushed the others off. He now stood on a little mound of stones he had built for himself and stared at the implacable smoking gray stuff creeping slowly beneath his feet.

Chapter 18

THEY got to the eastern shore of Lake Nicaragua at sunset. The lake was so huge—forty-five miles wide and one hundred long—they found it hard to believe this was not the Pacific Ocean. They had little time or inclination to admire the magnificent sunset over the waters, and headed wearily south along its shore. The moon's first quarter gave them sufficient light to continue after dark, and Mike decided to make as much progress as they could under cover of night. He reckoned they were one-third of the way down the lake's eastern shore, about seventy miles from the Costa Rican border and freedom. This would be a two-day trek at the minimum, over rough land, a period which would give the Nicaraguan authorities adequate time to ensure their capture. He had to find a quicker and less exhausting way to travel.

When they saw a small town ahead on the lakeshore, Mike ordered a halt. Rowboats, some with outboard motors attached, were pulled up on the land before the town. Such boats would certainly beat walking. They could travel all night on the lake and reach the border sometime tomorrow. But offshore there was something better yet—by moonlight they could see the white shape of a launch about thirty-five feet long, anchored, without lights.

"Bob, you're our boat expert," Mike said. "Think you can start her?"

Bob nodded.

Mike pointed to Lance, and all three of them stripped to their shorts and buckled on belts holding a sheathed Marine Corps combat knife.

"If you see any triangular fins," Mike told them with a smile, "they're for real. I've heard this lake is crawling with freshwater sharks. The lake was once an inlet of the sea and got cut off by a volcano or an earthquake, so the sharks became landlocked."

"I promise not to feed them," Bob said.

The others stayed where they were. Andre would signal by flashlight when they got the launch under way, and they would bring it inshore to pick them up. Mike entered the water where they were, in spite of it being a half-mile swim, because he felt they could not risk being seen by townspeople. One person seeing them could spoil the whole thing, since the townspeople could move faster in their small boats than the mercs could swim.

The water was calm, there were no currents, and it was pleasantly warm, so they made good time out to the anchored launch. All three hung on to one of its two anchor ropes. The ropes were thin and made of nylon. They would not be easy to climb. It would be simpler to go up over the side of the launch.

They swam to its side, which loomed about three feet over their heads, and listened. They heard no sound but that of wavelets slapping against the timbers of the boat. The cabin windows and navigation lights were dark.

Mike treaded water, fists forward and elbows held in at his sides. Lance and Bob grabbed an elbow each and heaved upward simultaneously, lifting Mike out of the water as they sank beneath him, displacing his weight. Mike clutched the gunwale with both hands and hauled himself up so that he balanced on his belly with his legs still over the side.

A soldier with a Kalashnikov across his legs sat huddled against the opposite gunwale fast asleep. If Mike had come up on the opposite side of the boat, he would have been right on top of him! Mike balanced where he was for a moment, ready to push back into the water at a second's notice, while he scanned the foredeck and peered into the darkness beyond the open cabin door.

Then he wiped the wet hair out of his eyes, eased himself over the gunwale, drew the knife from the sheath on his belt and tiptoed, dripping, across the afterdeck toward the sleeping soldier. He clamped his left hand over the man's mouth and drew the blade of his combat knife across his throat.

The soldier drummed his heels on the deck as he struggled in Mike's grip and as his lifeblood gushed down over his uniform. Mike released the limp body, put down his knife on the deck and grabbed the Kalashnikov. He cocked it and stood by the door of the dark cabin. He barged in suddenly, ready to spray anything that moved or made a sound in the darkness. The cabin was empty, so he came back out and helped Bob and Lance aboard. He and Lance dumped the body in the water while Bob started the marine diesel engine.

Like many diesels, this one was a bitch to start and noisy as hell when Bob did get it going; but the diesel was easy on fuel, and Bob was of the opinion they had plenty in the tanks to last them their voyage. Some lights in the town started to come on as the engine stuttered and failed over and over again. By the time it roared to life, they could see the flashlights of men climbing into small boats to come out to the launch.

"They probably think the soldier is drunk or loco," Mike said.

Lance cut the two anchor ropes and Bob swung the launch northward and parallel to the shore. The men in the small boats were shouting to them. Andre flicked on and off his beam, and the team waded out waist-deep to be helped aboard at the prow by Mike and Lance, while Bob kept the engine running and the screw turning out in the deeper water.

When they passed the town again, heading southward, the whole place was lighted up and the men in the small boats opened up on them with automatic rifles.

Mike sighed. "Not as quiet a start as I had hoped for, Bob. Better sail her without running lights."

When they were well under way, Harvey took the wheel, and Sally, who had been insisting that she be assigned duties like the others, took first watch. She noticed Mike's bloody combat knife where he had left it on the afterdeck and fetched a plastic basin of water from the galley so she could clean it for him as she kept watch on the foredeck.

"Next thing, you'll be washing his socks," Harvey sneered at her from the wheel.

Sally was stung. "What is it with you, Harvey? I get the feeling you don't much like women."

"Women are okay till they start picking up after me, dusting and washing things."

If any of the others had said what Harvey had said to her, she would have laughed. But Harvey's tone of voice caused a surge of anger in her, so she ignored him, kept watch and washed the knife in the basin.

The diesel began to develop a stutter, and after a while Harvey tied the wheel in place and went aft to tinker with the engine. Sally, sitting on the foredeck, which was also the cabin roof, saw a figure come out on the afterdeck behind Harvey. Bored with Waller's uncouth company, she looked curiously to see which of the team it was, hoping that it might be Mike.

Whoever it was, he stood just outside the cabin door, facing aft, a few paces from where Harvey was bent over the throbbing engine; all she could see from where she sat was the top of his head. As a joke, she reached down and grabbed him by the hair.

He yelled with fright and twisted his head out of her grasp. He looked up at her, and she saw he was a stranger. A Nicaraguan soldier. With a machete in his right hand. He raised the blade to slash at her, then stiffened suddenly; his eyes popped and his mouth opened.

Harvey stood behind him, supporting him with a knife buried in his right kidney. The machete dropped from the soldier's hand, and Harvey walked him across the after-deck like a drunk being escorted by a bouncer out of a tavern, and let him fall over the side.

After Harvey had rushed into the cabin to make sure the sleepers were all right, he returned to the wheel and said to Sally, "Not bad. You're really getting the hang of things."

"Wh-where did he come from?" Sally stammered with fright.

"Good point," Harvey acknowledged approvingly. "We're getting careless. That bastard probably heard Mike and the others come on board and hid in a sail locker or inside a bulkhead somewhere. Wake Mike and have him search this tub."

The norteamericanos had taken a battered old launch with a big diesel engine loud as a bus. Esteban smiled to himself and sat back in the captain's chair on the bridge of the naval cutter, smoking a cigar and watching the technicians monitor their night-navigation equipment. This time he had Mad Mike outmaneuvered.

If Paulo had known in the first place he was up against Mad Mike Campbell, he would have done things differently. For one, he would never have delegated so much responsibility to Manuel. In hindsight, it was laughable to have sent in Manuel with those airborne assault troops to stop someone like Campbell. They mentioned that they had sent for Manuel's dental records to see if he could be identified from the bones in the lava. Paulo was sorry to lose a loyal servant, but he could see now that the result had been a foregone conclusion. In sending Manuel, Paulo had sent a boy on a man's errand.

But from now on, it was going to be a different ball game. Paulo knew now whom he was contending with. The intelligence data had been radioed from Havana and decoded. Paulo was even amused by his instructions to take Mad Mike alive if possible, along with Senorita Sally, while the others were "disposable." Paulo thought he detected in this Fidel's curiosity to meet Mike.

To declaw the tiger and deliver him harmless in a cage to Havana to amuse Fidel . . . now that was something Paulo could enjoy anticipating. He was a big man and had a hearty appetite.

At dawn the mercs found themselves trapped by the naval cutter in a cove near San Carlos and the San Juan river. The San Juan drained the lake into the Caribbean, and about thirty miles down its length, the river became the border between Nicaragua to the north and Costa Rica to the south. Eden Pastora's "good guy" contras were said to control the river with their speedboats armed with machine guns and explosive charges known as "piranhas." But the mercs had no chance of slipping into the river now, trapped a few hundred yards offshore by a naval vessel that had three times their speed, plus four-inch guns and radar.

Paulo Esteban addressed them once again over the ship's speaker. Not only would he guarantee a safe-conduct down the San Juan for the launch and its crew in exchange for Sally Poynings and Mike Campbell, he now promised that Sally and Mike would be handed over to American authorities in Holland—after they had been presented as living evidence of United States aggression in Nicaragua at the World Court in The Hague.

"What more could you ask for under the circumstances?" Esteban wanted to know. "Senorita Sally goes home, and all of you survive to fight again, although you do not deserve to."

"I don't want to be selfish about this," Mike said, "but if any of you think you can save your skin—"

Andre laughed. "Anyone who believes Esteban would honor a safe-conduct for us out of Nicaragua after what we've done to them, take one step forward."

No one did.

"Think of something, Mike," Sally said in an adoring voice.

They all laughed and joined in.

"Yeah, Mike, think of something."

"What do you want us to do, Mike?"

"Come on, Mike."

Mike held up his hands, grinning. "Don't start getting loony. All right, listen to this. These bastards would have blown us out of the water by now if they didn't need to take Sally alive. For some reason, it seems they want to take me alive too. But Sally is our trump card. So long as she's with us and it looks like we can't escape, they won't shoot. They have to figure time is on their side. The more time we give them, the more troops they'll be able to move in on top of us. So what do we do? If we swim for shore, they'll blast us with their big guns. They'll kill Sally rather than let her escape. In short, we have one obvious choice— we sail out of here and they remain behind."

They all waited while Mike went below and returned with a roll of steel cable.

"As our nautical consultant, Bob," Mike asked, "do you think I could wrap this around the cutter's propeller?"

Bob looked serious. "She probably has twin screws, Mike. You might succeed if you had me to help you. There's masks and flippers below, but no oxygen."

"Let's go," Mike said.

They went over the shore side of the launch and swam under it. They had to surface for air on the way to the cutter, which was difficult for them to do unseen because of the calmness and clearness of the lake water.

Unknown to the mercs, they had been seen going over the side of the launch. Esteban shouted for frogmen. There were no frogmen on board the cutter. Then crew members. Half the crew did not know how to swim, and those who did had never dived . . . so they said.

"If I find you've lied to me," Esteban warned them, "I'll have you shot. I need volunteer divers. Fast."

No one volunteered.

Esteban grabbed a mask, flippers, spear gun, extra spears. He expertly went over the far side of the cutter, came beneath it and swam fast with his loaded spear gun extended before him.

Paulo saw two divers swimming through the water. The second carried a roll of cable and hung back behind the first, hampered by his load. Paulo decided to test the spear gun on the easier target.

The divers hadn't seen him, so he took his time aiming, and released the spear which had no attached line to slow or deflect its flight.

The spear gun shot slightly to the right of aim, so that Paulo harpooned the diver through one leg instead of in the trunk.

The first diver saw immediately that the second was in trouble, swam back and raised him to the surface for air. Paulo searched for a good shot, but then was forced to surface for air himself.

Panicked by Mike's shouts, Sally grabbed a rusty shotgun from a cabin rack and climbed up on the foredeck. Lance and Joe had dived in the water and were swimming out to help Mike with Bob. Andre and Harvey stood on the afterdeck with their automatic rifles, scanning the water.

Sally searched in the opposite direction. Almost beneath the prow of the launch, she saw Paulo Esteban's head out of the water with the mask raised from his face. He took a deep breath, winked at her and replaced the mask. He dived before she could blow his head off with the shotgun. She knew she was too late, but she was in such a rage she fired anyway.

The buckshot caught Esteban in the ass as he dived, reducing his broad posterior to a bloody pulp. He surfaced immediately, maskless, roaring with pain.

"Sally, Sally, help me!"

She looked away. Andre and Harvey were helping Bob aboard. She winced when she saw the spear through Bob's leg. But Andre snapped it quickly and pulled it out.

Sally knew her job. She ran below deck and collected bandages and disinfectant. She heard the launch's diesel stutter and refuse to start. After a few more tries, it roared like an Indianapolis racer and they were on their way. She brought the bandages out on the afterdeck, but none of the men were paying any attention to Bob's wound, including Bob himself. They were all looking back over the water. The crewmen lined the deck rail of the Nicaraguan cutter.

Paulo Esteban was in the water. He was being circled by three blue-gray fins. He shouted and splashed the water and the fins veered away, then began to circle him again. He swam toward the cutter until the sharks got too close to him again, when he frightened them off by splashing. But the blood scent in the water was too strong and they came in to circle him again, moving faster now and making feints at him.

Paulo was no more than twenty yards from the cutter by this time, and its crewmen had lowered a small boat into the water and four were shimmying down ropes into it. Others fired rifles from the deck at the circling fins.

When one shark made a lunge at him, Paulo somehow managed to kick it away, and the three beasts resumed their rapid circling.

Then one shark rolled on its side, and they all saw the white of its belly and the rows of teeth on its extrusible jaws as it swam just beneath the surface, seized Esteban by the middle, shook him from side to side and dived deep with its bloody burden.

The two other sharks dived also, and the water surface was disturbed by their feeding frenzy beneath, as they tore the food from each other with their toothed maws.

"You want to know if it's true that I was the one who killed Paulo Esteban?" Sally said into the phone. "Sure it's true. Though I had some help doing it." She listened some more, then the smile faded from her face and she replied sharply, "No. I had nothing to do with Clarinero's death. He was a good man."

After some more talk, she put down the phone and said to Mike, who was looking out the hotel-room window at the view of San Jose, the Costa Rican capital, "That was a call from New York. A guy from *People* magazine. They want to do a spread on me. They've been told I'm a government agent. Can you believe my father? Telling everyone that. He calls you my backup team. I hope you're not offended."

"Amused," Mike said.

He had kind of figured that Dwight Quincy Poynings would have spent his time plotting some sort of cover-up. Which was okay with Mike. Except the less said about him and the team, the better.

"I never told you, Sally," he said. "Clarinero gave me a message for you. He wanted you to know that he loved you."

"Really?" Her eyes brimmed, and a tear trickled down her cheek. "I thought I loved him too at the time. It's only since then I've realized I was deceiving myself."

Mike looked at her inquiringly.

"No," she confessed, looking him in the eyes, "I never knew what real feeling was until I met you."

Mike edged toward the door.

But Sally was quicker than any leftist guerrilla, and overcame the merc before he could escape.